A
DAUGHTER'S
TRUTH

Also by Laura Bradford

Portrait of a Sister

THE TOBI TOBIAS MYSTERIES

And Death Goes To . . .
30 Second Death
Death in Advertising

Published by Kensington Publishing Corporation

A
DAUGHTER'S
TRUTH

LAURA
BRADFORD

KENSINGTON BOOKS
www.kensingtonbooks.com

KENSINGTON BOOKS are published by

Kensington Publishing Corp.
119 West 40th Street
New York, NY 10018

All Kensington titles, imprints, and distributed lines are available at special quantity discounts for bulk purchases for sales promotion, premiums, fund-raising, educational, or institutional use.

Special book excerpts or customized printings can also be created to fit specific needs. For details, write or phone the office of the Kensington Sales Manager: Kensington Publishing Corp., 119 West 40th Street, New York, NY 10018. Attn. Sales Department. Phone: 1-800-221-2647.

Kensington and the K logo Reg. U.S. Pat. & TM Off.

BOUQUET Reg. U.S. Pat. & TM Off.

ISBN-13: 978-1-4967-1649-1 (ebook)
ISBN-10: 1-4967-1649-3 (ebook)
Kensington Electronic Edition: June 2019

ISBN-13: 978-1-4967-1648-4
ISBN-10: 1-4967-1648-5
First Kensington Trade Paperback Edition: June 2019

10 9 8 7 6 5 4 3 2 1

Printed in the United States of America

For you, my readers

Dear Readers,

With each new women's fiction novel I write, I strive to immerse you in a journey that feels oddly familiar to your own life. Yes, the backdrop I've chosen is an Amish community in rural Pennsylvania, but the story—the journey—is one I suspect we can all relate to in one way or another.

In my first novel, *Portrait of a Sister,* that journey was about choices and family and finding one's place in life.

Here, in *A Daughter's Truth,* it's about those moments in life that come out of nowhere and shake us to the core, leaving us to wonder who we are and how we will keep going. Sometimes, as is the case for Emma Lapp, that big moment comes at the hands of other people. Other times, those moments just happen—an unexpected loss, an illness, an act of nature, etc. Either way, though, when the proverbial smoke clears, we're all left standing at the same crossroad with the same big decision. . . .

Will the moment define me, or will I define the moment?

That's the question Emma must answer. And, at some point in our own lives, that's a question we'll likely have to answer as well.

When you've finished reading *A Daughter's Truth,* take a look at some of the book club questions I've included in the back. Many of them were things I found myself pondering as Emma took me along on her journey.

Happy Reading!

Laura

Chapter 1

Not for the first time, Emma Lapp glanced over her shoulder, the utter silence of the sparsely graveled road at her heels deafening. On any other day, the mere thought of leaving her sisters to do her chores would fill her with such shame she'd no doubt add their tasks to her own as a way to seek atonement inside her own heart. Then again, on any other day, she *would* be gathering the eggs and feeding the orphan calf just like always.

But today wasn't just any day. Today was her birthday. Her twenty-second, to be exact. And while she knew better than anyone else what the rest of her day would and wouldn't entail, this part—the part she'd been anticipating since her last birthday—had become her happy little secret.

Lifting her coat-clad shoulders in line with her cheeks, Emma bent her head against the biting winds and hurried her steps, the anticipation for what she'd find waiting atop the sheep-tended grass eliciting a quiet squeal from between her clattering teeth. Unlike her five siblings, Emma's birthday wasn't a day with silly games and laughter. It was, instead, a day of sadness—a day when the air hung heavy across every square inch of the farm from the moment she opened her eyes until her head hit the pillow at night. And while she wanted to believe it would get better one day, twenty-one examples to the contrary told her otherwise.

But this—

She rounded the final bend in the road and stopped, her gaze falling on the weathered gravestones now visible just beyond the fence that ran along the edge of the Fishers' property. There, on the other side of the large oak tree, was the reason for both Mamm's on-going heartache and the unmistakable smile currently making its way across Emma's face.

When she was four . . . five . . . six, it had been this same sight on this same day that had swirled her stomach with the kind of dread that came from knowing.

Knowing Dat would stop the buggy . . .

Knowing she and her brother Jakob would follow behind Mamm and Dat to the second row, third gravestone from the right . . .

Knowing Mamm would look down, fist her hand against her trembling lips, and squeeze her eyes closed around one lone tear . . .

Knowing Dat would soon mutter in anger as their collective gaze fell on the year's latest offering—an offering that would be tossed into an Englisher's trash can on the way to school . . .

It was why, at the age of seven, when she'd asked to walk to school with her friends, Emma told them to go ahead without her, buying her time to stop at the cemetery alone, before Mamm and Dat.

That day, she'd fully intended to throw the trinket away in the hopes of removing the anger, if not the sadness, from her birthday. But the moment she'd seen the miniature picnic basket nestled inside her palm, she'd known she couldn't. Instead, she'd wrapped it inside a cloth napkin and hid it inside her lunch pail.

Later on, after school, she'd relocated the napkin-wrapped secret to the hollow of a pin oak near Miller's Pond. In time, she'd replaced the napkin with a dark blue drawstring bag capable of holding the now fifteen objects inside—objects her mind's eye began inventorying as she approached the cemetery.

* The miniature picnic basket
* The pewter rose
* The snow globe with the tiny skaters inside
* The stuffed horse
* The picture of a dandelion
* The bubble wand
* The narrow slip of torn paper housed in a plastic covering
* The sparkly rock with the heart drawn on it
* The red and black checked napkin
* The plastic covered bridge
* The small, red rubber ball
* The yellow spinny thing on a stick
* The signed baseball she couldn't quite read
* The dried flower with the pale blue and pink ribbons tied around the stem
* The whittled bird

Emma savored the lightness the images afforded against the backdrop of an otherwise dark, lifeless day and quickened her pace. All her life, her birthday had been a day to hurry through in the hope Mamm's pain would somehow be lessened. There was always a cake with a handful of candles, but it was set in front of Emma with little more than a whispered happy birthday. There were presents, but they were always handed to her quietly, without the belly laughs and silly antics that were part of her siblings' birthdays. And when the sun sank low at the end of her day, she, too, was glad it was over.

But this? This stop at the cemetery had become the one part of her birthday she actually looked forward to with anticipation each year. Because even while she knew it was wrong to be drawn to a material object, the very act of guessing what it might be felt more birthday-like than anything she'd ever known.

Sliding her focus to the left, she surveyed the long, winding country road that led farther into Amish country, the lack of buggy traffic in keeping with the hour. Morning was a busy time in the Amish community. It was time to tend to the animals and get about the day's tasks. In the spring, summer, and fall, those tasks entailed work in the fields for those, like Dat, who farmed. In the winter months, as it was now, there were still things that needed tending—fences that needed reworking, manure to be spread in the fields, repairs made to aging structures, and assisting neighbors with the same.

A glance to her right netted the one-room schoolhouse where she'd learned to read and write as a young child, and where three of her younger siblings still went. At the moment, there was no smoke billowing from the school's chimney, but she knew that would change in about an hour when the teacher arrived ahead of her students.

Seeing nothing in either direction to impede her adventure, Emma stepped around the simple wooden fence separating the cemetery from the Grabers' farm to the south and the Fishers' farm to the north, eyed the gravestones in front of her, and, after a single deep breath, made her way over to the second row. She didn't need to read the names on the markers she passed. She'd memorized them during her visits there with her parents, when, as a new reader, she read everything she could.

* Isaac Yoder . . .
* Ruth Schrock . . .
* Ruth's twin brother, Samuel . . .
* Abram King . . .
* And, finally, Ruby Stoltzfus, Mamm's younger sister and the aunt Emma had never met

Instinctively, she took in the date of death in relation to the date of birth even though she already knew the answer.

When she was little, and she'd come here with her family, the numbers on the markers she passed hadn't really registered. But as she'd developed math skills and a perspective on life over the next few years, she'd begun to truly understand the reason behind Mamm's grief. Eighteen-year-olds weren't supposed to die. They just weren't. And when she, herself, had inched closer to—and eventually surpassed—the age her aunt had been at death, the whole occurrence took on an even more tragic undertone.

Shaking off the sadness she felt lapping at the edges of her day's one joy, Emma dropped her gaze from the simple lettering to the stark winter earth peeking out from the dormant grass below. An initial skim of the usual places where the various objects had been left in the past turned up nothing and, for a brief moment, her heart sank. But a second, more thorough look netted a brief flash of light off to the left.

Sure enough, as she moved in closer, she saw it, her answering intake of air bringing an end to a neighboring bird's desperate hunt for food in between and around the next row's grave markers. There, wrapped around a medium-sized rock, was a—

"Levi said he saw you out here!"

Whirling around, Emma turned in time to see her best friend waving at her from the other side of the fence. "Mary Fisher! It is not polite to sneak up on a person like that!"

"Sneak?" Mary echoed, shivering. "I-I d-did not s-sneak!"

"I didn't *hear* you. . . ."

"You did not hear Levi, either."

At the mention of Mary's brother, Emma looked past her friend to the Fishers' fields, a familiar flutter rising inside her chest. "Levi? He saw me?"

"Yah. That is how I knew you were here." Mary climbed onto the bottom slat of the fence and leaned across the top, her brown eyes almost golden in the early morning rays. "Happy birthday, Emma!"

"You remembered. . . ."

Mary's brows dipped. "Of course I remember. We've been best friends since we were babies, silly."

Slowly, Emma wandered between the graves and joined her friend at the fence. "Sorry. I guess I just thought maybe you'd forgotten."

"I didn't." Mary ducked her chin inside the top edge of her coat, muffling her voice as she did. "So . . . it is not any different?"

"It?"

"Your birthday. You know, with your mamm. . . ."

Emma didn't mean to laugh, she really didn't. But somehow it took more effort to refrain. "Thinking my birthday this year will be any different than it's been for the first twenty-one is like thinking your brother would ever notice me in the way he notices Liddy Mast."

"Please . . . Liddy Mast . . ." Mary grumbled on an exhale. "Do not remind me."

"What? Liddy is . . . *nice*."

"I suppose. Maybe. But she blinks too much."

"Blinks too much?"

"Yah."

Emma closed her eyes against the image of the dark-haired Amish girl who'd shown up at one of their hymn sings three weeks earlier and set her sights on Mary's brother almost immediately. "Levi does not seem to mind this blinking," she whispered.

"Levi is . . . well, *Levi*. The only things I know for sure about my brother is that he eats as if he has not seen food for days, he likes to put frogs in places I do not expect to see frogs, his constant hammering gives me a headache, and I would really rather speak of your birthday at this moment."

"There is nothing to speak of. It is just another day."

Mary's brown eyes disappeared briefly behind long lashes. "She lost her *sister*, Emma. That has to be hard."

It was the same argument she had with herself all the time. But . . .

"When Grossdawdy died last year, Mamm and Dat said it was God's will. And when Grossmudder passed in the fall that, too, was God's will. Shouldn't—" Emma stopped, shook away the rest of her thought, and forced herself to focus on something, anything else.

Mary, being Mary, didn't give up that easily. "Her sister was younger than you are now, Emma. And it was so sudden."

"But that's just it, Mary. I don't know if it was sudden or not. Mamm won't talk about it. Ever. She is just sad on this day."

"Maybe you should ask to celebrate your birthday on a *different* day," Mary suggested. "Maybe then there could be smiles and laughter on your special day, too."

She opened her mouth to point out the oft-shared fact that Mamm rarely smiled around Emma at all, but even Emma was growing tired of the subject. Some things were just a certainty. Like her brother Jonathan's rooster announcing the arrival of morning as the moon bowed to the sun. Like the answering gurgle of her stomach every time she pulled a freshly baked loaf of bread from the oven. Like the cute dimple her sister Esther shared with Mamm. Like the way Jakob's footfalls sounded identical to Dat's on the stairs each night. And like the surprise she knew she'd find beside her aunt Ruby's grave that morning . . .

Stepping off her own perch atop the bottom slat, Emma motioned to Mary's farm. "You should probably go. You do not want to upset your mamm by not doing your chores."

"I have a few minutes before I must be back."

Anxious to get back to the rock and the flash of silver she'd spied just as Mary called her name, Emma patted her friend's cold hand. "I am fine here. Alone."

"But it is your birthday, Emma! You should be doing happy things like talking to me instead of standing at . . ." Mary's words quieted only to drift off completely as she, too, stepped onto the ground. "I will leave you to pray alone. I should not have interrupted the way I did."

She met her friend's sad eyes with a smile. "I am very glad you did, Mary. Truly. I-I just . . ."

"You want to pray alone," Mary finished. "I understand."

Unable to lie to her friend aloud, Emma let her answering silence do the work.

"Well, happy birthday, Emma."

"Thank you."

She remained by the fence, watching, as Mary made her way back across her dat's field and, finally, through her parents' back door. For a moment she let her thoughts wander into the Fisher home, too, Levi's warm smile greeting her in the way it had Liddy Mast at the last hymn sing . . .

"Oh stop it, Emma," she whispered. "Levi does not see you any more than anyone else sees you."

Shaking her head, she picked her way back to Ruby's grave, her gaze quickly seeking and finding the shiny silver chain peeking out from around a nearby rock. Mesmerized, Emma dropped to her knees and slowly fingered the chain from the clasp at the top to the thick, flower-etched—

The air whooshed from her lungs as she lifted the chain from its resting spot and set the heart-shaped pendant inside her palm. She'd seen jewelry before many times—on English shopkeepers in town; on the driver Dat hired when they needed to travel outside normal buggy range; on Miss Lottie, the elderly English woman who lived out near the Beilers; and even on her own wrist for a very short time during her Rumspringa when she was sixteen—but nothing so delicately beautiful as the necklace in her hand at that moment.

"Who would leave something so pretty on the ground?" she whispered. "It does not make any . . ." The words fell away as her eyes lit on a thin line around the outer edge of the heart. A line just wide enough to wedge her nail inside and—

With a quiet snap, the heart split in two and she slowly lifted the top half up and back, her answering gasp echoing around her in the cold morning air.

There, nestled against a pale pink background, was a heart-shaped photograph of an Amish girl not much younger than Emma. . . . An Amish girl with brown hair and eyes so like Mamm's. . . . Yet, with the exception of those two things, everything else about the girl was a mirror image of . . . *Emma*?

Confused, Emma pulled the open locket still closer as, once again, she studied the face inside. The same high cheekbones . . . The same slender nose . . . The same wide, full lips . . . The same tiny freckles . . . In fact, with the exception of the hair and eye color, she'd actually think she was looking at a picture of *herself*.

Closing her fingers around the locket, Emma rose to her feet and began to run, the steady smack of her boots against the cold, dry earth no match for the thud of her heart inside her ears.

She was nearly out of breath when she reached Mary's driveway but she didn't slow down. Instead, she ran faster, her attention ricocheting between the house and the barn while simultaneously trying to work out where she'd be most likely to find her one and only true friend.

Her first stop was the barn, but other than a quick glimpse of Levi mucking a stall in the back corner, and Mary's dat gathering together tools atop a workbench, there was no one else. Spinning around, she ran farther up the driveway to the simple white farmhouse with the wide front porch. When she reached the front door, she made herself stop . . . breathe . . . and knock in a way that wouldn't startle everyone inside.

Still, she knew she had to look out of sorts when, a few

moments later, Mary's mamm opened the door and almost immediately furrowed her brow. "Good morning, Emma. Is-is everything okay at home?"

She followed the woman's gaze down to her hands—one clenched tightly around the unseen necklace, the other nervously fiddling with the edge of her favorite pale blue dress. Realizing the sight she must be, standing there on the Fishers' porch, still panting slightly from her run, Emma made herself smile. "I . . . I was hoping maybe I could speak with Mary for a few minutes?"

"I thought you spoke. Outside."

"We . . . did. But . . ." She stopped, swallowed, and willed her voice to remain calm even as her fingernails threatened to draw blood from her palm. "I will not take too much time. I . . . I just forgot to tell her something."

"Very well." Mary's mamm stepped back, motioned Emma inside, and then closed the door against the winter morning. "Mary is making some dough for bread in the kitchen."

She followed the woman down the narrow hallway to the back of the house and the large, yet simple kitchen that was nearly identical to Emma's. Only here, at the Fishers', the table was positioned in the center of the room whereas at home the table was off to the left where Mrs. Fisher kept her sewing table.

"Mary, Emma has something she forgot to tell you." The woman smiled again at Emma and then swept her hand toward the basket of laundry at the base of the steps leading to the second floor. "I'll start putting away the laundry while you girls talk."

"I'll be up as soon as we're done, Mamm." Eyeing Emma with a mischievous grin, Mary spread a cloth over the dough bowl and carried it to a sunny spot in the corner of the room. "You've been running, haven't you?"

"Yah. I—"

"I know we do not see my brother the same, but to run all

the way here just so you will look at the ground when he speaks to you? I do not understand you, birthday girl."

"I did not come to see Levi," Emma rasped. "I came to see you."

Mary's left eyebrow arched with intrigue. "But you just saw me. At the cemetery."

"Yah." Emma pointed to the long bench beside the table and, at Mary's nod, sunk onto the wooden seat, looking toward the stairs as she did. When she was satisfied Emma's mamm was no longer within earshot, she pulled her fisted hand to her chest and looked up at her friend. "I-I have to show you something. It is why I ran all the way here."

Mary took a seat on the opposite bench, her gaze locked on Emma. "What? What do you want to show me?"

"*This.*" Emma lowered her hand to the table, opened her fingers, and held out her palm to reveal the locket.

Confusion darted Mary's eyes between the necklace and Emma. "What is that?"

Thrusting her hand forward across the table, Emma swallowed. Hard. "Open it. Please."

"*Open it?* Open *what?*"

"I will do it." Emma popped open the delicate silver heart and wordlessly held it out toward Mary once again.

This time, Mary leaned forward, disgust registering across her round face a split second before infusing its way into her voice. "Emma Lapp! The Bible says, 'Thou shalt not make unto thyself a graven image!' "

"I didn't," she whispered.

"You are not to *pose* for one, either!"

Emma met and held her friend's eye before leading it back down to her open palm. "It's not me, Mary. Look again."

"What do you mean it's not you?" Mary snatched the necklace from Emma's hand. "Of course it's . . ."

Emma waited as Mary's eyes chronicled the same features she, herself, had noted back at the cemetery. Sure enough, as she watched, the disgust her friend had worn only seconds earlier began to dissipate, replaced, instead, by first confusion, and then curiosity.

"Who is this?" Mary finally asked, looking between Emma and the locket. "She looks just like you. . . . But with light brown hair . . . And eyes that are brownish green, instead of blue."

She opened her mouth to speak but closed it when there were no proper words to be found.

"Emma?" Mary repeated. "*Who* is this?"

Aware of her friend's probing eyes, she swallowed around the lump in her throat. "I-I don't know. That is why I came here. To see you."

"But how can you not know? You're holding it. . . . And she looks just like you. . . ."

"I found it."

Mary pulled a face. "You *found* a necklace with a picture of an Amish girl that looks just like you?"

"Yah."

"Emma, this doesn't make sense."

"I thought it would be like all the other things—little and shiny, or even just silly. But it wasn't." She took the necklace from Mary's open palm and stared down at the image again. "It was *this*."

"What do you mean *like the other things*? *What* other things?"

"The presents I find at my aunt Ruby's grave every year."

Mary's head whipped around toward the stairs only to return to start with widened eyes. "Presents?"

Nodding, Emma set the locket at her spot on the table and swiveled her legs over the bench until she was able to stand. Then, beckoning to Mary, she led her friend over to the kitchen window and its view of the cemetery in the distance. "Every year, since I was one, I imagine, Mamm and Dat would stop out at Aunt Ruby's grave on my birthday. We would not stay long, but we went every year. Every year, Mamm would start out sad, but soon she, like Dat, would be angry."

The sadness she saw in Mary's eyes at the beginning of her explanation ebbed into confusion. "I don't understand . . ."

"Someone leaves a present on Aunt Ruby's grave each year. On the day of her death. I don't remember what the presents were back then, but I remember Dat did not like them to be there." She leaned her forehead against the cold glass and lingered her gaze on the area where she knew the cemetery to be. "He would take the present and he would throw it into the first trash box we would see. I did not understand why these things were there, I just knew I did not like to see Mamm hurt even more than she already was on my birthday.

"That is why, when I was seven and able to walk to school alone, I told Luke Graber, Elizabeth Troyer, and the other children I walked with, to go ahead—that I would catch up."

Mary's quiet gasp pulled Emma's focus off the scenery outside the window and fixed it, instead, on her friend. "You went to the cemetery alone? On your birthday?" Mary asked.

"Yah. I wanted to get the silly thing before Mamm and Dat were to see it." Swallowing back against the emotion she felt building, she willed herself to remain calm, to hold back the memory-stirred tears. "But when I saw the miniature picnic basket sitting on the ground, I—"

"Miniature picnic basket?" Mary echoed.

"Yah." Bringing her hand up between them, Emma separated her thumb and index finger by about an inch. "It is just like a real picnic basket, but it is *this* small. It even opens . . . but there is nothing inside."

"I imagine it was hard to throw such a thing away."

"That is why I didn't." She shrugged away Mary's renewed gasp and wandered back to the table with her friend in tow. "I put it in my lunch pail and kept it there until the school day was over. Then, on the way home, I hid it out by Miller's Pond."

Mary's eyes brightened with excitement as, once again, she peered toward the stairs and dropped her voice to a whisper. "Do you think it could still be there even now?"

Lowering herself to her seat next to the locket, Emma fingered the chain. "It *is* still there. In a bag. With fourteen other things. This"—Emma closed her hand over the locket—"will make fifteen things."

"You saved them all?" Mary glanced back at the stairs. "In the tree?"

"Yah."

"Can I see them?"

"Maybe. One day."

"Why did you keep them?" Mary asked.

"Going there, to see what was left at Ruby's grave, is the one part of my birthday that feels . . ." Emma stopped, took a breath, and made herself continue despite the emotion that was beginning to choke her words. "*Special*."

Mary took a spot on the same bench and rested her head on Emma's shoulder. "Oh, Emma, I don't like that your birthday is always so sad. It doesn't seem right."

"Mamm did not ask God to take her sister."

"I know, but still . . . It was God's will."

"I know that, and you know that, but Mamm is still sad."

"I understand that, but it is like you said earlier. It was twenty-two years ago."

"Yah." Emma held the locket to her chest. "I know it's wrong to say, but I began to see these things at the grave as birthday presents for me. They were something to get excited about each year. But I don't know what to think about"— Emma opened her palm to the locket again—"this one. It is the only one with a picture."

"A picture that looks just like you," Mary reminded, straightening up.

The sound of approaching footsteps had Emma closing her

fist around the necklace once again. Together, they looked toward the stairs in time to see Mary's mamm appear with an empty laundry basket in her hands.

The same shame that cast Mary's eyes down to the table also propelled her onto her feet. "I did not mean to be so long, Mamm. I am sorry." Then, to Emma, she said, "It is time for me to get back to my chores."

"I understand."

"We will talk again soon." Mary lingered her gaze on Emma's hand and then gestured toward the stairs. "Now, I must sweep."

She watched her friend disappear up the stairs and then turned to find Miriam Fisher watching her closely. "I am sorry I took so long with Mary. I did not realize how long we had spoken."

"It is all right, Emma. Sometimes friends just need a little extra time." Miriam led the way toward the front door but stopped just shy of it. "You are twenty-two today, aren't you, Emma?"

"Yah."

"Happy birthday."

"Thank you." Emma reached for the doorknob only to stop and turn back to the woman. "You grew up with Mamm, didn't you?"

"I did."

"So then you knew *her*, too, right? You knew *Ruby* . . ."

Miriam Fisher's dark brown eyes dropped to the floor.

"You knew Ruby . . ." Emma prodded again.

Mary's mamm lifted her gaze and fixed it on something just beyond Emma's shoulder. "I knew Ruby."

"Was she like Mamm?"

Miriam's focus snapped back to Emma's. "Ruby and Rebeccah? No, they were very different. Rebeccah was always so serious. She was selling quilts by the time she was fourteen. And her chores were always done. Always."

"And Ruby?"

"She did her chores, too, of course. But always much later than she was supposed to that last year."

Something about the tone of the woman's voice intrigued her and she leaned forward. "Why? What was she doing?"

Miriam started to speak, shook her head, and then motioned over her shoulder toward the kitchen. "I'm sorry, but I really should get back to my own chores. There is much to be done before lunch."

"But—"

"Emma, you must go."

Disappointment sagged her shoulders, but she knew the woman was right. She'd already taken enough of Mary's time. To do so with Miriam, as well, would be wrong. Still, there was one thing she had to know—one thing she knew she couldn't ask Mamm without intensifying a pain Emma's very existence seemed to stoke.

Readying her hand on the door once again, she waited for Miriam's gaze to return to her. When it did, the question she'd wondered her whole life blurted its way past her lips. "How did Ruby die?"

Miriam jumped backward as if she'd been slapped. "*H-how did Ruby die?*" she echoed.

"Yah. Was she ill with fever?"

"No."

"Was she in a buggy accident?"

"No."

"Did she fall down or get hurt by an animal on Grossdawdy's farm?"

"No."

There was no denying Miriam's growing discomfort as Emma cycled through the various scenarios she'd imagined in her head over the years, but she needed to know the truth. If she knew, then maybe things would be different between her and Mamm, somehow. . . .

"Was there a fire?"

"No."

"Then, how?" she pleaded. "How did Ruby die?"

"She just died, Emma. That is all. Now, I really must get back to my chores and—"

Emma reached out, stopping the woman's retreat back to the kitchen. "I know she did not *just die*. That is why I am asking you to tell me what happened."

"Ask Rebeccah."

"Talk of Ruby makes Mamm sad. Especially today, on the day Ruby died. It is why I am asking *you*."

"Emma, please. I really must get back to—"

"The Bible says, 'A false witness shall not be unpunished, and he that speaketh lies shall not escape.'" Emma willed herself to breathe, to keep her voice steady and polite. "So you cannot say Ruby *just died* . . ."

Pressing a fist to her mouth, Miriam pinched her eyes closed, her audible inhale whooshing its way past her fingers. "She died in childbirth."

Chapter 2

She was halfway down Mary's driveway when she realized she hadn't said goodbye or thank-you or anything one should say after visiting. But she couldn't turn back. Not now, anyway. Not unless she wanted to run the risk Levi would step from the barn and see her looking as lost as she felt.

For as long as she could remember, she'd wanted to know how her aunt Ruby had died, but she'd been too afraid to ask lest she upset Mamm. When she was old enough to know what death was, she'd imagined the teenager's last breath coming while in bed with the flu. When she'd been old enough to understand conversations between grown-ups, she assumed the death had been tied to Rumspringa and an experimentation of the English world gone wrong. And when she'd attended the funeral of someone her own age in a neighboring district six months earlier, she'd seen Mamm's quiet tears over the tragic buggy accident as evidence that the long-grieved death had been because of something similar.

But to learn that Mamm's little sister had died during childbirth? It was—

"No . . . It must be a mistake," she murmured, stepping onto the roadway and heading east toward home. It couldn't be. . . . Miriam Fisher had to be wrong. . . . One only had to look in the cemetery to know that.

If Ruby had died during childbirth, the dead infant would have been buried beside her, the birth date matching that of death. Instead, to the left of Ruby's grave was Abram King, a man who lived to be eighty-two. And to the right was Hannah Troyer, her childhood friend's grandmother.

No, the only baby born that day was—

She stopped.

"Nooo . . ." Her whispered rasp echoed in the still January air only to be chased off by the hitch of her own breath.

Was it possible?

Was *she* the child that . . .

Feeling her legs begin to give out beneath her, Emma stumbled over to the edge of the road, to the fence that kept the Grabers' pigs from venturing into town. She grabbed the upright closest to her body and closed her eyes against the unmistakable sense of dread snaking its way across every ounce of her being.

The dimple little Esther shared with Mamm . . .

Jakob's tall, lanky build so like Dat's . . .

Sarah's and Annie's hair the exact same shade of brown as Mamm's, while Esther, Jakob, and Jonathan shared Dat's slightly darker hue . . .

Her own dark blond hair and big blue eyes . . .

The pretty sparkle in Mamm's eyes as she looked around the dinner table at the other children . . .

The way that same smile dulled as it came to rest on Emma . . .

She tried to calm her strangled breaths, but it was no use. Instead, she made her way back onto the road, each step she took bringing with it another memory, another certainty.

All her life, she'd felt as if she never quite fit. Not in the classroom or on the playground as a child, and not at hymn sings or other friendly gatherings now that she was older. But never did that sense of always being a step behind hurt like it did at home, where her childhood antics had drawn wary smiles, her thoroughness with her chores earned little more than a labored nod, and her smiles had never been returned with quite the same conviction as which they'd been given.

Was this why?

Because she was actually Ruby's—

Unfurling her fingers from their near death grip on the latest gravesite present, Emma stared down at the heart-shaped locket and the strangely familiar face inside—a face that looked like, yet wasn't, her own. The pronounced cheekbones were the same, and the shape of the eyes was the same, but that didn't necessarily mean anything, did it? Ruby was, after all, Mamm's sister. There was no reason Emma couldn't look like her. And besides, Emma's eyes were blue like—

No one's.

A flurry of footsteps off to her left broke through her thoughts in time to see her five-year-old sister, Esther, running in her direction, a sweet smile stretching the child's cheeks wide. "Emma! Emma! I helped Mamm bake a cake! For your birthday!"

She forced herself to smile as she squatted down for the hug the little girl liked before heading off to school each day. "I bet it will be a wonderful cake."

"You cannot eat it until tonight!" Esther wiggled free in favor of pointing at Emma's hand, the excitement over her cake-baking adventures replaced by a sudden bout of solemnness. "Mamm said we are not to take pictures."

Closing the locket back inside her hand, Emma stood, her gaze inching past Esther to a rapidly approaching Annie and Jonathan. "Did you forget something?" she asked, looking back at Esther.

"No."

She pointed the little girl's attention toward the driveway and their eight-year-old sister. "Seems Annie is carrying two lunch pails when she only has one tummy."

Esther's eyes widened. "Oh. I forgot."

"Yah." She tapped Esther's nose with her index finger. "It is your job to remember your lunch, not Annie's, right?"

Shame led Esther's eyes down to the ground. Curiosity lifted them back to Emma. "Why do you have that in your hand?" Esther asked, pointing at Emma's now closed fist.

"Because I do. Now go get your lunch pail from Annie and make sure you walk together to school, okay?"

For a moment she thought the little girl was going to protest, but, in the end, Esther simply ran back to Annie, liberated her lunch pail from Annie's hand, and then waved for her siblings to follow her onto the road toward school. "Bye, Emma. Happy birthday!"

"Happy birthday, Emma," Annie and Jonathan said in unison as they passed.

"Thank you."

Annie paused and glanced back. "Mamm is looking for you, Emma."

She bit back the *I'm looking for her, too,* that was on the tip of her tongue and, instead, mustered a smile and an answering wave as the trio set off in the direction of the one-room schoolhouse.

Seconds turned to minutes as she stood there, watching them, her mind's eye filling with memories of her own walks to school—her feet always slowing as she approached and then passed the cemetery. A few classmates had noticed over the years, but they never said anything. Then again, other than the teacher and her brother Jakob, most of the kids hadn't said a whole lot to Emma to begin with. Everyone had always been polite, of course, but no one had ever sought her out to chat or play the way they had with one another. Except, of course, Mary.

She yanked her attention back to her siblings only to discover they'd made it past the bend in the road that claimed them from her sight. Squaring her shoulders, she looked again at the locket, breathed in every ounce of courage she could find, and then headed up the driveway toward the house, the distant tap-tap of a hammer letting her know Jakob was working on another section of fence, while a peek at the chicken coop showed Sarah gathering eggs into a basket.

When she reached the porch, she walked up the steps and into the house, letting the door flap closed in her wake.

"Surely you are not already done collecting the eggs—oh, Emma. I did not know it was you."

Stopping briefly just inside the kitchen doorway, Emma took a moment to catch her breath. When she did, she crossed to the sewing machine and Mamm. With little more than a blink, she thrust her hand out, palm up, and watched as her mother's eyes dropped to the locket.

"What is that?"

With nary a word or even a sound, Emma wedged her finger against the locket's seam and pried it open, her mother's answering gasp echoing around the room. "Emma! Where did you get that?"

"At the cemetery."

Mamm jumped to her feet, her eyes ricocheting between the locket and Emma. "What were you doing at the cemetery?"

"That's what we do on my birthday, isn't it?" she countered, her voice shrill. "We go to the cemetery to visit your sister's grave, and you cry. It is a part of my birthday like a picnic is for Sarah's, a game of stickball is for Jonathan's, a walk to the pond is for Jakob's, a game of follow the leader is for Annie's, and bubble blowing is for Esther's."

Like a moth to an open flame, Mamm's gaze returned to the open locket, tears making their way down her colorless cheeks.

"I used to think your sadness was because Ruby died on my birthday. But it is more than that, isn't it?" Emma demanded. Then, before she lost the courage Mamm's tears were rapidly eroding, she added, "It's because *I'm* the reason she died, aren't I?"

She wasn't sure what response she'd been expecting. Maybe a gasp . . . Maybe a violent shake of Mamm's head . . . Maybe a frantic reach for Emma's hands while pleading for her to refrain from such silly talk . . . Whatever it was, though, it hadn't been this weighted silence that hung in the air like an impending storm.

Not knowing what to do or say, Emma looked again at the photograph of the girl atop her hand and willed the eyes she saw looking back at her to respond the way she'd wanted Mamm to respond. But as with Mamm, there was only silence.

Heavy, heavy silence.

The kind that was an answer all on its own.

"Please," Emma whispered past the emotion gathering inside her throat. "I-I need to know. Was . . . Was she . . ." She stopped, swallowed, and tried again, her voice reflecting the shake of her locket-holding hand. "Was Ruby my *mamm*?"

Slowly, Mamm lowered herself back onto her chair, her breath labored. Then, dropping her head into her hands, she released a tired sigh. "Yah."

On the walk home from Mary's, she'd known the truth. Deep down inside herself, she'd known the answer she would soon have. But still, hearing it confirmed aloud pained her in a way nothing else ever had. "I-I don't understand," she said between gulps of air. "Ruby was only eighteen when she died. She wasn't even . . ."

The rest of the protest faded from her lips as the reality of who she was and where she came from hit her like an unexpected kick from one of Dat's mules. Suddenly it made sense why Mamm never smiled at her in quite the same way as her brothers and sisters. . . . Why Dat had always held her at arm's length, preferring to nod his approval in her direction rather than pat her shoulder the way he did with Sarah, Annie, and Esther. . . . Why her classmates in school hadn't tried as hard with her as they did with each other. . . . Why she was the only girl at the hymn sings who wasn't courting yet. . . .

"I remind you of her," Emma whispered. "Don't I?"

Mamm's head snapped up, her eyes wet with tears. "You do! You have her smile and her cheeks!"

More than anything she wanted to believe that's all it was, that when Mamm looked at her it was like looking at Ruby. But she knew the reminder went deeper than that—to a shame that weighed on Mamm's shoulders every bit as much as any pain. "No, I remind you of her sin," she rasped.

"Emma! That's—"

"Did she get to see me?"

Mamm drew back. "Who?"

"Ruby . . . My mamm . . . I don't know what I'm supposed to call her!"

A flash of pain skittered across Mamm's face as, once again, she rose to her feet. "Emma—"

"Please. Just answer my question. Did she get to see me before she died?"

"Yah."

"And?"

"She smiled at you." Pressing her fist to her mouth, Mamm inhaled sharply only to let the same breath go in a slow, controlled whoosh. "And then she was gone."

Wandering over to the window, Emma looked out over Dat's winter fields. Even with the dormant earth, she could imagine the view come spring, when the corn and barley were starting to grow. Spring was a time of beginnings just like birth. Only, in her case, it had been different. Her birth had meant the end of Ruby's life and, in some ways, Mamm's—

She spun around. "What about my dat? I mean, my *real* dat? Why didn't he take me when Ruby died?"

"Because he was an Englisher!" Mamm closed the gap between them, grabbed the locket from Emma's hand, and shook it in the air. "He did not care that Ruby was Amish! He did not care that she had been baptized! He did not care about your mamm *or you* at all!"

"Is . . . is that why I have never fit here?" Emma asked, closing her eyes.

"What is *here*?"

"Here—in Blue Ball . . . In school . . . At hymn sings . . . When we go visiting . . ." She heard her voice growing hoarse, knew it was only a matter of time before she began to weep. But still, she had to know. "Here—in this house . . . In this family . . . Because everyone knows what I am?"

She waited for Mamm to break the silence, to argue that Emma *did* belong and always had, but those words never came. Instead, when Emma opened her eyes, she saw that Mamm's focus had moved to somewhere far beyond Emma. And in that moment, she knew the truth.

Chapter 3

Hugging her knees to her chest, Emma wiped the last of her tears against her dress sleeve and looked out over Miller's Pond. Even without Dat's mantel clock, she knew afternoon was beginning to fade into early evening. She also knew that by being here, instead of at the house as she should, Sarah and Jakob, and the younger ones, now home from school, were surely covering her chores and beginning to question where she'd gone.

She tried to imagine what Mamm would say. Would she shrug and change the subject? Would she redirect their attention to a chore that needed to be done? Or would she tell the truth—that Emma was really their cousin, not their sister?

Tired of the tears that had been her constant companion since fleeing the kitchen and Mamm's painful silence, Emma lifted her chin to the sun's waning rays and breathed in the cold, crisp air. For as long as she could remember, this pond, this rock, had always been her retreat of choice. When she'd been little, she'd liked it for its vantage point over the wildflowers that grew along the southern shore, and the squirrels and birds that hovered nearby, oblivious to whatever it was about her that made her peers shy away. When she'd gotten a little older and school was no longer part of her days, she'd venture here during a break in chores, to think and to dream. And, of course, every year on her birthday, she'd come here to hide yet another trinket inside the hollow of the oak tree she could just barely see from her favorite resting spot . . .

For what had to be the hundredth time that day, she opened her palm and gazed down at the eighteen-year-old face she'd all but memorized—a face she'd never known, yet shared in more ways than not. But it was the other stuff—the stuff she couldn't see in a tiny picture—that she most wanted to know about Ruby.

Like the sound of her laugh . . . Had it been hushed like Mamm's or—

"I figured I would find you here."

Dropping her knees back to the rock's surface, she jerked her gaze across her shoulder to the footpath. "Mary! Stop sneaking up on me like that!"

"That stick"—Mary pointed at the ground behind her feet—"and these leaves did not let me sneak. *You* let me sneak."

Emma swiped the residual dampness from her cheeks and scooted forward until her feet touched the ground. "How did *I* let you sneak?"

"By not seeing or hearing anything around you." Mary crunched across the last of the leaves separating the footpath from the rock and sat beside Emma, her brows dipped with worry. "Are you okay? Your face looks a little funny. Almost like you've been crying."

Pushing off the rock, Emma shrunk her neck farther into her coat and wandered over to the water's edge. "Why did you come?" she asked instead.

"I made something for you—for your birthday. But when I stopped at your farm to give it to you, Sarah said you were not home. When I asked if you would be back soon, she made a face and went back to feeding your dat's new calf." Mary, too, abandoned the rock and joined Emma at the edge of the pond. "I thought feeding the new calf was *your* job."

"It is."

Mary laughed. "It is good to have a birthday. It means less chores."

"I have been here since the sun was"—Emma swept her hand across her shoulder—"back there."

Mary's laugh hushed. "But you were at *my house* this morning . . ."

"Yah. And then I ran home and, after a little while, I ran here."

"You've been here this whole time?" Mary asked, drawing back.

"Yah."

"Doing what?"

"I have done some yelling, some stomping, some throwing, some thinking, and, yah, much crying."

"But why? It's your birthday and you found that pretty . . ." Mary's words trailed off as understanding traded places with confusion. "You showed it to your mamm, didn't you? That's why she looked so troubled when I went up to the house to see if she knew where you—"

"She is not my mamm," Emma whispered. "Her sister, Ruby, was."

"Emma Lapp, you are not to say such things! The Bible says, 'Lying lips are an abomination to the Lord!' "

"The Bible also says, 'God is a Spirit: and they that worship him must worship him in spirit and truth.' "

Mary's eyes narrowed on Emma's. "I do not understand what—"

"Ruby died *the day I was born,* Mary."

"In an accident or because she was sick or . . . however she died. That doesn't mean she was—"

"*Your mamm* told me Ruby died in childbirth."

The whoosh of Mary's breath as she sucked in her surprise echoed around them. "M-my mamm told you such a thing?"

"I asked how Ruby died, and she spoke the truth."

"She . . ." Mary stopped, swallowed, and tried again. "She told you Ruby was your mamm?"

"No. I figured that part out on my own when I left your house. It made sense—the day, the way Mamm would never speak of how Ruby died, the way she and Dat have always been different with me than Jakob and Sarah and the rest of the children, seeing her picture in the locket and knowing I look more like her than Ma—I mean, *Rebeccah* . . ."

Again, Mary stepped back, only this time, the heel of her boot touched water. "*Rebeccah*? Who—wait. What are you doing?"

"*Ruby* was *my mamm. Rebeccah* is *my aunt.*"

"Emma, you shouldn't talk like that!"

"Why? It is the truth! Mamm—I mean, *Rebeccah* told me!"

Mary's mouth opened, then shut, then opened again. "I-I don't know what to say."

"That is okay, because I don't know what to feel. Except anger and . . ." Emma glanced across the pond at the tree she'd yet to approach. "Questions. Many, many questions."

"But you know now, don't you? What more could there be to know?"

Spinning on the toes of her boots, Emma led the way back to the rock and the necklace splayed across its center. When she reached it, she lifted up the locket, the strands of the delicate chain brushing briefly against her arm. "I want to know where this came from! Why it was next to my real mother's grave!"

Mary looked from Emma to the locket and back again. "You mentioned other things you found, on other birthdays. That you've kept them . . ."

"Yah." She pointed across the pond with her free hand. "They are in a bag in that tree." Then, beckoning her friend to follow, she added, "Come. I will show you."

They trudged around the southern edge of the pond and headed in the direction of the half dozen oak trees that lined the western side. With quick feet, Emma led the way past the first and second tree. At the third tree, she circled around to the back and the hollow she'd long ago masked with a piece of bark.

With quick, deft hands, she maneuvered the piece of bark

from the hole, set it on the ground beside the trunk, and reached inside. Sure enough, with little more than a single pat to the left, she closed her cold fingers around the gathered edges of the bag and pulled it out, Mary's answering gasp barely audible over the sudden, yet familiar acceleration of her own heartbeat.

"How long has that been in there?" Mary asked.

"Since a few days after my seventh birthday—though, back then, there was only one thing in the bag. The next year there were two things . . . and then three things . . . and, soon"—Emma shook her locket-holding hand—"*sixteen*."

"The presents? They're all in there?"

"Yah. I will show you. Come." Once again, she led the way back around the pond to their starting point and the rapidly decreasing sunlight the rock still offered. When they reached her favorite spot, she set the locket down and reached inside the bag's drawstring top.

"This miniature picnic basket was the first one—or, the first one I got to before Dat." She pulled it out, held it up for Mary to see, and then set it on the rock beside the locket. "It is just like a real one, isn't it? Only tiny."

Mary sat down, ran her fingers across the wicker sides and handle, and then glanced up at Emma. "Why would someone leave such a thing next to a grave?"

"I don't know. I only know that they did." Again, Emma reached inside, and again she pulled out a trinket. "This one was when I turned eight. It is heavy for something so small."

Mary leaned forward, her breath warm against Emma's fingers. "That's a rose!"

"Yah. Here. Feel it." She handed the pewter flower to her friend and, at her friend's nod, pulled out one of her favorites— a tiny snow globe with even tinier skaters inside. Mary's answering intake of air made Emma smile. "I know, it is pretty, isn't it? And look . . ."

With practiced hands, she turned the clear-fronted globe

upside down, shook it gently, and then righted it for Mary to see.

"It's snowing!"

"Yah." Emma's smile morphed into a giggle as her thoughts traveled back through fourteen years' worth of birthday afternoons. "Every year, since I was nine, I have made it snow on the skaters."

"I would, too." Mary watched with fascination as the final flakes fell and then, with little more than the nudge of her chin at Emma's hand, added, "Can I try?"

Nodding, Emma handed the snow globe to Mary, watched her shake it, and then reached inside for the small brown horse with the black mane. "It is good I found this when I was ten instead of seven. It would have been hard to leave this in a tree."

"Oooh, that looks like Levi's horse, Hoofer, doesn't it?"

Emma turned the horse around in her hands. "You are right, it looks very much like Hoofer."

With great reluctance, Mary set the snow globe down next to the horse and pointed at the bag. "What's next?"

"A picture." She rooted around in the bag until she felt a familiar glossiness. "It is of a dandelion."

"A dandelion?" Mary echoed. "Why would someone leave *that*?"

Emma shrugged and handed it to her friend. "It's the puffing part of a dandelion . . ."

"Still."

Again, she reached inside. "*This* was when I turned twelve."

Mary traded the picture for the bubble wand. "What? No bubbles?"

"No bubbles . . ."

"You blew them all, didn't you?" Mary teased.

"No. It was just the wand."

Mary pulled a face. "Why?"

"I don't know." Emma returned to the bag and yet another odd item. "This one was there when I turned thirteen. I don't really know what it is except a piece of ripped paper inside a plastic covering . . ."

"Let me see." Mary took the plastic-encased paper and turned it over a few times. "It looks like it is part of a ticket. But I can't quite read what it—wait . . . It says—"

"Admit one," Emma finished for her friend. "I know. But I do not know what it is for." She reached inside the bag again and pulled out the small round rock she'd found on her fourteenth birthday. "This is pretty, don't you think?"

Mary's brows scrunched together. "It's a rock . . ."

"Yah, but look"—she spun it around for Mary to see— "someone drew a heart on it!"

They examined the rock and its drawing from several different angles and then added it to the growing menagerie atop the rock. Next up was the miniature covered bridge that reminded Mary of the one just past the grain mill on Route 35, the small, red rubber ball Emma caught just before it bounced into the pond, the yellow spinny thing on a stick that had Mary blowing so hard her cheeks turned bright red, the baseball with the name they couldn't read beyond the uppercase B and uppercase H, and the dried flower with the pale blue and pink ribbons Mary suspected had been a rose at one time.

"Wow. This is quite a lot of things," Mary said, sweeping her hand toward the rock.

"There is one more. From last year. When I was twenty-one." Again, Emma reached inside and pulled out the lone remaining object—a whittled bird.

Mary's hushed breath mimicked Emma's. "Wow . . . That is beautiful! And . . . it even has a worm in its mouth."

"Yah."

"It is a shame such things must stay in a bag in a tree."

"Dat would be angry if he saw them." Emma stepped

around Mary to place the bird alongside everything else. "He threw away the ones before these."

"Do you remember what they were?" Mary asked.

"Not really, no. Dat would scoop them up before I could see what they were. I knew only that they were small and that they made him angry."

Mary looked from item to item before looking back at Emma. "These were there every year?"

"Yah."

"Haven't you ever wondered why?"

"When I was little, yah. But I wondered more why they upset Dat and Mamm so. After that, when I would go to the cemetery alone before school, I mostly just wondered what the new thing would be." Aware of Mary watching her, Emma busied herself with gathering up the objects and returning them to the bag. "I know it is wrong to keep them, but they are too pretty to throw away—even the picture of the dandelion and the ripped ticket. It is as if they mean something."

"Maybe they do."

Emma paused her hand atop the stuffed horse and studied her friend. "What are you saying?"

"Maybe those things"—Mary pointed at the remaining objects still lined up along the top of the rock—"are from your father."

She pulled a face. "I told you. Dat didn't put them there. He got angry when he saw them, remember?"

"I'm talking about your birth father."

Clutching the bag to her chest, Emma stumbled back a few steps. "My-my birth father?"

Mary nodded.

"But . . . but Mamm—I mean, *Rebeccah,* said he didn't care about my mother or me," Emma sputtered. "That-that he left her to face her sin alone. That he was . . . *English.*"

Silence settled around them as Mary pried the bag away

from Emma and filled it with the last few items. When everything was safely inside, she pulled the bag closed and handed it back to Emma. "It seems to me there is only one way to know if that is true."

"What? That he didn't care about us?"

Mary's nod was slow yet unmistakable even in the growing dusk. "Find him, Emma. *Ask* him."

Chapter 4

"She brought them again."

Emma shifted her focus from the group socializing by the side of the Troyers' barn to Mary and waited for further explanation. Mary, of course, didn't disappoint.

"I tried to put yours in a spot everyone would see first, but I could not find them."

She sidled closer to the fire Benjamin Troyer had lit in an effort to ward off the dropping temperatures and rubbed her hands together. "I don't know what you're talking about. Who is *she* and what did she bring?"

Rolling her eyes, Mary dropped onto the vacant bench beside Emma. "Liddy Mast. She brought oatmeal cookies again. But it is okay, because her plate is still full and I did not see a single one of yours anywhere."

Emma glanced over her shoulder, surveyed the table of food, and returned her gaze to start. "Mine are still there."

"Where?" Mary asked, jumping to her feet once again.

"Right next to Liddy's . . ."

Mary marched over to the table and splayed her hands. "I don't see them, Emma."

"The chocolate chip ones are mine," she murmured.

"Chocolate . . ." Mary rested her hands on her hips and stared at Emma. "You always bring oatmeal. Because Levi likes them."

"Liddy Mast brought them to the last hymn sing. Because Levi likes them."

"So . . ."

"He will not notice that I did not bring oatmeal cookies. He will notice only that Liddy did."

"Maybe, if you went over and talked to him . . ."

Emma pointed her chin toward the male version of Mary and the pretty girl hanging on his every word, and waited for her friend to catch up. When she was certain Levi and Liddy's conversation was seen, Emma shrugged. "Levi will smile at me if he catches me looking, but he doesn't speak to me the way he speaks to Liddy."

"Have I ever told you about the time Levi tripped over his own foot and broke his nose?" Mary grabbed two cookies, fast stepped it back to the bench, broke off a piece of chocolate chip cookie, and held it out to Emma. When Emma declined, Mary helped herself. "Levi does not always see what he should see the first time."

"Just because he does not see *me,* does not mean he doesn't *see.*"

"He *broke his nose,* Emma. By *tripping over his own foot.* Who does that?" Mary joked before waving the rest of the first cookie between them. "This is very, *very* good. Maybe even better than the oatmeal ones."

She mustered a smile worthy of her friend's kind words and then dropped her own voice to a level only Mary could hear. "I thought about what you said at the pond on Monday."

"Good." Mary popped the rest of the cookie into her mouth and grinned. "About what?"

"About trying to find him."

Mary stared at her for a second. "Wait. You mean your birth father?"

"Shhhh . . ." Emma glanced toward Levi, Liddy, and the rest of their peers and, when she was certain they had not heard, returned her words and her focus to her friend. "Yah. My birth father."

Mary took another bite, eyeing Emma closely as she did. "How have things been going at home? With your mamm?"

She fought back the urge to correct Mary's use of the word *mamm* and, instead, shrugged. "I keep busy with my chores. Sometimes, I feel her watching me, but I do not say anything about it."

"You could ask *her* about your birth father."

Her answering laugh earned more than a few funny looks from their peers, but, as was always the case, they soon turned away, making it so she could turn to words, instead. "I told you the other day, Mary. She said he didn't care about my real mamm or me."

"That doesn't mean she doesn't know where he is . . ."

"I asked that night, after you and I spoke."

"And?"

"She told me I wasn't to speak of him. Ever."

Mary stilled the second cookie mere inches from her lips, her eyes wide. "Then what are you going to do? How are you going to find him?"

"I don't know. A stuffed horse and a bubble wand can't talk."

"It would be great if they could, wouldn't it?"

"Yah. It would be—wait!" She turned on the bench so fast, her knees crashed into Mary's. "You can see the cemetery from your fields! Perhaps you have seen someone there on the morning of my birthday . . . or maybe even the night before!"

Mary's brows furrowed. "I am not out in the fields at night or that early in the morning. That would be Dat or Levi."

Emma's gaze ricocheted off Mary's and onto the dark-haired man nodding his head at something Liddy was saying while looking at . . .

Emma?

Unsure of what to do or how to respond, she cast her eyes down at her lap, counted to five in her thoughts and, when she looked back up, found him focused on whatever Liddy was saying once again.

"I could ask him if you want. Or, *you* could ask him!" Mary suggested.

She watched Mary's brother for a few moments and then turned back to her friend. "He is busy. With Liddy."

"I can fix that." Returning to her feet, Mary tugged Emma up and on to her own. "Come with me."

When they reached the outskirts of the group, Mary relinquished Emma's hand a few steps shy of Levi. "Liddy? Could you help me with something over by the food table?"

Liddy's impossibly blue-green eyes widened behind even more impossibly long eyelashes as she stopped talking, followed Mary's finger toward the table, and, after a slight hesitation, nodded her assent.

"Now ask him," Mary whisper-hissed as she fell into step behind Liddy, in route back to the table.

Feeling her hands begin to tremble ever so slightly, Emma steadied them against the sides of her coat and glanced over at Levi. "Hi . . ."

"Hi." He stepped forward, cutting the space between them in half. "I did not see your cookies today."

"Liddy brings oatmeal now, so I made chocolate chip, instead."

"I will need to try one." Levi leaned against the tree at his side. "Did you have a nice birthday?"

Not wanting to lie, she used her sudden shiver to change the subject. "It is hard to think spring will come soon, yah?"

"Are you cold?" he asked, pushing off the tree. "Because we could go sit by the fire if you'd like."

"No . . . I mean, a little, but Liddy will be back soon and I don't want to take you away from—"

He reached up, readjusted his black hat, and then dropped his hand to his side. "I am sure she will find me wherever I am."

"But—"

"Let's sit."

Together, they moved over to the fire. When she was settled on the bench, he sat beside her, warming his hands as he did. "Are you having fun, Emma?"

She tried to nod, even tried to add in a smile, but neither felt normal. For years she'd wondered what it was about her that left her on the outskirts with Levi and the rest of her peers. And for years she'd scurried about trying to fit where she never would. But now, thanks to a heart-shaped necklace and the picture of an Amish girl, she knew her inability to fit in had nothing to do with her bent toward shyness as Mary had always guessed, or any other shortcoming she'd seen in herself.

No, her difference traced back to the very beginning—*her* very beginning. There was no changing that. For her, or for anyone else.

"You can see the cemetery from your fields, yah?" she asked.

Levi's brows traveled up toward the brim of his hat. "The cemetery? Yah. I can see it from Dat's fields. Why?"

With fingers that were suddenly fidgety, she smoothed down the part of her dress she could see sticking out from the base of her coat. "I . . . I was wondering if you can see people there sometimes."

"See people?"

"Walking around, visiting the graves, that sort of thing."

"It does not happen often, but yah . . ."

She could feel him studying her, clearly wondering about her questions, but she couldn't stop. Not yet. "Is it always Amish who come?"

"It is an *Amish* cemetery, Emma."

"I know. But perhaps English come sometimes, too?"

He looked from Emma to the fire and back again. "Sometimes the English drive by. Sometimes they slow down and look. I have seen some get out of cars and take pictures with their cameras the way they do our farms, and our buggies, and our school. They do not stay long. Except one."

She snapped her head left and stared at Levi. "One?"

"Yah. He does not take pictures. He does not stop at the school or pay me any mind in the field. He just comes to stand inside the cemetery."

"*H-he*?" she stammered.

"Yah."

"When? When does he come?"

"Every winter."

"E-every . . ." She wiped the ever-increasing dampness from her hands onto her black winter coat. "How do you know?"

"Because I remember the cold, and I remember his jacket. It is black like his truck. It is because of his truck that I see him."

"I don't understand . . ."

"It is hard to see things that early in the morning. A black truck is even harder to see. But I can hear his truck when he comes down the road, and I can hear him shut the door when he gets out, too."

"Does he *always* come in the morning?" she asked.

"Yah."

Gripping the edge of the bench, she willed the spinning in her head and the thumping in her chest to stop. It didn't. "Have you seen him yet this year?"

"Yah."

"When?"

She followed Levi's gaze to the stars twinkling in the night sky above. "It was just a few days ago."

Her answering and audible inhale pulled more than a few sets of eyes in their direction. "Do you happen to know *which* day? Like was it Wednesday or—"

"It was Monday."

"Monday?" she echoed. "Are you sure?"

"Yah. I am sure."

Monday . . .

Her birthday and the anniversary of her real mamm's death . . .

The day the locket with her birth mother's picture had been left at the grave . . .

Palming her mouth, Emma forced herself to breathe while mentally picking her way back through Levi's words. Surely it had to be the person who'd been leaving those gifts beside Ruby's grave all these years, didn't it? It was the only thing that made any sense.

"Emma? Are you okay?"

Was she? She wasn't sure. But either way, she needed more information.

"What does he do if he does not take pictures?" she finally asked.

"He bows his head for a long time."

"In prayer?"

"Perhaps."

"Does he say anything?"

After a brief pause, Levi shook his head. "Not that I can hear."

It was all so much to take in, so much to imagine. "Perhaps it is someone different each time?" she suggested.

Again, Levi shook his head. "No. It is the same person."

"How can you be so sure?"

"It is the same shiny black truck."

"There are many black trucks, Levi."

"Yah. But this one has a sign. On the door."

She drew back so hard, she would have toppled off the back of the bench if not for Levi's hand. "A sign? You mean with words?"

"Words and pictures."

"Do you remember what the pictures are?" she prodded. "Or what the words say?"

Slowly, Levi removed his hand from Emma's back and closed it around the edge of the bench, his gaze locked on hers. "I remember both."

"Tell me. Please."

"It is a construction company."

"A construction company? How do you know?"

"Because the sign says Harper Construction. And there is a picture of a hammer on one side and a toolbox on the other. The words and the pictures are white."

"But you said it is dark when he is there. How can you see pictures and read words?"

"He stays until the sun comes up."

Unsure of what to say, Emma turned back to the fire, its decreasing warmth a sure sign that the week's hymn sing was drawing to a close. Soon, the remaining food would be brought into the Troyer home, benches would be put away, and her peers would be getting into buggies and wagons for the drive home. Those who were courting would ride home together. Those who weren't would ride home with a sibling or friend.

"Emma? Is everything okay?"

"Is there anything else you can tell me?" she asked, her voice thick with emotion. "About this Englisher?"

"Yah."

Her gaze flew back to Levi's. "What? Tell me!"

"The sign does not just say Harper Construction. It says New Holland, too."

Chapter 5

She had felt Mamm watching as she'd collected the breakfast plates and carried them to the sink. She'd felt her watching as she swept the floor, and readied the children's lunch pails for the day ahead. In fact, once the little ones had left for school and Jakob and Sarah had headed out to attend to their respective chores, Emma had even caught her getting ready to speak in the reflection of the kettle, but when Mamm's mouth invariably closed without so much as a word spoken, she knew nothing would be forthcoming.

On one hand, she knew she could help ease the week-long tension by acting as if nothing had changed. But, on the other hand, everything *had* changed, and she simply couldn't pretend otherwise.

"Emma?"

Stilling the dishcloth atop the final plate, she glanced over her shoulder to find Mamm's worried face replaced by Sarah's. "Is something the matter, Sarah?"

"I don't know. You've been so different this past week."

She wished she could argue, but she couldn't. Sarah was right. She *was* different. It was as if the truth about her birth and her parents had wiped away her incessant urge to please. Sure, she still did her chores and everything that was expected, but now she stopped at that point rather than going beyond. Part of that was because she was angry, sure. But a far bigger part was finally knowing no amount of trying would ever change Mamm and Dat's feelings about her.

"Emma?"

She shook her thoughts back into the moment, added the now-dried plate to the stack inside the cupboard, and hung the damp towel across the stove's handle. "I am fine, Sarah."

"I heard you moving around in your room last night. Even after Dat's lantern went out last night," Sarah protested.

"I-I was thinking." Emma grabbed the broom from its resting spot beside the refrigerator and crossed to the table. "I am sorry if I kept you up."

"Did something happen when we were at the hymn sing? I saw you talking to Levi Fisher by the fire before it was time for us to leave."

"What would happen, Sarah?"

"Perhaps he wants to court you and you do not know what Dat will say?"

She didn't mean to laugh, nor could she stop it. "Levi will soon court Liddy Mast."

"Liddy Mast?"

"Yah. Liddy Mast."

"When did he start liking *her*?" Sarah asked, her nose scrunched.

"I imagine the first time he saw her at that hymn sing a few weeks ago."

"But—"

Stopping mid-sweep, Emma lifted her hand into the air. "Sarah, it isn't time to talk of such things. There is much work to be done—work I am doing but you are not." Then, with a peek at the clock, she added, "If I am not here when it is time for lunch, please see that the meal is ready when Dat and Jakob come in from the field."

"If you're not *here*? Why, where would you be?"

Emma glanced toward the stairs and then the window before bringing her attention back to her sister. "I need to use your scooter. My tire is flat."

"*My scooter?*"

"Yah."

"But why?" Sarah asked. "Where are you going?"

"I just need to go into town."

"Does Mamm know you are going?"

She lifted her chin in defiance. "No. I am twenty-two. I can go into town when I wish."

"Emma!"

"It is true, Sarah. I am not a little girl. My morning chores are done. I am going into town."

Sarah's eyes widened. "Does Dat know?"

"No." Emma pulled the broom handle tightly against her chest and did her best to rein in her growing irritation. "Please, Sarah. There is just something I have to do."

"What am I to say if Mamm asks where you've gone?"

"If you are busy, she won't ask. If that doesn't work, just tell the truth—you don't know where I went."

After a few moments of utter silence, Sarah nodded, pivoted on the toes of her boots, and headed upstairs to the day's waiting laundry. Emma, in turn, eyed the last few crumbs on the floor, returned the broom to its spot beside the refrigerator, and made her way out to the side yard and Sarah's waiting scooter.

She tugged the scooter's handle from its resting spot against the dormant apple tree and walked it toward the driveway, her gaze skittering between the barn and the fields. The telltale ting of a bucket against the ground let her know Jakob was inside the barn, likely getting ready to fill the animals' water troughs. She was curious where Dat was, but to linger any longer than necessary made no sense, especially if she didn't want her plan upset by additional tasks or chores. Besides, the longer she took to get to New Holland and back, the more difficult she made it for Sarah to keep from answering questions.

Stepping her left foot onto the scooter, Emma propelled herself forward with her right, the responding smack of cold air on her cheeks and hands making her wish she'd grabbed her coat on the way out the door. Still, she pressed on—down the driveway, past her neighbors' farms, and onto the main thoroughfare toward town, the occasional buggy-only sighting giving way to one that included cars and trucks, too.

At the traffic light by the Amish eatery popular with the English on vacation, Emma spotted an Amish teenager stacking boxes on the back step. "Hello," she called, scootering to a stop just inches from where he stood. "Do you know New Holland well?"

"Yah."

She pulled her hands from the handles, wiped them down the sides of her dress, and then backed up a few feet in the hope it might minimize any chance he could hear her heart galloping inside her chest. "Have you ever seen a black shiny truck that says Harper Construction on the side?"

"Sure." He pointed to a large tree near the back of the parking lot. "Parks back there most of the time."

She stared at the boy. "You've seen it here?"

"Yah. It is here often—Friday afternoons, mostly." Setting the last box atop the pile, the boy eyed her from head to toe. "He comes in here for lunch after it is busy."

"He?"

"The Englisher who drives the truck."

"Do . . . do you know his name?"

"He told me to call him Harp."

"*Harp?*" Emma echoed.

The teenager shrugged, then jerked his chin toward the restaurant's back door. "I better get these inside before—"

"Wait!" Tightening her hold on the handles, Emma stepped off the scooter and inched closer. "Is there a building that goes with the truck? You know, like a barn where he builds the things he builds."

"He builds houses. *Big* houses. He shows me his drawings sometimes when he's waiting for his food to come." The boy wrapped his hand around the bottom box and hoisted the entire pile off the ground. "He said I'm pretty good at reading a floor plan—least that's what he called his picture."

She laid her scooter on its side and then fast stepped it over to the door in an effort to help. "Okay, so maybe he doesn't use a barn for what he builds, but maybe he has an office or something where he draws his pictures?"

The boy maneuvered the boxes through the narrow opening her assistance afforded and then stopped. "He has an office. It's in the old bank building."

She followed the direction indicated by his chin. "Old bank building?"

"Yah. Not far from Otis's Buggy Tours."

Emma wasn't sure how long she'd been there. An hour? Maybe two? All she knew for certain was that the black shiny truck with the Harper Construction sign Levi had described hadn't moved from its spot outside the back door of the old bank building since she entered the parking lot. Well, that and the fact that the only other car in the lot—a small brown two-door—hadn't moved, either.

Yet every time she tried to tell herself it was time to head home, her feet wouldn't budge from their hiding spot behind the old shed on the edge of a neighboring property. From that spot she could see both the truck and the back door, as well as two different windows that revealed little more than interior lights.

When she'd left the farmhouse, bound for New Holland,

Emma's only real goal had been to find Harper Construction. Once she did, the goal shifted to catching a glimpse of the man Levi had seen at the cemetery the morning of her birthday. But the longer she waited for that glimpse, the more agitated she found herself getting.

All her life, she'd believed there was something wrong with her—something she needed to try to change in order to make Mamm smile, or the kids at school include her, or boys want to court her. Maybe she could be a better quilter, do her chores faster, bring just the right cookies to share, or even learn to bat her eyelashes like Liddy Mast. When her efforts fell short as they always had, she tried harder and harder and harder.

But none of it had mattered. None of it was ever going to matter. Because in the end, it wasn't about what she did or didn't do, or how she looked or didn't look. All that mattered was the actions of two people she'd never met—one who died during her birth, and one who hadn't cared enough to even look in on her as she grew.

And then there was Mamm and Dat, or, rather, the people she'd *thought* were her mamm and dat. Unlike Emma, they'd known the truth. They'd known why she hadn't fit inside their home and community. They'd known that her prayers to be like everyone else were never going to be answered the way she'd hoped. Yet they'd said nothing.

Fisting her hands at her sides, she shifted her focus from the building to the truck. How could someone have a child and not care? How could he go about his life, building houses, and never wonder if his child was even happy? How could he—

She stepped out from the shadow of the shed and headed toward the very door she'd all but memorized from her hiding spot. So much of her life had already been wasted not knowing. Today, that ended. Today, she was going to get the rest of the answers she needed.

With determined steps, Emma made her way around the building and through the front door, the contrast between the late-afternoon sun and the electric lighting that greeted her, momentarily jarring. A few quick blinks, however, helped her eyes adjust enough to be able to pick out an older woman seated at a desk, talking on a telephone. From somewhere beyond the woman's desk, she could make out a deeper, male voice.

"I'll be right with you, Miss."

At Emma's nod, the woman returned to her call, freeing Emma to peruse the framed photographs lining the wall to her right. Although the background in each picture changed, one person remained the same. Leaning closer, she studied the English man's dark blond curly hair, defined chin, wide lips, and eyes the exact same shape and shade of blue as Emma's. . . .

"I'm sorry for that delay. My name is Sue Ellen, how can I help you today, Miss?"

She thought back on the times she'd sat at the dinner table, looking around at her parents and siblings, noting the similarities each sibling had with either Mamm or Dat—similarities she'd always been hard pressed to find in herself. Yet, there, in the picture, she saw her own eyes. . . . Saw their same smile-born crinkle . . . Saw the—

"Miss? Is everything all right?"

The scrape of the woman's chair against the wood floor snapped Emma back to her surroundings long enough to point at the closest picture. "Who is this man right here?"

Sue Ellen peeked around a large potted plant on her desk. "That's Brad, of course."

"Brad?"

"Brad Harper. President of Harper Construction and"— the woman swiveled her chair just enough to indicate the open office a few feet from her desk and then swiveled back to start—"my boss."

Emma took one last look at the picture and then strode the rest of the way to the desk. "I need to see him."

"Who? Mr. Harper?"

"Yah."

Dropping her chin nearly to her chest, Sue Ellen looked at Emma across the top of her glasses. "Can I ask what this is about?"

"I just need to see him."

"If you tell me what this is regarding, I could make an appointment for you to come back tomorrow." The woman shifted a pile of papers to her left and opened a small black calendar-style book. "He's booked tomorrow morning with a new client, but he has a little time after lunch—say . . . maybe two o'clock?"

"No, I need to see him *now*. It won't take long."

Sue Ellen paused, took in Emma's kapp and plain Amish dress, and stood. "I'll see if he can spare a moment after he's done with his call."

She considered waiting, but the moment Sue Ellen started for the open door, Emma knew she had to follow.

"Brad? There's someone here to see you."

"Not now, Sue Ellen, I just got off with the foreman out on the Hanson property and the two new guys he hired didn't show up today." The brown leather chair creaked ever so slightly as it swiveled slowly in their direction. "Which means they're gonna fall behind out there if we don't find a pair of brick layers who can step in real quick and get—"

The hitch of her own breath cut short the man's sentence and pulled his gaze past Sue Ellen and onto Emma, his eyes widening a split second before his face drained of all discernible color. "Ru . . . *Ruby?*" he rasped.

"Actually, it's *Emma*." She pushed her way past Sue Ellen, thrust out her hand, and opened it to reveal the locket with Ruby's picture. "Did you leave this on my mamm's grave last week?"

"Your-your mamm's grave?" Grabbing hold of his desk for

support, the man stood. "No. I left it by . . . no. I-I mean . . .
This can't be. . . . Ruby has been dead for—"

"Twenty-two years this past Monday," Emma finished,
her chin raised.

He drew back so fast, his chair banged against the window
behind his desk. "How do you know that?" he demanded.

"Because having *me* is what killed her!" And, just like that,
the anger that had brought her to that moment gave way to a
steady stream of tears she tried, unsuccessfully, to blink away.

Chapter 6

Brad steadied himself against his desk and, when he seemed confident enough he could stand alone, waved Sue Ellen from the room. Seconds turned to minutes as he stared at Emma and then, unseeingly, at something outside the confines of his office walls. Eventually, he shook himself back into the room, back to Emma. "I . . . I don't know what to . . ." His words trailed away, his eyes pained, his lips trembling. "I-I don't understand. How . . . how can this be? You . . . I mean, I thought . . . I was *told* you died, too."

Emma wiped away the last of the pesky tears. "If that were so, I would not be here."

"I realize that, I just . . ." Stepping backward, he took her in from the top of her kapp to the tips of her boots before bringing his full attention back to her face. "You have her same cheekbones . . . And the same curve right *here.*" He touched the center of his own top lip only to let his hand drift back to his side. "But your eyes are different. Hers were this pretty brown that sparkled when she smiled. Yours are blue just like . . ."

He covered his mouth with his hand as he took a single step forward and then a half step back. "I-I don't know what to say. I . . . I mean I can't believe this. It doesn't make any sense."

"You did not know?" she rasped.

"Know? Know what?"

"That I lived?"

"No! I thought you died with her!" Raking his fingers through his hair, Brad took off across the office toward his desk, reversed course to the window, and then spun back around toward Emma, the confusion he'd worn just moments earlier morphing first to anger and then . . . *joy?*

When he reached her, he gathered her hands inside his own and held them tightly. "I don't know what to say . . . You're my-my . . . *daughter—Ruby's and my* daughter . . ."

"Yah. I mean, *yes.*"

"I can't believe this. It's just . . . I don't know . . . I don't know what to say." He led her over to his desk and invited her to sit in the chair across from his own. "I keep thinking Sue Ellen is going to walk back in here and tell me this is some sort of bad joke. That this is going to end up being just like all my other dreams."

Slowly, Emma lowered herself to the edge of the chair, and after a moment or two of trying to decide what to do with her hands, she simply laid them in her lap. "Other dreams?"

"That Ruby didn't die . . . That *you* didn't die . . . That I got to build the house we wanted, for us."

She stared at him. "You wanted to build us *a house?*"

"I did. *We* did."

"But Mamm—I mean, *Rebeccah*—said you didn't care about my real mamm. That you didn't care about *me.*"

A darkness not unlike a summer storm cloud passed across his face. "Rebeccah, as in Ruby's sister?" At Emma's nod, he pushed off the edge of the desk, pulling a hand down his face as he did. "That's where you've been this whole time? At Rebeccah and Wayne's place?"

"Yah."

"I sat out on the road, outside their farm so many times after Ruby died, wanting to talk to them, wanting to know something about her death—*your* death. But Wayne wouldn't let me onto the property. Said Rebeccah had been through enough and my being there was an unnecessary reminder. So I stopped."

A noise much like that of an injured animal followed his words, only to be smacked away by the thump of his fist against his desk. "I stopped! But you were there . . . inside . . . the whole time!"

"Yah."

Clenching his hands into fists, he strode over to the window. "They were wrong! Wrong about my feelings for Ruby, and wrong to keep you from me!"

She looked from the window, to her hands, and back again, her throat constricted by so many emotions she didn't know where to start. "So, it is not true? You *did* care about her . . . and me?"

"Emma, you . . ." He closed the gap between them with several long steps and then dropped into a squat beside her chair. "My feelings for your mother were like nothing I'd ever felt before—or since. And the word *care* isn't even in the same universe in terms of my feelings for her. I *loved* her, Emma. With everything I was and everything I wanted to be. And when she told me about you—that you were coming? I wanted nothing more than to give you a good life, a good home, a loving family."

She considered his words and the emotion with which he said them against everything she knew thus far—which wasn't much. It all sounded good but . . . "If you loved my real mamm the way you say you did . . . and you wanted me the way you say you did . . . then why weren't you there when I was born? Why didn't you know I *lived*?"

The cloud was back. Only this time, instead of ushering in an outward rage, she sensed a storm brewing behind his eyes. She decided she was right when his hand left hers to wipe at a lone tear. "I want to answer that, Emma, I really do. And I will. But right now, I want to sit with *this*, with"—he swept his damp fingers toward her face—"*you*, with *all* of this. You're . . . alive. You're my-my *daughter*."

Her lips trembled their way into a smile as she, too, wiped at her own tears. "Yah."

"You look so much like her, Emma. Even now, when you're crying. It's like my life has rewound back some twenty-two years and she's actually here, sitting in the office I told her we'd have one day . . . Only it's not her. It's you. . . . And you have *my* eyes and"—he leaned forward, his brows knitted— "my mother's chin."

Emma flew her hand to her chin and fingered it gently. "Your mother's chin?"

"Yup. My mom—*your grandmother*—has that same chin. One of her best features, in fact."

She knew she shouldn't be surprised to hear of a grandmother. It made sense, actually. But she'd been so thrown by the truth surrounding her birth, she hadn't let her thoughts move beyond Ruby and . . .

"I-I don't know what to call you," Emma whispered. "You are my real dat, but you are not Amish."

He returned his hand to hers and held it close. "We don't have to figure all of that out right now. We have tomorrow, and every day after to decide all of that."

Tomorrow . . .

A glance at the window and the waning daylight brought her to her feet. "I-I have to go. It is getting late and my scooter cannot be seen on the road when it is dark."

"Whoa. Whoa." He straightened to a stand. "Slow down. I'll drive you home if that's where you want to go. But if you don't, I can bring you back to my place or to my mom's if that would make you feel more comfortable. And I—"

Palming his mouth, he stepped back, his eyes wide. "My mom is going to freak when she sees you."

"No . . . I have to go back to the farm." Again, Emma looked at the window. "I-I told my sister Sarah that I would be back. I have already left her too long. Now she will have to give answers she should not have to give."

"But—"

"Please. I-I must go." Emma turned toward the door but stopped before she'd gone more than a step. Glancing over her shoulder, she soaked up the sense of belonging she found in his face and the unfamiliar flash of confidence it gave her in return. "I could come back tomorrow, if that's okay?"

"*If that's okay?*" He grabbed his keys off the top of his desk and fairly ran back to her side. "Trust me, Emma, there is nothing in this entire world that would make me happier than that."

He pulled her scooter from the back of his black shiny truck and set it on the ground next to her feet, the happiness he'd worn on the way out to the farmhouse now concealed by a wariness in everything from the way he moved, to the way he looked from Emma to the driveway and back again. "Are you sure I can't take you all the way up to the house?"

"Yah."

"Because there is a lot I want to say to them—to *both* of them."

"Yah. But not today. Today, it is for me to say." She followed his gaze past the maple tree to the corner of the barn she could see from where he parked. There was no visible sign of her brothers, but she knew they were near, likely inside, finishing up with the animals before dinner. "Jakob, Sarah, Jonathan, Annie, and Esther do not know the things I have learned since my birthday. I do not want them to find out this way."

"Those are Wayne and Rebeccah's children?"

Wayne and Rebeccah's children . . .

It sounded so odd to hear them described that way. Without

her own name in the mix. And, for a split second, the sudden tightness in her throat almost led to her correcting him. But she couldn't. Wayne and Rebeccah were not her parents. And Jakob, Sarah, Jonathan, Annie, and Esther were not her siblings.

Closing her eyes against a flurry of memories that had her holding a newborn Esther, teaching Annie to make a pie, hugging Jonathan after he scraped his knee when he was not more than four, helping Sarah with her quilts, and playing with Jakob by the pond, she willed herself not to cry.

Everything she'd ever known to be true was now different. *She* was different.

"Emma?"

"Yah." She parted her lashes to reveal the barn once again. "They are Wayne and Rebeccah's children."

"Jakob is the oldest?"

"No, I . . ." She stopped, inhaled, and wrapped her hands around the handles of Sarah's scooter in preparation for the ride up to the house. "Yah. Jakob is the oldest. Esther is the youngest. She is five."

"How old is he?"

"Jakob?" At Brad's nod, Emma swallowed. "He is twenty-one."

Cupping his mouth with his hand, Brad rocked back on his heels. "I wonder how many times, when I'd sit down here on the road, hoping to talk to Rebeccah those next few years, that the child I'd seen her holding had actually been you."

"Me?"

"Yeah. I mean, I was younger than you are now. I hadn't been around babies, so I had no idea how big they should or shouldn't be at different ages. Wayne never let me get closer than where I'm parked right now, so when I'd see a little one in Rebeccah's arms on occasion, I assumed it was hers."

She could hear his growing anger, even felt some of her own beginning to press at the bout of sadness, but the sound of Jakob securing the latch on the chicken coop meant it all had to stop. For the moment.

"I really should go." Emma walked the scooter away from the truck but waited to actually step on. "Dinner will be ready for the table and I must help Sarah and Annie."

Brad shut the truck's rear gate with an echoing thump. "I will see you again, right? Tomorrow? Around lunchtime?"

A week ago, she would never have made plans during the height of the workday, certainly not without seeking permission from Mamm or Dat first. But it wasn't a week ago, it was now. "Yah. If you are not too busy."

His laugh punctured the evening air. "To get a second chance like I'm getting right now? No, I will never be too busy for you. In fact, if you're good with lunchtime, I'll get what I need to get done in the morning, and then I can turn it over to Sue Ellen in the office and to my foreman out in the field for the rest of the day."

She met his clear blue eyes and felt the answering shiver that moved its way up her spine. For the first time, she knew what her own eyes looked like in the light of early evening, and how they must look when she, too, was both excited and nervous all at the same time. "I do not need to take your whole afternoon."

"Yes, you do. You need to take many, many of my afternoons." The thin graveled road popped beneath his work boots as he drew closer. "Emma, we have twenty-two years of time together to make up for. And I have twenty-two years of your life to catch up on. I don't intend to rush that."

"Should I come to the same place tomorrow?"

"Yes, or you could call me and I'll come get you."

She pulled a face. "I am Amish. I don't have a phone."

"That's right . . ." He led her focus down the street toward the next closest farm. "What about the phone that used to be in that little wooden shack between this place and Weaver's? Did they pull that out or something?"

"No, it is still there. But it is for business and emergencies."
She studied him for a moment, a dozen questions suddenly
filling her thoughts. "Did Ruby use that phone to call you?"

His nod was slow, distant. "Sometimes, yeah." Then, shaking off the memory, he turned back to Emma. "I could just be
out here waiting at a certain time, if that's easier."

"No, I'll come to you."

"That's a long way to go on a scooter, Emma. Especially at
this time of year. Besides, I'd feel better knowing you're
safe."

"It is not too long, and I have scootered to town many
times," she protested.

"Emma, they have to find out at some point. One way or
the other."

He was right. They did. But dealing with anger, as she was
where Mamm and Dat were concerned, was somehow easier
than the hurt that would come from sharing the truth with
her siblings.

"You didn't create this situation, Emma. Remember that.
Rebeccah and Wayne did. With their lies." Reaching into his
pocket, he extracted the locket she'd shoved at him in his office and unhooked the clasp. "When I left this for you, I
never thought I'd actually be able to put it around your
neck."

Confusion pushed her chin back. "You didn't leave it for
me. You left it on Ruby's . . ."

And then she knew.

The gifts she'd been stashing away in the hollow of the
oak tree by Miller's Pond since her seventh birthday had, in
fact, been for her all along. Left by a man who'd clearly believed she'd been buried in her mother's arms.

"I-I'm sorry you didn't know," she whispered.

"So am I, Emma." He set the locket on his palm and
opened it to the picture inside, the answering pain in his eyes
unmistakable. "There's not a day that goes by that I don't

think of her. And there's not a day that's gone by that I didn't think about you, mourn you, imagine you—all of it. Sometimes, clients bring their kids to a meeting. And while they're talking about stuff like closet size and window seats, I'm looking at their kids, trying to figure out how old they are and what you might have looked like at that age. Funny thing is, no matter what age they were, the face I always saw in my mind was a variation of Ruby's."

Emma sucked in a breath. "Did you know I was a girl?"

Glancing up from the locket, he met and held her gaze. "I did. That was the one thing Wayne told me when he came out of the house that day."

"*What* day?"

"The day you were born. I stood right there"—he pointed to the part of the driveway that met the road—"and waited to hear how Ruby was. How *you* were. And after a few hours, Wayne came out and told me the two of you were gone." He looked again at the locket, his voice thick, raspy. "I remember feeling as if someone punched me in the gut. I couldn't breathe, I couldn't think. But when Wayne started to walk away, I managed to pull it together enough to ask him what you were."

At a loss for what to say, Emma took the locket and chain from his hand and gazed down at the face so like her own. "I-I really do look like her, don't I?"

"Spitting image, minus your blue eyes and blond hair. But even being blue, your eyes are the same shape."

"I wish I could have known her," she managed past the lump she couldn't seem to dislodge no matter how hard she swallowed or how many times she tried to clear her throat. "How she spoke, the kinds of things she liked to do, the things that made her smile, and if she was excited to have me."

"She was *very* excited to have you. We both were."

"Then . . ." Emma stopped, blinked at the tears beginning to dapple her lashes, and tried to steady her breath enough to continue. But just as she was beginning to doubt she could, her hand and the locket disappeared inside his.

"There is so much I want to tell you, Emma. Things I want you to know, to experience, to believe with your whole heart. And you will, because I'm going to tell you and show you everything." His blue eyes, a mirror image of her own, were waiting when she looked up. "Starting tomorrow."

Chapter 7

She leaned the scooter against the tree and quickly smoothed her hands down the front and sides of her dress. Jakob's voice from somewhere in the vicinity of the barn let her know supper hadn't started. Yet.

Still, the position of the sun in the western sky told her it wasn't far off.

Inhaling the cold winter air, Emma made her way onto the porch and over to the front door, her ears perked for anything that might indicate Mamm's or Dat's exact location. If she were to guess, Dat was in the barn finishing up a few final tasks with Jakob and Jonathan, and Mamm was preparing the dinner plates while Sarah, Annie, and Esther waited to set them on the table.

The thing she couldn't quite guess was what Mamm's reaction would be when Emma strolled into the house after an unexplained absence of nearly six hours. Would she be angry? Would she be upset? Would she be silent?

Shrugging off the imagined answers she wasn't sure she even cared about, Emma let the screen door bang closed at her back and made her way toward the beckoning smells of homemade bread and chicken stew.

"I'm here," she called, wiggling out of her coat.

A sharp intake of air pulled her gaze from her coat's hook to the table in time to see Sarah finish with the napkins and practically run to Emma's side. "Emma! Where have you been? I did not want to tell Mamm that you had gone, but when you were not here to help with lunch or to bake the bread for tonight, Mamm asked me if you'd left. I could not pretend I did not know."

"I know. I wouldn't expect you to lie, Sarah." Emma motioned toward the counter and the stew bowls that stood stacked and waiting to be filled. "Where is she?"

"Who? *Mamm*?"

It was on the tip of her tongue to correct Sarah by inserting *Rebeccah* in place of *Mamm*, but she settled, instead, for a simple nod. Now was not the time or place.

Sarah swept her hand toward the stairs. "She has not been down since Dat and Jakob went back out to the barn after lunch."

"But that was hours ago," Emma protested. "It is Monday! There was bread to be made and—"

"*I* made the bread. And I sent Annie next door to the Weavers' with a loaf as Mamm always does."

"That is good, but it is not like her to be upstairs for so long."

"I do not think she is feeling well," Sarah said.

Emma stared at her sister. "Have you checked to see if that is so?"

"Yah."

"And?" Emma prodded.

"She said she was not sick and that I was to come down here and make the bread. But she did not look well."

Emma cocked her ear for any sound of life coming from the second floor, but there was nothing. "Is everything ready for dinner?" Emma glanced out the window at the gathering dusk and then back at Sarah, waiting.

"Yah."

"Then as soon as Dat and the boys come inside, start filling the bowls."

"What are you going to do?" Sarah asked.

"I will go upstairs and check on her." Slowly, Emma made her way up the same staircase she'd climbed since she was old enough to walk, each step delivering up a crystal-clear memory from a life that had been lived around a lie. There were the races with Jakob that had always ended with him reaching the top step first. . . . There were the creaky steps she'd tried to avoid while sneaking downstairs in the hope she might catch a glimpse of whatever new animal had come into the world. . . . And there was the anticipation that had accompanied her up the steps to her parents' room every time a new sibling had been born. . . .

Only they hadn't been siblings.

They'd been cousins.

And Rebeccah and Wayne hadn't been her mamm and dat.

Ruby had been. And Brad *was*.

At the top step, Emma turned left, clenching and un-clenching her hands at her sides. She knew she should be concerned about the woman at the end of the hall—a woman she'd called Mamm her whole life. But she wasn't. What she was, was angry, and it was an anger that was only growing stronger, if the unfamiliar heat in her face was any indication.

She'd seen anger before. She'd stood next to it each of her first seven birthdays. And even though she'd been small and hadn't understood its underlying origin, she'd felt its power.

Now, that anger was hers.

It was raw and it was intense and she had no desire to push it away for anyone, least of all the woman responsible for its presence in the first place. Still, a lifetime of habit had her knocking on the partially open door rather than pushing her way inside.

"Sarah and Annie have everything ready," Emma said through the opening. "They will put the stew into the bowls when Dat and the boys are ready."

She turned back to the stairs, only to stop at the sound of her name. Part of her wanted to ignore it, to simply go down to the kitchen and wait for dinner to begin. Another part wanted to ignore it and bypass the kitchen altogether in favor of shutting herself away in her own room, away from everyone and everything connected to the first twenty-two years of her life. And still, another part wanted to heed the invitation into the room if for no other reason than to share the details of her day—a day that had started with questions she never should have had, and ended with answers that changed everything. Including her feelings for the woman on the other side of the door.

The pull of the latter won.

Pushing her way into the room, Emma felt the immediate hitch to her breath as her gaze fell on the lone figure in the room—a figure who, with the exception of Emma's birthday, had always seemed so strong. Yet there, standing beside the window with stooped shoulders and red-rimmed eyes, *strong* was not the word she'd pick for Rebeccah Lapp.

"I was worried about you, Emma. You did not tell me you were leaving."

"You are right. I did not."

Rebeccah crossed to the bed she shared with her husband and sat down. "You were gone a long time. Jonathan said you were not at Miller's Pond."

"You sent Jonathan to look for me?"

"Yah."

Nodding, Emma claimed the now vacant spot at the window. A precursory look at the barn straight ahead, and the road in the distance, quickly bowed to her overwhelming need to shock. "I saw him today," she said.

"Him?"

"My father. My *real* father."

And just like that, any natural color drained from Rebeccah's face, taking with it the strained yet muted aura that had filled the room just moments earlier. Before the woman could speak, though, Emma continued. "He was surprised to see

me. To hear that *I*"—she touched the front of her chest—
"am *alive*. To know that I did not die with Ruby the way he
had been told. By *you* and by *Wayne*."

"Emma! What have you done?"

Dropping her hands to her sides, Emma stepped forward,
her eyes locked on the pair staring back at her as if *Emma*
was in the wrong. "What have *I* done?" she spit back. "I am
not the one who did this! You are. You and your husband!"

"Emma—"

"No! I never got to know my mamm. I knew her only as
your sister, Ruby. Every year we would go to the cemetery
and you would be sad. But she was not just your sister. She
was my mamm. She died having me. But I didn't know because you didn't tell me. And then, when I found out and
asked about my birth father, you said he didn't care. That he
didn't care about Ruby or me. But you were wrong! I know
this now because I *found* him and he *told* me."

"He *didn't* care about you—either of you!"

Anger propelled her forward, closing the gap between
them to mere inches. "You do not speak the truth! You
haven't for twenty-two years!"

"Emma!"

"You did not speak the truth to me, and you did not speak
the truth to my real father. But *now* he knows. Because *of
me*! Because *I* found him! Now he knows I did not die with
her. . . . That I lived right here in this house the whole time."

Rebeccah dropped her head into her palms. "Oh, Emma,
what have you done?"

"I told the truth! And now, because I did, *I* will finally
know the truth. About my real mamm. About my real dat.
About the way they loved each other and—"

"He should not have been with my sister," Rebeccah thun-
dered back, looking up. "*He* is why she is dead!"

The words drew tears Emma fought to blink away. "No. *I*
am why she is dead. And because of that, I will never know
her. But I can know *him*, and I will. Starting tomorrow."

Rebeccah's answering gasp echoed around the room. "Emma, you can't!"

"Can't what? Get to know the man who would have raised me if you hadn't told him I was dead?" Wiping her face, Emma made her way back to the door while her words, her thoughts remained in the room. "For twenty-two years, you kept me from him. You told him I had died, and you let me believe I belonged here—with you. But I *didn't* die, and I *never* belonged here."

"Of course you belonged—"

Emma whirled around, hand up. "The Bible says, 'The lip of truth shall be established forever, but a lying tongue is but for a moment.' But the Bible is wrong! Twenty-two years was not *a moment* for me. It was my forever. But no more. To-morrow, my life—the life I should have had all along—will start. With my father."

Chapter 8

The sudden flash of sunlight across the trio of smiling faces propelled her gaze toward Sue Ellen and then onto the back-lit figure making haste through the front door of Harper Construction.

"I'm here.... I'm here.... The woman behind the deli counter was new and so it all took a lot longer than it..." The deep voice trailed off, returning, seconds later, peppered with hesitation and uncertainty. "Where is she? Where's Emma? I saw her scooter parked out back."

Swiveling her chair to the right, the receptionist's smile directed Brad's gaze through his office doorway and onto Emma. "Ta da!"

"You came." He set two plastic bags atop Sue Ellen's desk and then closed the gap between them with three slow yet deliberate strides. "I was afraid they wouldn't let you."

"It is not for them to choose." Returning her attention to the framed photograph at her shoulder, Emma pointed at the young family depicted. "Are they your friends?"

"Clients, actually."

"They look so happy," she said, staring, again, at the face-splitting smiles worn by the three-member family.

"That's because it was a very big day for them."

"A big day?"

"The day they moved into their first real home."

Confused, Emma looked back at him. "They did not have a home before this?"

"Not a house, no. They lived in an apartment in the city."

Again, she looked at the picture, but this time she focused beyond the exuberant faces to the pale yellow house with a wide front porch and a pillow-topped swing. On the top step, leaning up against a white spindled rail, was a small brown teddy bear and a bright blue suitcase. "An apartment is small, yah?"

"They can be. Especially in cities. Theirs had two bedrooms, but there was not much room for the little girl to play. The mother loved to cook and bake and wanted to involve the little girl in that, but the kitchen was so small she could barely fit by herself. But the house changed all that. The little girl got a yard and a playroom, and the mom got a big kitchen. And now there's another little one in the third bedroom."

Brad nudged her attention toward the next framed photograph and the elderly couple sitting peacefully on the back deck of a home with more windows than Emma had ever seen. "The Donnelsons, there? They downsized. Their kids are grown and so they decided to build a smaller home here, and get a vacation condo at the beach. They spend a lot of their time out on that very deck, reading, chatting, and singing."

"Singing?"

"Well, technically, *she* sings. *He* plays the guitar—something he loved doing as a kid but gave up when it came time to get married and raise a family. Retiring and downsizing gave him back that time." Rocking back on his heels, Brad ran his fingers along his jawline. "I love that shot because it encapsulates their reason for building—to slow down, to breathe, to soak up life. Whereas, with the Regans"—he swept his hand toward the shot of the family in front of the yellow house—"you get the feeling they can't wait to get busy with their new life. Two very different ends of the spectrum in a lot of ways, yet both ended up being really memorable projects for me."

"For you?"

His blue eyes met and held hers. "I designed and built both of those houses, Emma. It's what I do. What Harper Construction—my company—does."

Unsure of what to say, Emma dropped her focus to the floor and swallowed. "I-I did not know."

The feel of his hand around hers pulled her focus back. "Hey . . . You not knowing things about me, and me not knowing things about you, is not our fault, kiddo. But we're going to change that, starting now. Okay?"

She was pretty sure she nodded, although it was possible she just imagined it. Either way, he squeezed her hand ever so gently and then hooked his thumb toward Sue Ellen's desk. "I wasn't sure what you like to eat, so I just got a little bit of everything until I figure it out. The picnic table in back works for me unless there's somewhere else you'd rather go to eat?"

"I don't know about a picnic table."

His shoulders rose and fell with a shrug. "We could go to a real restaurant if you'd prefer, but I thought, since it's not all that cold today, that maybe eating outside would be nicer. You know, less distractions and stuff while we get to know each other—"

"Boss?"

Emma followed Brad's attention to the doorway and the woman standing inside it. "Yes, Sue Ellen . . ."

"The picnic basket is packed and ready to go."

"Thanks, Sue Ellen." He returned his smile to Emma. "So are you good with the picnic table in back, or would you prefer a park somewhere?"

His question hovered in her thoughts as she looked back at the picture of the young family.

The woman's pure joy . . .

The man's arm wrapped casually, yet protectively, around his wife and child . . .

The little girl's squeal of excitement you didn't have to hear to know . . .

They were people Emma had never met. People she saw only through a picture frame. Yet standing there, looking at them, she felt as if she'd known them her whole life.

The joy . . .

The protectiveness . . .

The squeals . . .

Only for Emma, they had been part of a dream she'd tried to shake off more times than she could count—convinced her thoughts were a sign of an ungrateful heart.

"Emma?"

She looked past the family to the yellow house, her mind's eye soaking up the suitcase, the teddy bear, and the front door that stood open and waiting. The image blurred as she imagined herself stepping inside, the sound of laughter guiding her feet down the hall. In the kitchen, she saw the woman placing cookies on a plate she then carried over to the little girl seated at the table. Soon, their comfortable chatter and warm laughter beckoned the man inside.

Every time she tried to conjure up a topic for them to talk about in her thoughts, it faded against the simple sound of laughter and . . . *ease*. The way it did when you truly belonged somewhere.

"Emma? Is everything—"

Breathing in a sudden burst of clarity, she turned, the location for their first lunch together practically rolling off her tongue. "I would like to have our picnic at Miller's Pond."

Emma settled onto a corner of the blue and black checked blanket and carefully arranged the hem of her dress across the upper edge of her black boots. "It is the first time in many days that I do not see my breath when I am here. Perhaps it will be an early spring."

"I take it you come here often?" Brad leaned against the trunk of the oak tree and slowly unwrapped his sandwich.

"Yah." Pulling her sandwich onto her lap, Emma looked out over the pond, her thoughts wandering to her favorite rock on the other side of the tree. "It is where I come to think and to feel . . . *better.*"

He balled up the wrapper and tucked it inside the empty basket. "You come here, to Miller's Pond, when you're sick?"

"No. When I am sick, I stay close to home."

"Then what did you mean when you said you come here to feel better?"

She dropped her focus to her lap and slowly began to unwrap her own lunch. "Sometimes it is nice to not have to try so hard to be me. I do not have to think of different ways to get a smile or what I must change to make people like me. I can just come here and be me."

For a long moment, he said nothing, his eyes searching her face the way she might search the henhouse for any missed eggs. When he finally spoke, his voice, his words, his interest seemed to still the air around them. "You should always be you, Emma. Always."

She listened to the echo of her laugh as she looked at the pond once again. "When I was in school, I would wonder why the other children did not wave me over to play games like they did with each other. So I would put extra cookies into my lunch pail—to make them like me. It did not work. At the hymn sings I go to, I see the smiles and hear the happy shouts when people win a volleyball game. So when *I* play, I work hard to help my side win. But when it is time to be silly after we win, they are silly together. Without me. And at home, the other children can make Mamm smile with her eyes. I cannot. Doing extra chores and having Englishers want to buy my quilts at the road stand does not change that."

Returning her attention to her sandwich, she unwrapped it and took a bite, the ham and cheese she'd finally settled on proving to be a good choice. "But now I don't have to wonder why these things are so, and I don't have to keep trying to think of different ways to fit. Because I won't. Not here, anyway."

"You lost me, kiddo. You won't what?"

"Fit." She plucked off the part of the cheese overhanging the edge of her bread and popped it into her mouth. "Cookies and quilts can't change how I was made."

Brad leaned forward. "How you were *made*?"

"Yah. My real mamm, Ruby, was Amish. You are English. There was no marriage. When people look at me, they see something bad—something wrong."

Pushing his sandwich off his lap, Brad parted the fruit and chips from their resting place in the center of the blanket and scooted forward. "I loved your mother, Emma. Loved her with my whole heart. I wanted a life with her. I wanted a life with *you*."

She liked how it all sounded, she really did. But—

"How did the two of you meet?" she asked, taking yet another bite of her sandwich. "Was it during her Rumspringa?"

A slow smile gathered at the corners of his mouth as his gaze traveled somewhere far beyond her face. "I was working for my uncle that first summer. Picking up nails, moving material, fetching drinks for the crew, that sort of thing. It wasn't necessarily how I *wanted* to spend my summer, but schoolwork wasn't really my strong point and my mom wanted to start exposing me to things I could do to earn a living in the future. She let me choose between working with my cousin or my uncle. Being around guys who were repairing things sounded infinitely more appealing to me than cutting grass, so I opted for my uncle's fix-it business instead of my cousin's lawn service."

Brad cupped his hand across his mouth, only to let it slide back down to his thigh. "I remember the day I first laid eyes on Ruby like it was yesterday. I was out on a job site not far from here. Woman's front porch was sagging and it needed shoring up. My uncle had moved on to the steps and needed a level he'd left in his truck. Since I was essentially his gopher for the summer, it was up to me to drop what I was doing and go get it for him. I walked down to his truck, popped open one of his toolboxes, didn't find the level he wanted, and moved on to the second toolbox. Took some rummaging, but I found the right one and put everything else back inside the box. I was just stepping away from the truck when I saw her walking up the road. She had a plate of cookies in one hand, and a loaf of bread in the other. And when I waved, she gave me the prettiest smile I'd ever seen. Felt a reaction clear down to my toes."

Shaking his head quickly, he scooted his way back across the blanket and reclaimed his sandwich. "I'd seen Amish hundreds of times. Can't live in Lancaster County and not see them. Never paid much attention, really. They lived in their world, I lived in mine. But that day? Standing there next to the truck, looking at Ruby? There was only one world that mattered and it very definitely had her in it. So I stepped down to the road and I asked her name. Only the first time she told me, I was so busy looking at her it didn't really register. She was wearing this pale green dress, and just *this* part of her hair"—he touched his hairline, then pointed at Emma's— "was showing underneath her kapp. The sun was hitting it in such a way, it sparkled. And her eyes? They were this pretty brown, but in the sun, as they were that day, there were these little flecks of gold, too."

He took a big bite and then another as he leaned back against the tree. "I know I had to have looked like a fool at that moment, just standing there, staring at her. But I couldn't help myself. Fortunately for me, the sound of my uncle yelling for the level got me back on track. And that's when I realized I hadn't caught her name. So I asked again. And she answered again. I asked her where she was going and she told me she was bringing the bread and the cookies to the woman whose porch my uncle was fixing.

"Next thing I knew, we were walking side by side up the driveway. To this day, I can't remember handing my uncle that level. I know he was sitting up, looking mighty grumpy when we approached, but I didn't care about anything except Ruby. And when she went inside to deliver the cookies and the bread, I kept that front door in my sight so I'd know the second she came back outside."

He took another bite, grinning as he chewed. "And you know what? When she finished up inside, she came out with an oatmeal cookie wrapped inside a napkin for me. Best cookie I ever had, I'll tell you that."

"So what happened next?" she asked, her curiosity piqued as much by his words as the joy he wore while speaking them.

"I walked her back to the road. And even though the driveway was pretty short, I made the most out of that walk. I found out she was seventeen, that she had one sister and three brothers, and that she worked at a little ice cream shop out on the county road on Wednesdays, Fridays, and Saturdays. And before I was ready, we reached the road and she said she had to get back home to help her sister with dinner. So she headed back in the direction she'd come and I just stood there, watching. She turned around a few times, and every time she did, I waved. After about the fifth time of her turning and me still standing there, she tried to shoo me toward the driveway. When I didn't budge, she laughed. And, Emma? The second I heard that sound, I knew I had to see her again."

Intrigued, Emma swapped her sandwich for a chip and slowly nibbled her way around the outer edge. "Did you get in trouble for standing there so long?"

"You mean with my uncle? Nah. Said he knew I was smitten the moment the two of us walked up the driveway together."

"Your smile is so very big right now."

"That's because I'm thinking about your mother. But really, you should have seen *her* smile. There were so many things I loved about Ruby, but her smile? It was the best. Distracting as all get-out, but *wow*."

Emma brushed the residual chip crumbs from her hands and then hugged her knees to her chest. "Tell me more. Please."

And so he did. He talked of borrowing his mother's car to drive out to the ice cream shop where Ruby worked that Friday, and how he kept swapping places with other people in line until he was sure it would be Ruby who would take his order.

"I still remember that moment when she looked up from the ice cream case and she realized who I was." Interlacing his fingers between his head and the tree, Brad lifted his chin until he could see the sky through the bare branches. "She was halfway through the same *can I help you* I'd heard her say at least a half dozen times while I was playing leapfrog in line, when her eyes widened, the words stopped, and that smile I hadn't been able to forget since the previous day was trained squarely on me.

"For a minute, I actually forgot there was a line of people behind me. All I could do was just stand there, smiling back at her. The longer I stood there, smiling, the pinker her cheeks got until the girl working the case next to her said something in Ruby's ear, prompting Ruby to ask me for my order."

"Was it hard to leave?" Emma prodded, fascinated.

"It would've been, sure. But I didn't leave. I gave her my order, which I still remember—vanilla with this peanut butter hard shell stuff—and watched her scoop it into the cone. When she handed it to me, I gave her the money and found a small table in the corner where I could eat it. . . . Though it pretty much melted down my hand on account of the fact I spent more time watching her than actually working on my cone."

"Did she know you were still there?"

"At first, no. But after a while, the girl she was working

with looked up, spotted me watching Ruby, and whispered something to her. Next thing I knew, Ruby's cheeks were all red again, and she was peeking at me, peeking at her." Brad's laugh cut through the still air. "After a while, I couldn't keep sitting there, you know? My ice cream was gone and people wanted my table. . . . So I moved outside and sat on a bench. Two hours later, when her shift was up, I was there, waiting."

Emma reached for a cookie and rested it atop her knees. "Was she surprised?"

"She was. She was even more surprised when I offered to drive her home. But she accepted and we talked all the way back to her parents' farm."

"What did you talk about?" Emma asked. "Or do you not remember any longer?"

"I remember everything about my time with Ruby . . . *everything*." Dropping his hands back to his lap, Brad reached for his drink and took a sip. "I asked her about being Amish. She explained to me that she was getting ready to be baptized soon. She asked me about school and my summer and why I'd been at her English neighbor's house the previous day. So I told her about my job with my uncle and how my mom wanted me to learn a trade. When we passed the turnoff to this very spot, she pointed it out to me and told me how it was one of her favorite places to go and think."

Emma drew back. "Ruby came here? To think?"

"She did." He pointed her attention to the large rock Emma knew all too well. "She liked to sit right there and look out over the pond at all different times of day, but mostly late afternoon, when the sun's position made it so the top of the pond was—"

"*Covered with sparkles*," Emma finished in a gasped whisper. "I-I sit on that same rock! And I like that part of day best, too!"

Draping his hand atop hers, he squeezed. "Like mother, like daughter, it appears."

It was a lot to take in. A lot to digest. Still, she wanted more. Needed more. "So what happened when you got to Grossdawdy's house?"

"Grossdawdy? Who is that?"

"That means grandfather. But he would not have been Ruby's grossdawdy. He was her dat."

"Ahhh, okay." Brad tugged at a blade of dead grass beside the blanket and, when the ground released it, wrapped it around his finger. "Here I thought I knew everything there was to know about the Amish, yet that is a word I did not know."

She broke off a piece of her uneaten cookie but stopped short of taking a bite. "That is because Mamm and Ruby's grossdawdy went to the Lord when Mamm—I mean, *Rebeccah*, was not much older than my sister Annie."

When he reached the blade's end, he unwrapped it and tossed it back onto the earth, his eyes returning to hers. "When I dropped Ruby off that night, I knew I had to see her again. When I said that to her, her cheeks grew red again, but she did not say no. She said only that Sunday was the Lord's day—that it was a day of worship and, later, a hymn sing with friends. So I reminded her Sunday was still two days away. That Saturday came first. When she did not say anything, I thanked her for telling me about Miller's Pond and that I was going to check it out the next afternoon with my fishing pole. And then, when I drove away, I said a prayer— something I didn't do much of as an eighteen-year-old boy who was too busy being an eighteen-year-old boy."

"You said a prayer? Why?"

"That Ruby would show up."

"And she did." Emma didn't pose it as a question. She didn't need to. Her very existence on this earth made the statement safe.

This time, when Brad smiled, it was both happy and sad all at the same time. "That day was our first date as far as I'm concerned. I remember it all. I remember the feel of the sun on my left cheek as I stood right there." He pointed to the edge of the pond closest to them. "I remember the way my heart started thumping the second I heard the crunching of old leaves behind me. Because when I did, I knew my prayer had been answered. And I remember the way her hands were trembling when I turned around."

"Why were her hands trembling?" Emma asked, wide-eyed.

"She was nervous. I was nervous. We knew why we were both there—I wanted to see her, and she wanted to see me." Raking his fingers through his wavy blond hair, Brad exhaled a burst of air at the memory. "I thought about asking her if she wanted to try fishing, but I didn't want to spend our time together worrying about whether anything was biting on the line. So I suggested a walk. And that's when she pointed to her—and now *your*—rock and said maybe we could just sit. And talk."

He brushed away crumbs from the blanket between them and then took another bite of his sandwich. "I learned about her family, she learned about mine. She told me she enjoyed painting on milk cans, and I told her my favorite part of working with my uncle was when I got to build things—steps, decks, sheds. Told her I wanted to build whole houses one day. And, after a while, she told me about Samuel Gingerich."

Emma stared at Brad across her half-eaten cookie. "*I* know Samuel Gingerich. He lives on the other side of the Beiler farm. He and his wife, Hannah, have six children and a seventh on the way . . ."

"Seven kids," Brad mumbled. "Wow."

Pushing off the blanket, he wandered over to her favorite rock. Emma, in turn, abandoned the rest of her cookie and followed.

"How do *you* know Samuel Gingerich?" she asked.

"I don't." Brad ran his fingers along the flattest part of the rock, closing his eyes briefly as he did. "Not really, anyway. Ruby told me this Samuel guy had driven her home from the previous hymn sing. And with me being English, I didn't really register what she was saying, at first. I mean, I gave female classmates lifts home after school all the time. But as we sat and talked, she explained to me how courting works. How, once she was baptized, the next step in her life would be marriage. Samuel Gingerich was looking to be the one she'd start courting and then marry."

Shaking off the memory, he retracted his hand from the rock and slowly lowered himself to the very spot where Emma often sat. "I tell you, Emma, hearing that was like getting hit with a two-by-four or something. I know I'd literally only met her two days earlier, and even with that, I still didn't know her beyond a few conversations, but the thought of her getting married? To someone else? I couldn't do it. . . . I couldn't let it happen."

Mesmerized, Emma sat down on the far end of the rock, Brad's ability to make her feel as if she was at the pond, with him and Ruby, like nothing she'd ever experienced before. "What did you do?"

"I asked her to give me a little time to get to know her." His gaze skirted the pond and their food-strewn blanket before settling back on Emma. "She told me about her upcoming baptism and what it meant. That she couldn't just take up with me, an Englisher. So I asked her about the way she kept looking back at me that first day, and about her reaction to seeing me at the ice cream shop the next day, and about her being there, with me, at the pond at that moment. And then, before she could answer, I told her why *I* had stood there, watching her walk away that first day. . . . Why *I* went to the ice cream shop and waited to drive her home afterward . . . And why *I'd* prayed that she would come to the pond that day . . ."

"Why *did* you do all those things?" Emma asked.

"Because the moment I saw her, I knew Ruby was the one for me."

She didn't know what to say, so she stayed silent, the man's words, and the raw honesty with which they were spoken, in direct contrast to Mamm's regarding Brad's feelings for Ruby. Unless . . .

"What did Ruby say?"

"At first, nothing. But just as I was starting to think I'd made a complete fool of myself, putting my heart on the line like I did, she told me she felt it, too. And that she was scared."

"I would be scared, too," Emma said, her voice suddenly hoarse. "You are an Englisher, and she was planning to be baptized."

Nodding, he repositioned himself on the rock so as to face Emma directly. "I didn't really know what that meant for the Amish—the part about being baptized. I didn't realize what was expected by her community and what she, herself, would have to eliminate from her life moving forward. I just figured her biggest worry was about me being English. That she was scared because she didn't know my world all that well. So I told her we'd take it slow. That we'd get to know each other on dates."

"*Dates?*" Emma echoed.

His answering laugh filled the space between them. "Oh, Emma, sometimes, when I look at you, I feel like I've re-wound back twenty-three years and . . ." He waved away the rest of his sentence only to gather his next breath in time with his exit from the top of the rock. "She wasn't baptized yet, so that was a plus in our corner. So, too, was the fact she was still technically on Rumspringa. But she'd already made the decision to be baptized the next time the bishop did one and so we had to get creative about how and when we'd see each other. I didn't want to just always come here. I wanted to take her out, get rid of her fear about the English world, and get to know everything about her that I could.

"Sometimes those dates came during the time she'd have been riding her scooter home after work. Instead of her spending all that time getting home, I'd throw her scooter in the back of my truck and we'd use that time to do something together. Sometimes those dates happened when all her chores were done and her parents thought she was working, but she wasn't. And sometimes—"

"You mean, Ruby . . . *lied*?"

"No. She just didn't correct them when they assumed she'd been at work."

"But she would not have had money to give her dat on days she did not really work."

"*I* gave her money. From *my* job."

"But that is not work," Emma protested.

"Trust me, kiddo, it was worth every penny and then some. Because it meant Ruby and I could spend time together—real time, on real dates." He stopped, his smile draining from his face. "I've replayed every moment we ever spent together hundreds—no, *thousands*—of times over the past twenty-two years. In fact, I'm not sure I'd still be here right now if it wasn't for those moments . . . and you."

She recovered her gaped mouth. "*Me*?"

He held his hands out to her and, when she took them, pulled her to her feet, the emotion in his blue eyes surely reflected in her own. "I wanted to be the kind of man my little one would've been proud of. If she'd lived."

"I *did* live," Emma whispered.

"Thank God for that."

Chapter 9

She was just rounding the final bend in the road between Miller's Pond and the farm when the clip-clop of an approaching horse and buggy forced her thoughts into the moment. Lifting her hand as a shield against the late-afternoon sun, Emma stepped to the side of the road and waited for the charcoal-gray buggy of her brethren to draw close enough she could identify the horse or its driver.

Yet just as the white marking between the mare's eyes was starting to click into place, Mary's round face peeked around the edge of the buggy cover. "Emma, hello! Isn't this a wonderful surprise!"

Relieving her hand of sun-shielding duty, Emma waved to her friend and waited for the buggy's shadow to engulf her. When it did, she mustered the closest thing she could to a smile, lifted her gaze to her friend, and wobbled a hairbreadth at the second face peeking out around Mary's.

"Hello, Emma."

She shifted her weight across her boot-clad feet and waited for the sudden flapping inside her chest to stop or, at the very least, slow enough to let her think straight. "Levi . . . Mary . . . hello."

Levi's large brown eyes held hers for a moment before the quiet jut of his chin sent her focus in the direction she'd just come. "It is getting cold."

"Yah."

Rolling her eyes toward the buggy's ceiling, Mary jumped in. "So where are you coming from and where did you get *that*?"

She followed her friend's finger down to her own hand and the last of the black and white cookies Brad had insisted she take as he headed back to his office. "I just got them, is all."

A glance back at Mary yielded a raised brow—a raised brow Emma knew meant more questions were near if she didn't head them off. Fast. "Would you like a cookie?" Emma asked, holding one out to Levi. "They are very good."

"Very good are your oatmeal cookies."

The unexpected praise scurried her gaze toward her boots. The sudden loss of the cookie from her fingers redirected it back to Mary.

"I am not picky about *my* cookies." Mary's grin receded long enough to take a bite of the vanilla side of the cookie. "Yah, it is as good as it looks."

"Mary!" Levi scolded.

"What? You turned it down! It is not my fault if you are ferhoodled." Again, Mary rolled her eyes before bringing her full attention back to Emma. "So where are you coming from?"

"Miller's Pond."

"With cookies?"

"Yah."

"Why were you there?" Mary asked, the cookie all but forgotten.

"I . . ." She cast about for something to say short of the truth she didn't want to share in front of Levi. In the end, she settled on being as vague as possible. "I had something to do."

The second the words were out, she knew she'd chosen the wrong response. Vague didn't work with Mary. Vague with her friend was like dangling a mouse in front of one of the barn cats and expecting it to walk the other way.

In short, it didn't work.

Turning to her brother, Mary gestured outside the buggy. "If it is okay, I would like to walk with Emma to her farm. When she is there, I will start home and you can pick me up when you are done at Bishop King's."

"I can walk alone, Mary," Emma protested. "It is still plenty light out."

"Yah. But if I walk with you, it is less time in the buggy with"—Mary pointed at her brother—"*him*."

His eyes on Emma, Levi addressed his sister. "I have a much better idea."

"This should be good . . ." Mary teased.

"Perhaps *you* should walk, and *Emma* shall ride with me."

"Hmmmm . . ." Mary's grin moved from teasing to something that made Emma's cheeks grow even warmer. "Perhaps that would be good. But not today. Today, I will walk with Emma. She has much to tell me, don't you, Emma?"

She wanted to protest, but the truth was, she did want some time with Mary. So much had happened since they'd last spoken, so much she wanted to share. Before she could even nod, though, Mary was out of the buggy and standing beside her, the girl's arm snaking its way around Emma's.

"There is no need to hurry, Levi," Mary instructed. "If I make it home before you do, I will think about setting a spot for you at the dinner table."

"Mary!"

Levi's soft laugh led Emma's widened eyes back to his. "It is okay, Emma. I am used to my sister. But she forgets the many things I find in the barn that I could put in her room if she is not nice."

"Levi Fisher, you would not dare!"

With a wink directed solely at Emma, Levi urged the horse on its way with a firm click of his tongue that was quickly drowned out by Mary's answering huff. "If Levi so much as puts a mouse in my room, he will not eat for days."

It felt good to laugh, and laugh she did. "I don't think your mamm would let Levi go hungry, Mary."

"Maybe not. But I could do something to his food to make it taste bad."

"You wouldn't."

Mary's answering shrug made Emma laugh even more. "You are right. *Maybe*. But it is fun to think about sometimes. Just as it is fun to think of you being my sister one day."

Emma stopped, mid-step. "How could I be your sister?"

"When you and Levi marry."

This time, her laugh was more of a snort as she wiggled out from her friend's hold and reclaimed her earlier pace. "You are talking nonsense today, Mary."

"No, I'm not."

"*Liddy Mast* will be your sister one day." Emma stopped, spun around, and batted her eyelashes until Mary caught up. "And when she *is*, Liddy will do this"—she batted them harder—"across the table at you every time she and Levi come for supper."

Mary held up her palm. "Please. Do not say such things."

"Why? I am not like *them*. I am like *him*. *I* speak the truth."

"Not like them? Who is . . ." Mary's eyes widened, narrowed, and then widened again. "Wait! You are like *him*? As in—"

"As in my birth father. My *real* dat." Propelled forward by Mary's answering gasp, Emma met and surpassed her earlier pace, the crunch of the sparsely graveled road beneath her boots rescinding against the memory of the past two days.

Mary ran to catch up. "How can you say that? You can't know if you are like him!"

"I can, and I do."

"How?"

"Because I have met him. And we have spoken."

Mary's boots skidded to a stop while Emma continued walking. "Wait. You have? When? Who? How? And, more importantly, why did I not know?"

"It just happened. Yesterday. And it is because of Levi that I found him."

"*Levi?*" Mary echoed. "As in *my brother,* Levi?"

"Yah!"

This time when Mary caught up, it was to grab Emma's arm and pull her over to the fence that separated the Weaver farm from the county road. "Talk to me, Emma. Please! What did my brother do?"

"He told me what he saw the morning of my birthday." Turning toward the empty field, Emma rested her forearms atop the fence. "That he saw the same thing on many of my birthdays."

"Meaning?"

"You were right. It was my real dat who put those things on Ruby's grave each year. Levi saw his truck *and* him from your dat's field."

"He did not say anything to me."

Emma shrugged. "You did not ask. I did."

"Did Levi speak to him? Is that how you knew who your real dat was?"

"No. But Levi described his truck and the name of the English company it said on the truck's door. I figured out the rest."

"English company? I don't understand . . ."

"Yah. It is a construction company. In New Holland. Harper Construction—that is my real dat's name. Brad Harper."

Mary hoisted herself up onto the bottommost rail and thrust her upper body forward enough to afford a view of Emma's face. "You went to New Holland?"

"Yah."

"By yourself?"

"Yah. On Sarah's scooter."

"And you saw him?"

"Yah. At first, I did not know it was my real dat. I knew only that he'd been at the cemetery on my birthday. So I waited behind an old shed to see him come out to his truck. But when he didn't, my anger led me inside." She took in the barn and farmhouse in the distance, the cows grazing in the foreground, and, finally, her friend. "The minute I saw his picture on the wall, I knew he was my real dat. His eyes are the same blue as mine. His hair is the same color, too."

"Was he mad that you came to his work?" Mary asked.

"He was *shocked*."

"That you found him?"

Closing her eyes, Emma revisited the exact moment her birth father looked up and saw her, his blue eyes rounding and then widening, his skin draining to the color of her kapp, and the raspy sound of his voice as he said her birth mother's name.

"He was shocked that you found him?" Mary repeated.

Emma shook the memory from her thoughts and met her friend's eyes through her own parted lashes. "No, he was shocked that I was alive."

"But . . ." Mary stepped down off the rail. "That doesn't make any sense. Why would he be shocked about that?"

"Because they told him I died with her."

Mary's mouth gaped, closed, and gaped again. "Who would tell him such a thing?"

"Who else? Wayne and Rebeccah."

"Your mamm and dat?"

"No, *Wayne* and *Rebeccah*. Ruby and Brad were—I mean, *are*—my real mamm and dat."

"But you did not die with Ruby!"

"I know. They lied to him, just as Rebeccah lied to me when she said Brad did not want Ruby and me. He *did* want us. He *did* want me."

Mary, too, looked out at the field but not for long. "So? What happened?"

"We talked and then he drove me home. And then today, we spent many hours together at the pond, having a picnic and talking."

"That is where that cookie came from?"

"Yah."

"Your mamm—I mean *Rebeccah*—was *okay* with you spending time with him like that?"

"I did not give her a choice." She could feel Mary studying her and turned to meet the inquiry head-on. "She *lied*, Mary. To my real dat and to me. She should be shunned for what she has done. Dat, too."

"Shunned?" Mary echoed. "Are . . . are you going to tell Bishop King?"

"I don't know. I-I haven't thought about it. But why shouldn't I? They lied. For *twenty-two* years." She pushed back from the fence and returned to the road, her anger-filled pace making it so Mary had to run to catch up once again. "They were wrong to do that, Mary. Wrong to keep the truth about Ruby . . . and Brad . . . and *me*. It was not for them to choose!"

"Maybe there was a reason, Emma. Something you don't know. Something they will tell you if you ask."

"I'm not asking them!"

"Why?"

Emma whirled around. "Don't you get it? They've been lying to me for twenty-two years! Why would I ask them anything? If I did, they would just tell more lies!"

Mary opened her mouth to speak, yet said nothing, her worried eyes searching Emma's as the silence between them dragged on.

"I should have known, Mary," Emma insisted, her voice hoarse. "Ruby was my mamm! And Brad—he . . . He really loved her!"

Slipping her arm inside Emma's once again, Mary set their pace at a speed more conducive for talking. "Did he explain what they all meant? The scrap of paper? The bubble wand? The—"

"You mean the presents?" She shrugged away Mary's answering nod. "I didn't ask about them. I wanted to listen to him talk about meeting Ruby." And it was true. She'd been so caught up in hearing the story about how her parents had met, she'd forgotten all about the bag of trinkets stowed in the hollow of the tree on the other side of the pond.

Mary slowed. "Don't you want to know what they mean?"

"Of course. That is why I will ask tomorrow."

Once again, Mary stopped, necessitating a stop on Emma's part as well. "You will see him again tomorrow?"

"Yah."

"But why?"

She tugged her arm free and turned to face her friend. "There is much to learn. For both of us."

"But he is English," Mary warned.

"Yah. Perhaps I would be, too, if he was not told I was dead."

"Emma Lapp, don't you talk like that!"

"Why? It could be the truth."

"*Could be* does not mean *should be*!" Mary said, stamping her foot. "And you have been baptized!"

It was on the tip of her tongue to share what she'd learned about her birth mother, but, in the end, she kept Ruby's history to herself. Everything was so new, so fresh. And really, she just wanted to sit with it herself, to digest everything she'd learned at her own pace and in her own time.

Still, the knowledge that Mary's concern was born out of friendship helped tone down some of Emma's anger. "When you look across the table at your mamm and dat, you see parts of you. You know that your smile is like your dat's, and your laugh is just like your mamm's. You know that you have that funny spot on the back of your head like your gross-dawdy has.

"All my life I have seen parts of my brothers and sisters in Ma—" She paused for a lengthy inhale. "In *Rebeccah* and *Wayne*. But not me. Never me. I want to fit somewhere, too,

Mary. Just like you and Levi do. And just like Jakob, Jonathan, Annie, Sarah, and Esther do."

"You fit with *me*, Emma. You always have. Since we were very little."

"Getting to know my birth father does not change that, Mary."

"I pray that you are right."

She heard Mamm's footsteps crest the top of the stairs and pause outside Emma's door, waiting no doubt, for something to indicate Emma was still awake. Emma, in turn, sat perfectly still on the edge of her quilt-topped bed, waiting, anxiously, for the steps to continue down the hall and the faint glow of Dat's bedside lantern beneath the door to finally disappear.

The nightly ritual, save for the part that had her praying Mamm wouldn't come into her room to talk, had always been so routine. So . . . normal. Or so she'd always thought. Yet now that she knew her place in this home had been a lie from the start, she couldn't help but feel as if she were suffocating.

How many times had she sat there, in that same exact spot, wishing Mamm would come inside her room, sit on the edge of her bed, and talk to Emma the way she did sometimes with Annie and Esther. But it never happened, leaving Emma to rationalize the reason the same way she did so many other aspects of her life—she was odd, she didn't try hard enough, she'd done something poorly . . .

Yet now that she knew the real reason, Emma wanted nothing more than to be left alone. To think. To feel. To look forward to the next day and more time with her real dat.

Still, she couldn't quite shake the guilt she felt when she'd turned away from Mamm in the kitchen earlier in the evening only to spy Esther watching them, wide-eyed. Emma wasn't entirely sure how long the little girl had been there as Emma had silenced Mamm's every attempt to talk with a raised palm, but it was clear her behavior had caused confusion and fear—feelings she never intended the five-year-old to share.

Clutching the sides of her dress with renewed anger, Emma looked at the gap beneath her door, the shadow of Mamm's feet a reminder to remain still, to keep her breath quiet. Finally, mercifully, the shadow rescinded, followed soon after by all vestiges of light as Mamm joined Dat in their bedroom.

It took a moment to adjust her eyes to the total darkness, and another moment to cross to the window, lift the dark green shade into its daytime position, and look out over the dormant moonlit fields. Just last week, she'd walked those same fields with Sarah and Annie, working to rid them of the rocks and pebbles that always seemed to mysteriously appear in the months following the autumn harvest. It was a task they did every year in preparation for the tilling Dat and the boys would do as February became March.

Closing her eyes, Emma imagined the golden-yellow wheat stalks that would soon grow so tall their soft beards would tickle her cheeks. Spring was her favorite time on the farm. There was something exciting about green replacing brown, food for the animals growing in one field, crops Dat would sell in another, Mamm's vegetable garden behind the house springing back to life, and the insistent moo of yet another new calf through the open barn doors.

She willed her nose to conjure the smells of freshly plowed soil, spring flowers from the garden, and Mamm's apple pie cooling on the kitchen windowsill. . . .

Mamm.

Emma turned and surveyed her room—the quilt-topped bed, the chest of drawers, the porcelain bowl and pitcher she used to wash her face at night, the plain dresses that hung from hooks to the right of her closed door, and, finally, the heart-shaped silver locket and chain resting beside the glass of water on the small bedside table. On quiet stocking-clad feet, she made her way back to the bed, her fingers closing over the locket as she settled against her moon-drenched pillow.

For a few long moments, she simply lay there, soaking up every part of the necklace. The heart shape . . . The delicate flowers etched around the edges . . . The way it shone in the moonlight . . . The featherlight feel of the chain as it snaked across her wrist . . . The smooth simplicity of the locket's underside . . .

Slowly, carefully, she worked her thumbnail into the tiny slit she could just barely make out by sight and popped open the locket, the audible whoosh of air that had marked her first and every subsequent peek at the picture it contained echoing against the plain white walls of her room.

It didn't matter how often she looked at the young girl inside, or how she mentally prepared herself for what she'd see when she did. The near mirror image of herself stunned Emma every single time. In fact, sitting there in a room lit only by the moon, the differing hair and eye color was difficult to discern. Yet as she continued to study the woman who had been her mother, another difference emerged—a difference that was suddenly so glaring she didn't know how she'd missed it until that moment.

Ruby's smile was like nothing Emma had ever seen or felt on her own face. It was all encompassing in the way it drew Emma's gaze in before sending it skittering upward to the girl's cheeks and eyes. She tried to imagine a time she might have looked like that, too, but every time her mind started to search her memories, the face nestled inside her palm pulled her back.

All her life, she'd known Ruby as one thing: Mamm's younger sister. Beyond that, she knew only that Ruby had died at eighteen—on the same day Emma was born, making the day a painful one for the woman she'd been raised to believe was her mamm.

But what Ruby was like? The things she'd liked to do? The moments that had made her smile as she did in the picture?

Those were the things Emma didn't know. Those were the things Emma had never dared to ask lest the very subject upset Mamm.

Yet this girl, this sister, this person who'd died on her birthday was Emma's real mamm. She'd given birth to Emma and then died. At eighteen. And now, thanks to Brad, the name she could never so much as mutter as a child was beginning to take shape as a person in her thoughts. A person whose smile had made her real father take notice. A person who had strayed from the life she was supposed to lead and died because of it.

Because *of her.* . . .

Tugging the locket to her chest, Emma finally gave in to the tears she could no longer hold back.

Chapter 10

Emma heard the telltale crunch the moment his work boots hit the leaves. It was quiet, even a little tentative at first, but as she lifted her head from her knees and their eyes met, it became faster and more purposeful.

"There you are." Brad strode toward her rock. "I was worried when you didn't come to the office as we planned, so I took a chance you might be here. At your spot. And . . ." His words trailed off momentarily as he studied her face. "You okay, kiddo? You look a little worn out."

"I'm just tired. I-I did not sleep well."

Slowly, he lowered himself to a vacant spot beside her. "So why didn't you come to the office like we talked about?"

"I thought better of it."

"Better of it? I don't understand. . . . Do you not want to spend time with me?"

She looked out over the pond, willing her voice to remain steady. "I do. It's just that . . . I don't know. I just thought this would be best."

"There's nothing *best* about not seeing you, Emma. Nothing at all."

"But you loved her," she protested around the ever-present lump lodged halfway down her throat. "I mean, really truly loved her."

"Ruby? Yeah, I loved her. Still do. Always will."

Pushing against the invisible yet almost crushing weight pressing down on her shoulders, Emma stood. "Then I do not think you want to spend time with *me*."

Brad, too, rose to his feet, only instead of looking out over the water, he looped around until they were standing face-to-face. "I can't imagine why on earth you'd think that. You're all I've been able to think about since I saw you standing in my office the other day. All I've been able to talk about—ask Sue Ellen. She's had to clap her hands in my face at least a dozen times when I go from talking about site plans and blueprints, to the way you look so much like Ruby."

"Why must she clap her hands?"

"When a client calls, and I'm too buried in my thoughts to pick up the phone. . . . When I've been mid-order with a supplier and start thinking about all the places I want to take you and all the people you need to meet. . . . When she's trying to ask me a question and I haven't heard a word out of her mouth . . ." He scrubbed at his chin and then reached for her hands, holding them gently inside his own. "Do you know how hard it is waiting to tell my mom until she's back from her trip to see her sister? She's going to be absolutely beside herself, Emma!"

Tugging her hands free, she sidestepped him and made her way closer to the water, the answering crunch of leaves letting her know he wasn't far behind.

"Emma, talk to me. What's wrong? Are they giving you a hard time about seeing me? Because I could have them—"

She shook off his words. "No. It's not that. I will see you when I choose. They cannot stop me. But I don't know why you'd *want* to see me."

"Emma, you're *my daughter*. *Ruby's* and *my* daughter."

"I'm also the reason she's dead," Emma whispered as the tears that had soaked her pillow during the night made their way down her cheeks once again. "I'm . . . the . . . reason . . . you don't have her . . . anymore."

Silence greeted her raspy cry and renewed sniffling, but only for as long as it took Brad to suck in his own breath and spin her around. "Whoa. Don't ever say that again. *Ever.* You are the best thing that's happened to me in more than twenty-two years. Losing Ruby tore me apart, it really did. And I still haven't fully recovered from her death, either—not sure I ever will. But she made up her mind.

"But you? Being here? That's a gift. An *unbelievable* gift that I've thanked God for more times than I can count these past few days."

Lifting her watery gaze to his own emotion-filled eyes, Emma marveled, again, at the ability to finally see part of herself in another person. "You are sure?"

"I'm sure." He released his grip on her arms and stepped back, sweeping his hand in the direction of the road. "So, what do you say we get in the truck and head into town? We can grab a bite at the deli, or order in some lunch to my office. I know you want to hear more about your mother."

Emma paused, mid-nod. "Actually, if it's okay, maybe we could stay here again today? I-I have some things I want to ask you about."

"Okay, yeah, sure. We can do that. But let me call Sue Ellen and let her know I found you. I suspect she was worrying along with me when you didn't show."

"I'm sorry. I did not mean to make anyone worry."

Reaching into his pocket, he pulled out his phone, swept his finger across the screen, and then grinned. "I still can't believe this—*any* of this."

"This?"

"Yeah. That I'm standing here at Miller's Pond, talking to my twenty-two-year-old daughter . . . That I'm about to call my secretary to tell her I tracked you down and we're going to hang out together here for a little while . . . That I'm going to be able to call my mother tomorrow morning and tell her she has a granddaughter . . . It's a little surreal, quite frankly."

"Yah." Emma nudged her chin toward the rock but remained in place as Brad prepared to make his call. "I will meet you at the rock. There is something I must get first."

He paused his finger on the phone's touch screen. "If you need to go somewhere first, I can take you."

"I just need to get something there"—she pointed to the opposite side of the pond—"and then I will bring it to you. I will be back before you are done with your call."

She smiled away the question in his eyes and shooed him toward the rock, his answering laugh soon followed by the sound of his secretary's name. When he was safely in route to their chosen meeting spot, Emma turned and made her way around the outer edge of the pond, her mind's eye skipping ahead to the drawstring bag housed in the oak tree on the other side.

For so long, she'd imagined the trinkets she'd snuck off Ruby's grave every year as a sort of birthday present. She'd always wondered who left them and why Dat had gotten so upset by them, but those questions had always shifted to the background against the fun of the new item. When she'd still been in school, she'd hidden the surprise in her lunch pail until it was time to walk home past the pond. When she completed her schooling, there had been no reason to hide the item as she'd always go straight from the cemetery to the pond. But no matter her age or the route in which she took to get to her secret tree, she always spent time on the rock with the new gift. She'd turn it over, study it, try to imagine its significance, and then carefully add it to the bag.

Now, though, because of the locket and everything it had led her to over the past nine days, she was about to learn what everything meant and why Brad had been putting them there every year on the anniversary of her birth mother's death—details she both wanted and maybe even dreaded a wee bit, too. Everything about her life had been a lie thus far. Except those presents. They'd made her feel special on a day that never was. Yet, in hearing the truth about each one, she'd have to say goodbye to yet another part of her childhood—a part filled with silly little stories and games she'd made up while carrying each new present to its home inside the tree.

The crunching beneath her boots slowed as she reached the tree, her heart suddenly torn between knowing and not knowing. Slowly, she lifted her chin until all she could see in front of her was the early February sun peeking over the tips of the tree's bare branches, its answering warmth on her cheeks quieting her heart. Three deep breaths later, she lowered her attention back to the tree and the hollow her seven-year-old self had disguised from the world with a piece of old bark.

With practiced fingers, she removed the loose bark, set it against the base of the tree, and then reached inside for the dark blue drawstring bag she'd smuggled out of her room fifteen years earlier. Year by year, item by item, she'd filled the cotton bag and kept it hidden in this exact spot. And with the exception of Mary the other day, Emma had never shared its existence or contents with anyone.

She ran her hand across the bag's lumpy innards, her mind's eye filling in the coordinating item.

* The stuffed horse . . .
* The red rubber ball . . .

A second feel had her changing the rubber ball to the baseball before moving on.

* The snow globe with the skaters . . .
* The whittled bird . . .

The other things were harder to feel through the cloth, but she knew they were all present. Clutching the bag to her chest, she peeked around the trunk to the Englisher on the other side of the pond. She took a moment to soak him in, to try to catch her heart up to everything she knew thus far.

For twenty-two years, Wayne and Rebeccah Lapp had been Dat and Mamm. She never really saw herself in them the way she did her siblings, but they were Dat and Mamm. Now, she knew better.

Now, she knew that her real mamm, Ruby, was buried not far away, and her real dat, Brad, was an Englisher with Emma's same hair and eyes.

Mamm said Brad hadn't cared about Emma and Ruby, that he had left Ruby to deal with their sin, alone. Yet everything Brad had told her so far about his relationship with Ruby didn't match Mamm's words. In fact, the stories couldn't be more different.

So, who was right?

And where, exactly, did that leave Emma?

Glancing down at the bag, she gathered her breath and headed back around the pond, her need to know about the contents pushing its way past a whole different set of questions about herself and her birth parents—questions that seemed to multiply by the hour. She could feel him watching her as she maneuvered her way around downed limbs, through piles of old leaves, and across the plank of wood that served as a makeshift bridge from one side of a tiny inlet to the other. When she finally reached the rock, she saw him wipe the back of his hand across his eyes.

"Is . . . is Sue Ellen okay?" she asked.

He dropped his hand to his thigh and nodded. "She's fine. Glad to hear you're okay and that I found you. Why?"

"You look . . . I don't know . . . a little unhappy, I guess."

"I'm happy, Emma." He patted the part of the rock she'd claimed earlier, and, when she accepted the nonverbal invite, he pointed a lazy finger in the direction she'd just come. "Watching you just now? Walking around the pond? It was like watching Ruby. You're about the same height and there's

so much about the way you move, the way you carry yourself, that is just like her."

"I'm sorry."

His focus snapped back to her face. "No! Don't be! It's a
good thing, Emma. It's as it should be. You're Ruby's daughter. *My* daughter." He nudged his chin in the direction of her
lap. "I'm pretty sure my call to Sue Ellen took less than a
minute—two at the absolute longest. Either way, it wasn't
time for you to go home."

She followed his questioning gaze to the bag now resting
in her lap. "I-I didn't need to go home to get this. I keep it inside an old oak over there. It has been there for many years—
fifteen, in fact."

"You've kept a bag inside a tree for fifteen years? Why?
What's in it?"

"I was kind of hoping you could tell me." She inched her
fingers up to the top of the bag and then yanked on the drawstring opening. "Every year, on my birthday, we would start
the day with a visit to the cemetery. To Ruby's grave. Mamm
would get very quiet and I knew, when I looked up at her,
there would be tears on her cheeks. I also knew, in those
early years, that when I looked up at Dat, I would see anger."

"Anger?" Brad barked.

"Yah. He did not like the things we would find on Ruby's
grave each year."

"He didn't *like* the things?"

"Yah. He would throw them in the English trash can when
we would leave." Sensing Brad's growing irritation, she jumped
to the part that mattered most at that moment—the part that
got her to the bag. "The first time I went to the cemetery alone,
I was seven. I stopped at the grave before school, and I put
the little picnic basket in my lunch pail. I meant to throw it
away as Dat had all the others, but I couldn't. My birthdays
were never like they were for the other kids. There was cake
and some sort of present, but there were no smiles, no laughter, no special hugs. It was a day I didn't get excited about the

way my brothers and sisters did. But that day, when I went inside the gate at the cemetery, I was excited to see what was on Ruby's grave. It was as if someone had left a present for me . . . for *my birthday*. So that day, on the way home from school, I hid it in the oak tree. And when I was able to, I came back with this bag." She lifted it up just long enough to give it a little shake. "I did the same the next year with the silver rose, and the year after that with the snow globe and the tiny skaters inside, and—"

"The stuffed horse, the picture of the dandelion, the bubble blower thing, the torn ticket stub—"

"So, it *is* a *ticket*?" She reached inside the bag and slowly removed each item, arranging them on top of the rock in the order in which she'd found them. When she got to the torn slip of paper housed in the clear plastic covering, she took in the details she'd all but memorized and then looked up at Brad. "What was it a ticket for?"

"I took her to a carnival. The ticket was for her first ride on a Ferris wheel . . ." He fingered the clear plastic covering and, at Emma's nod, took the torn ticket in his hand. "I left these things for you, but I never dreamed you actually got them."

"I know now that these things were for me, that what I pretended for so long was actually true, but I don't understand why. Why would you leave presents for me if you thought I was dead?" she asked.

"Because I had to. To get through the day. I never got to see you, or hold you, or tell you I loved you. So I did those things the best way I could with"—he waved the ticket stub at the items spread out between them—"these things. Every year. On your birthday. My mom suggested it as a way to help me through the pain. And it worked. At least a little. It helped me feel connected. Like I was getting to celebrate your special day with you from down here.

"Even when I was away, still lashing out at the world

around me, I always came back in time to leave your next gift. Never missed a single one."

Pulling her knees to her chest, Emma considered his words, the quiet relief they allowed warming her from the inside, out. "So they really were meant for me. . . ."

"Every one of them." He rolled a thin stick between his fingers before chucking it onto the ground. "They were my way of telling you about your mom and me. The way we were, the way we loved each other. Looking back, I think getting to stand there by the grave, telling you about them, helped validate all of it for me somehow. My feelings, the relationship, all of it."

She rested her chin atop her knees. "Validate it? How so?"

"Ruby and I were seventeen and eighteen when we started up. People don't take that seriously. They call it young love and puppy love and all sorts of demeaning terms. And maybe that's the case for a lot of teen relationships, I don't know. But I know ours was real. I know my love for Ruby was real. I know I wanted a future with her and with you. And I know my world was forever turned upside down when I lost her, and then you, too."

Emma dropped her legs back down to the rock, and picked up the miniature picnic basket that had started her fifteen-year collection. "I remember peeking inside my lunch pail many times that first day. I would peek to make sure it was still there, I would peek to make sure no one else had found it, and I would peek just so I could see how pretty it was. I even wished I could take it home and play with it, but I knew I couldn't."

A darkness dulled his eyes. "And you say Wayne threw some of my gifts away?"

"I do not remember anything about my first, second, or third birthdays, but I know he did on my fourth, fifth, and sixth." She looked again at the tiny basket between her fingers. "Tell me about this first one. . . . Why a picnic basket?"

Brad met and then followed her gaze down to her hands, the anger she had sensed in him just moments earlier chased away by a soft laugh. "We had a handful of cookie picnics, Ruby and me. Most of them here, at the pond. On this very rock, in fact. She'd fill an old lunch pail with cookies she'd made. Her oatmeal ones were my favorite."

"I make oatmeal cookies! Levi likes them a lot, too—though Liddy Mast makes them for him now."

He studied her closely. "Levi? Is he your boyfriend?"

"N-no," she sputtered. "He . . . he's just a boy I know. His sister, Mary, is my best friend. I go to hymn sings with them."

His jaw tightened. "Ahhh, hymn sings. I remember those. It's where you go to find someone to court."

"It's not really like that. We go to be with others our age. But yah, many do court after meeting someone suitable at a hymn sing." Emma turned the basket over in her fingers one last time and then set it back down on the rock. "So, the basket is because you had cookie picnics?"

Shaking his head ever so slightly, he picked up the basket and studied it from all sides. "No. The basket is for the full-fledged picnic I put together for us one afternoon. I wanted her to see what an English picnic is like with the fancy basket, the traditional blanket with the red and black squares, sandwiches, grapes, chips, brownies, and Frisbee."

"Frisbee? What is that?"

"It's a round plastic disc that's about the size of a dinner plate that you can throw in the air." His grin spread into an all-out smile. "Ruby hadn't ever seen one before, either. But by the time we had to call it quits so she could get home, she'd actually gotten quite good. That's the way she was, you know. She had a way of picking things up quickly, and picking them up well."

Emma tried to imagine the game as he described, but without ever having seen it herself, she couldn't be sure she had it right. Instead, she took the conversation back to more familiar ground. "And the food? Did she like it?"

"She did. Very much. And even if she hadn't told me that again and again on the drive back to our drop-off spot, I'd have known simply because of the way her eyes sparkled the whole time."

Nodding, she moved on to her eighth birthday and the tiny rose. "What about this?" she asked, holding it atop her open palm. "Why did you give me *this*? What does it mean? And how is something so small so heavy?"

His laugh reddened her cheeks. "It's heavy because it's pewter."

"Ruby liked pewter?"

"No. I didn't give this to you because of what it's made of. I gave it to you because of what it is—a rose. Pewter just meant it wouldn't die like a real flower." He took it from her hand and held it close to his nose. "I bought her a rose once. On Valentine's Day. She said it was the prettiest flower she'd ever seen. I told her that made sense since she was the prettiest girl I'd ever seen. Because she was—the prettiest. Until I saw *you* standing in my office the other day, anyway."

Emma held her hands to her flushed cheeks and shook her head. "I'm not pretty. I'm Amish. We're *plain* people."

"Funny thing is, I used to think that about Amish girls, too. To me, they all dressed the same, covered their hair the same, didn't use makeup like the girls in my high school, didn't wear rings or necklaces or anything like that. And then I met Ruby. She didn't need that red garbage on her cheeks or all that stuff on her eyes. All she had to do was smile at me. Or laugh at something I said. Heck, even when she cried she was beautiful."

"Ruby cried with you?" At his slow, labored nod, she drew back. "Why? Was it because of me? Because I was coming?"

"No, Emma. It wasn't because of you. It was because . . ." He glanced across the pond, seemingly oblivious to the pewter rose he still held between his fingers. "Sometimes life just seems a little uncertain. A little scary, you know? Some people deal with it by yelling or stamping around. Others get quiet or cry. It's life."

"The Amish are not to yell and stamp around."

Closing his hand around the rose, he sighed. "I know."

She waited to see what else he'd say, but, when he remained silent, she moved on to the present that had marked her ninth birthday.

"I loved this one." Scooping up the tiny snow globe, she took a quick look at the skaters inside, shook her hand, and grinned as snow fell down around the couple inside. "I know it is silly, but I would pretend it was me in there skating. Only I would pretend the girl was wearing a kapp and a dress like me."

"She did."

Startled, Emma looked at him across the top of the clear, plastic dome. "I don't understand."

"The girl *did* wear a kapp and dress." Turning Emma's hand so he, too, could see inside, Brad continued. "I took Ruby skating one afternoon. I borrowed some skates from a girl at school and I took Ruby to the pond next to my house. While we were there, it started snowing just like this."

Emma returned her attention to the figures now covered with white flecks. "Did she like it?"

"She loved it. Took her a little while to get the hang of it, but by the time we were done, she was trying to make patterns in the ice by turning in little circles." He dropped his hands to the rock and leaned back. "Whenever I hear her laugh in my thoughts, it's from that day."

"I wish *I* could hear her laugh," Emma whispered.

"I do, too, kiddo."

Again, she looked at the skaters. Only this time, instead of the happiness they'd always stirred inside her, there was a sadness she didn't want to feel. Not with him—

"Emma? Are you okay?"

Setting the globe back on the rock, she shrugged off his question in favor of her tenth birthday gift—the stuffed horse. "It took me the whole walk here that day to come up with just the right name for her, but I did." Emma ran her fingers down the toy's silky mane and then handed it to Brad. "I called her Sugar. Still do."

"*Sugar* . . . I like that." He turned the horse over, inspected it from all angles, and then set it back down.

"Her color made me think of the cinnamon sugar Mamm— I mean, *Rebeccah*—sometimes puts on the top of her apple pie. If she forgets, someone is always quick to remind her."

Brad's jaw noticeably tightened, yet he said nothing.

"One time, last year, when Esther had just turned four, she was helping me make an apple pie. She was standing on the bench so she could see what I was doing and she noticed I hadn't put the cinnamon sugar on yet. When my back was turned doing something else, she dumped the whole jar onto the top." Emma's laugh echoed in the cool winter air. "*That* was too much sugar. Even for Esther."

"My mom—your grandmother—makes a great apple pie. It even won a ribbon at the county fair one year. She would have loved getting to teach you how to make it." Brad pushed forward, raking a hand through his hair as he did. "*If* she'd had the chance, of course."

She stilled her hand just shy of her eleventh birthday gift and swallowed. "I am sorry I did not find you sooner. I did not know."

"*You're* sorry?" he echoed, his voice thunderous. "*You're* sorry? For what? For being told you belonged to someone who had no right to claim you? For having no reason to believe you'd been lied to? For living the lie that had been forced on you and forced on me? Please, Emma. There are only two people who are responsible for this situation and it's not you and it's not me. They're the ones who should be sorry—*will* be sorry, if I have anything to say about—"

The telltale snap of a twig from the direction of the road brought Emma to her feet. "Shhh. Did you hear that? I think someone is . . ." Her words faded off as a quick flash of blue pulled her gaze toward a gnarled tree not more than two buggy lengths away.

"Who's there?" Brad called out as he, too, stood.

Seconds later, a familiar round face peered around the tree, causing Emma to stumble back a half step. "Esther!"

The single crunch that had guided their focus toward the child turned into a series of crunches as Esther covered the distance between them in short order.

"Hi, Emma!" A bright smile pushed the five-year-old's cheeks nearly to her eyes just before she wrapped her arms around Emma's legs. "I looked and looked for you and now I found you!"

Prying the little girl's arms away, Emma squatted down. "Esther, what are you doing here? And where is"—she looked toward the road—"Annie or Sarah or whoever you're with?"

"It is just me! Annie and Sarah are home with Mamm."

She sucked in a breath. "Esther! You are not to come so far by yourself!"

"But I had to share my school cookie with you!" Esther opened her hand to reveal a crumbled cookie half and then slid her attention off Emma and onto Brad. "Hi! What's your name? Are you Emma's friend?"

"My name is Brad and I'm Emma's—"

Grabbing hold of Esther's free hand, Emma stood, her face warm. "Every morning, I-I put two cookies in Esther's lunch pail for her to eat. But each day, she brings half of one back home to me."

"It is a very good cookie," Esther said, her expression earnest. "Here, Emma. Eat it."

"Okay, okay." She took the cookie, offered some to Brad, and, when he declined, popped it into her mouth. "Mmm . . ."

Satisfied, Esther wiggled free and ran to the rock. "Emma, look! It is like a store!"

She followed the tip of the child's finger to the now empty bag and the contents she'd lined up in a row beside it. Before

she could think, let alone speak, Esther scooped up the bubble wand and gazed up at Brad. "Did you bring bubbles, too?
'Cause I love bubbles!"

"No! He didn't." Mouthing an apology across the top of
her sister's head, Emma gathered up all of the gifts, stuffed
them inside the bag, and handed it to Brad. "I need to get her
back to the farm. She's too little to be out here alone."

He looked from Esther, to the bag, and, finally, back at
Emma. "But we have more to go through, more to talk
about."

"I know. And we will. Tomorrow."

Chapter 11

She allowed Esther one final wave at the shiny black truck and then captured the little girl's hand inside her own. "Come now, Esther. It is time to get you home. Mamm will be worried if she discovers you are not in the barn."

"*You* are not in the barn."

"I'm older than you are. I don't have to be in the barn."

The crunch of gravel beneath Esther's feet slowed as she looked over her shoulder and then back up at Emma. "Is that man your friend, Emma?"

"No, he's..." She squeezed her eyes closed, silently counted to ten, and then opened them to find the five-year-old staring up at her, mouth agape. "He is just someone I am getting to know—someone I should have known long before now."

"Can I know him, too?"

"Perhaps. Maybe. I-I don't know." Desperate for a change in topic, Emma pointed at the Weavers' horse rooting around the dormant field and worked to infuse a lightness into her voice that she didn't feel. "Now, is that one *Dolly* or is that one *Molly*?"

Esther's gaze followed Emma's to the upcoming fence line and the solitary mare. "That is Molly."

"How can you tell?"

Esther tugged her hand free and ran over to the fence, her finger pointing. "See her eyes? She has black in the middle. Dolly doesn't have black. Only brown. Like the man's horse."

"What man's horse?" she asked, motioning her sister back to the road for the final stretch of their walk.

"The man you are getting to know."

She stopped, mid-step, as Esther ran back to her side. "Brad does not have a horse," Emma corrected. "He has a truck."

"It was on the rock! It was brown, like Dolly."

And then she knew. Esther was talking about Sugar, the stuffed horse Brad had left at Ruby's gravesite on Emma's tenth birthday. Scanning the Weavers' field to the left, she searched for yet another way to distract Esther, but before she could settle on something, Esther began hopping up and down.

"He drawed a heart on a rock."

"*Drew,*" she corrected as her own thoughts returned to the pond and the present she'd found on her fourteenth birthday.

"Why did he drew on a rock?"

Leaning down, Emma tapped her sister on the nose. "Actually, that time it's *draw.* And I don't know why. You showed up just as we were getting to the—"

"He had a red ball that was very dirty!"

"It wasn't dirty," Emma protested. "It is just old, and someone wrote on it."

Emma pulled a face. "Balls are for throwing, Emma. And rocks are for touching. Paper is for writing."

"That is true. But I am sure there is a reason. We just didn't get to those things yet." She held out her hand and, when Esther took it, began walking again. "Why did you leave the farm, Esther? You know you are not supposed to do that."

"I had to share my cookie. But you were not there to share it."

"That's right, I wasn't."

"But you're *always* home to share my cookie, Emma."

"I know, sweetie, but things are different now."

Esther peered up at Emma. "Why? Don't you like sharing cookies with me anymore?"

"Of course I do. I-I love sharing cookies with you. But, well, I need to figure out some things is all and—"

"I can help you, Emma! I am learning lots of things at school! Watch!" Esther pulled her hand free and hurried into Emma's path. "A, B, C, D, E, F, G . . ."

Emma grinned. "Come on, what's next?"

Esther tapped her chin, once, twice, and then squealed. "H! I, J, K, L, M, N, O, P!"

"Very good, Esther!" Emma clapped her hands and then squatted down for a big hug. When Esther stepped into her arms, she lingered a kiss against the little girl's kapp. "That's four more letters than last week! You will know the whole alphabet soon!"

"When I do, I can help you figure out things!"

Oh how she wished it were that simple. If it were, maybe she wouldn't feel so alone, so unsettled.

"Mamm's eyes look like that, too," Esther said, pointing at Emma's face.

"Like what?"

"Sad."

She fought against the familiar worry trying to gain a foothold in her heart and made herself shrug, instead. "No, my birthday is over, sweetie. Mamm only gets sad on my birthday. You'll get used to it. *I* certainly did."

"Mamm made me wet *here*." Esther reached into her shoulder through the open neckline of her black coat. "But I got dry before I came to find you with your cookie."

"Slow down a minute. Mamm made you *wet*?"

"Yah. She hugged me like this"—Esther wrapped her arms

around herself and then dropped them to her side—"and her tears got me wet."

Emma drew back. "Mamm was crying?"

"Yah."

"Why?"

Esther's little shoulders slumped beneath her coat. "I don't know. Maybe her tummy hurts."

Or maybe she is worried she will be shunned for her lies . . .

Standing, she reached for Esther's hand again. "Maybe. Now come on, sweetie, it's time I get you home."

They were just passing the barn when the bang of the farmhouse door pulled Emma's gaze off the baby calf she and Esther were laughing about and fixed it on the woman hurrying down the porch steps.

It was a sight she'd seen many times during her life, yet suddenly nothing about it was the same. Now, instead of thinking *Mamm,* she thought *Rebeccah* and *liar.* And now, instead of hurrying her own feet in response, she stopped, tightened her hold on Esther, and fisted her free hand at her side.

"Esther Lapp, where have you been, child? Annie is searching the fields looking for you, and I sent Sarah to the Troyers' to see if you'd chased a barn cat onto their farm." Mamm's brown eyes bore into Esther's before lifting upward to meet Emma's. "Emma? Was she with you?"

"She found me." Emma lifted Esther's focus off the ground and back to her face as it had been off and on for most of their walk home. "Go on. Tell her."

Toeing the ground, the five-year-old stepped closer to Emma, her cheeks red with shame. "I . . . went to . . . the pond. To find Emma."

"Esther Lapp!"

"I always give her the rest of my cookie," Esther protested, her voice shaky. "Emma was not in the house or the barn. I founded her at the pond."

Emma squeezed the little girl's hand, gently. "*Found*."

"Found," Esther corrected.

Uncertainty guided the woman's gaze back to Emma. "Were you at the pond alone?"

Esther brightened. "I said hi to her friend, Mamm! He said hi, too!"

When Esther pulled her hand from Emma's, Emma folded her arms and nodded. "That's right. She met Brad. My real—"

"Esther, you are to go inside. I need to talk—"

"His horse looks like Dolly, Mamm!"

Surprise propelled the woman back a step. "The Englisher has a horse?"

Giggling, Esther shook her head. Hard. "Not a real horse, Mamm. A toy! And he had a red ball, too! A dirty one. But Emma said it is not dirty. She said someone writed things on it. Isn't that silly, Mamm?"

Emma opened her mouth to correct her sister's grammar but let it go as the little girl began to hop up and down. "He had lots of toys, Mamm! And he isn't little, like me. He is great big like Dat!"

"Toys?" Rebeccah echoed.

"Yah. The ones *he*"—Emma pointed toward the bearded and hatted man in the farthest field they could see—"did not throw away. The ones I got to first."

Esther stopped hopping. "*Dat*?"

Squatting down, Emma redirected Esther's attention toward the eight-year-old walking across the dirt, searching. "You know what? You should go tell Annie that you are home so she can stop looking for you. Then go with her to the Troyers' to tell Sarah. I think they have spent enough time looking for you, wouldn't you say?"

Shame reddened Esther's cheeks once again. "Yah."

"Good. Now go."

Emma watched the little girl run across the driveway and into the field, Esther's kapp strings flopping against her tiny shoulders. When she was certain Annie saw Esther, she stood and turned back to Rebeccah. "Ever since I was seven, I have gone to the cemetery before breakfast. That first year, I did it because I wanted to make the day better for you and for"— again she gestured toward the far field—"*him*. I knew I could not stop your tears for the sister you lost, but I thought I could keep Dat from getting angry. I tried to throw the trinket away, but I could not. It made me happy, the way someone should be on their birthday—the way Jakob, Annie, Sarah, Jonathan, and Esther could be because your sister did not die on their special day. So I kept it in a bag in a special place, and I added to it each year."

"You should not have kept such things!"

"Why? They weren't for you or Dat. They weren't for Ruby, either. They were for me. *Me!*" She narrowed her eyes until she couldn't see Annie, Esther, the fields, or anything else beyond the pale-faced woman standing just inches away. "Brad thought I died with Ruby. No, he was *told* I died with Ruby. By you! Those things he left on the grave weren't for Ruby. They were *for me*. For *my birthday*."

She jerked back at the feel of Rebeccah's hand on hers. "Don't!"

"Emma, please. There are things Dat and I want to—"

"You mean *him*?" She pointed at the far field, once again. "Because that's not my dat. *Brad* is my dat. Or should I say *father* since he is *English*?"

"Emma, I know you're upset. But if you would just talk to me, to us, we—"

"Perhaps that is something you should have done many years ago."

"Emma—"

"What is there to say? That I should not go to Bishop King? That you did not mean to lie to me and to my birth father? That you and *Wayne* did not pretend to be my . . ." The squeak of the barn door stole the rest of her words and sent her gaze racing toward the barn in time to see Jonathan walking toward them, cradling something in the crook of his arm.

"Emma! Mamm! Look what I found near Mini's water pail."

She held Rebeccah's wary eyes for several beats and then found the smile the twelve-year-old sought as he stopped at Emma's elbow. Leaning forward, she patted his sleeve down just enough to afford a clear view of the tiny mound of white and gray matted fur. "Oooh, I see Bean had her babies . . ."

"She did. There's four more next to the water pail, too."

"And Bean?" Emma prodded.

"She's already licking them," Jonathan declared.

"Then you probably should get this one back before the new mamma gets upset." Emma stroked the tiny kitten between the ears. "I'll bring Esther in to see the new additions when she gets back with Annie and Sarah."

Jonathan's eyes disappeared beneath the rim of his hat only to reappear as he gazed back up at Emma. "Aren't you going to say it?"

She knew what he was asking. And why wouldn't he? She'd been greeting every newcomer to the barn the same way since before Jonathan was even born . . .

Not wanting to disappoint, she leaned across her brother's arm and planted a soft kiss atop the newborn kitten's head. "Welcome to your home, little one."

"That's not how you say it," Jonathan admonished as he headed back toward the barn. "You say, 'Welcome home.' Not 'Welcome to *your* home.'"

When he was safely out of earshot, she turned back to Rebeccah. "Soon we must tell them."

"Them?"

"The children."

"Emma, I—"

"They should know what I did not. They should know that this was never meant to be my home." Sidestepping her way around the woman she'd once believed to be her mamm, Emma willed her stoicism to remain as she gave voice to the last of her new truths. "And that I was never meant to be their sister."

Chapter 12

"I'm sorry that took so long, Emma." Sue Ellen deposited the phone into its base and quietly folded her arms across the top of her meticulously kept desk. "My job with your father is full of peaks and valleys."

Emma stilled her fidgeting fingers. "You are to climb sometimes?"

"Climb? No, I . . ." A knowing smile crept across the sixty-something's face. " 'Peaks and valleys' is an expression, dear. It means there are moments when I sit here twiddling my thumbs. And other times, I have customers in the office, suppliers on the phone, and contractors coming in and out, asking me this, that, and the other.

"Case in point, I was actually getting in a little reading not more than five minutes before you got here. But the second I noticed the door opening, the same supplier I've been trying to reach since yesterday afternoon finally decides to return my call."

"That's okay." Emma smoothed a small wrinkle from her lap and then pointed toward the open office behind Sue Ellen. "He's not here?"

"He had to step out for a little bit, but he won't be long. You can wait at his desk if you'd like."

She studied what she could see of Brad's office from her seat—the large desk, the fancy chair, the bookshelves filled with books and framed pictures—and shook her head. "No. If it is okay, I would like to sit here. I will not be a bother."

"You're not a bother, sweetheart! In fact, you're a breath of fresh air on an otherwise dreary, sunless day." Sue Ellen pushed back her chair, stood, and came around the desk, her pale green eyes narrowed on Emma. "Can I get you something to drink?"

"No thank you. I will just wait."

"If you change your mind, let me know." The woman wandered over to the row of framed photographs that had claimed Emma's attention during her phone call. "Your father is a good man, Emma. A hard worker. Built this company by himself. From the ground up. And it's only been six years."

Inching forward, Emma pointed to the center picture. "Why do so many people smile as he cuts a ribbon?"

"That was the ribbon cutting ceremony that started all of *this*." Sue Ellen splayed her hands. "It was the start of Harper Construction as you see it today. This building, the crews, my job, all of it. Now, there are Harper houses sprinkled all over Lancaster County, and we're getting ready to break ground on our first full-blown Harper neighborhood. It's all very exciting, Emma. And you're part of it now."

"Me?"

"Of course. Everyone in Brad's family is involved in some way. Brad's mom consults with customers on color schemes—countertops, appliances, paint, etc.; Brad's uncle helps with odds and ends as his health allows; and you? Well, I guess you two will figure that out. Together."

"But I . . . I'm . . ." She let the rest of her words go in favor of the obvious. An obvious that had her sitting in an English office in an aproned dress, black lace-up boots, and a white kapp.

Abandoning her position beside the wall, Sue Ellen crossed to the empty chair beside Emma, the animation she'd shown only seconds earlier all but gone. "I can only imagine what these past few days have been like for you, dear. Are you holding up okay?"

Was she? She didn't know. If she wasn't actively spending time with her birth father, she was wandering around in a daze, the near constant roar in her ears making it difficult to think through anything in its entirety.

"I don't know," she whispered, looking down at her lap. "Everything is different. My mamm and dat are not my mamm and dat. My aunt was not my aunt—*she* was my mamm. And my *real* dat is *English*."

Sue Ellen's gentle hand quietly stilled Emma's trembling one. "It's a lot for anyone to try to process. Your whole world has literally been turned upside down. But Brad will be by your side every step of the way, I know he will. And, for what it's worth, I'm here, too. I may never have walked in your shoes, Emma, but I'm a mighty fine listener and I've been told my hugs have a way of making things a little better."

"Your hugs?"

"My niece showed up in the middle of the night one time to get one of my hugs."

Emma drew back. "She was not sleeping?"

"She was cramming for one of her last exams at college and she needed an energy boost," Sue Ellen said, laughing at the memory. "When I opened the door and saw her standing there, I thought something bad had happened. But she just told me she was doubting herself in terms of the test and needed something to get her over the hump, so to speak. I reminded her that chocolate works beautifully for me in that regard, and that's when she told me my hugs were *her* chocolate. Tickled me to no end to hear that."

"Did the hug work?"

Sue Ellen nodded. "She aced the test."

"Is that good?"

The woman's momentary confusion parted in favor of yet another nod and laugh. "It means she passed the test with flying colors!"

The roar was still there, and everything was still as daunting as ever. But, for just a moment, something about Sue Ellen's lighthearted voice made Emma feel a little less alone. A little more—

"You're going to pass all of this with flying colors, too, Emma. I just know it."

She allowed herself one good, deep breath as she, again, met Sue Ellen's eye. "But I am not in college. I am not taking such a test."

"You're right. You're not." Pausing, Sue Ellen cupped Emma's cheek in her hand. "But when you're ready to make the leap into this world for good, who knows where you might go and what you might do in life. The sky's the limit for you now, dear. Your father will move heaven and earth to make sure of that."

Slipping his fingers inside the bag's narrow opening, Brad tugged outward until his entire hand could reach inside. "You're sure you're okay with going through the rest of your presents here at the office instead of back at the pond?"

Emma turned from the window overlooking the back parking lot and managed a nod. "Yah. It has gotten colder since I rode my scooter here."

"I'm sorry I was so late getting back here. My meeting went a little longer than anticipated." One by one, Brad set fifteen years' worth of birthday gifts across the top of his desk and then tossed the drawstring bag onto a nearby shelf. "So, did Sue Ellen take good care of you while you were waiting?"

She wandered back to her chair and lowered herself to its edge. "Yah, I—"

"Oh! I didn't tell you. . . . My mom is due back from her sister's sometime in the next"—he peered at his silver link watch—"three hours or so. I figure I'll either be there when she arrives, or stop by shortly thereafter, to tell her the big news."

"There is big news?"

He pulled a face only to let it dissolve into a smile. "Um, hello . . . My daughter—her *granddaughter*—is alive and well." He picked up the baseball and turned it over in his hands. "You could go with me, if you want. Really bring home the surprise."

Looking up at the ceiling, he shook his head. "Can you imagine? *Hey, Mom . . . The baby didn't actually die with Ruby. She's actually been living with her kidnappers for the past twenty-two years. And . . . ta da . . . here she is.*" He turned the ball over one last time and then deposited it back atop his desk. "Yeah, probably a bit too jarring, huh?"

She knew he was still talking. His facial expressions told her that. But her thoughts kept returning to one particular word and the way it made her stomach feel the way it did when she thought about Esther wandering away from the farm. "Wait."

His eyes lit on hers. "You okay, Emma?"

Pressing her hand to her stomach in an attempt to stop the sudden yet definitive swirl inside, she made herself breathe. "You called Mamm and Dat *kidnappers*."

"Because that's what they are."

"But . . ." She thought back over the many newspaper and magazine headlines she'd seen in the English grocery stores while growing up and, as her mind's eye narrowed in on a few, she gasped. "But kidnappers *steal* people!"

His blue eyes darkened. "That's right. They do."

"They . . . they . . ." She stopped, swallowed, and tried again, the swirling in her stomach growing all the more urgent. "They didn't *steal* me. They just didn't tell me I was Ruby's baby."

"And *my* baby." The wheels of his chair thumped against the floor as he stood. "I'm your father, Emma. That means you belonged to me—that I should have left that house with you that day. Only I didn't. Because Wayne told me you didn't make it and I believed him. And for the next twenty-two years they raised you as their own. Unbeknownst to me."

He stopped midway to the window and turned back. "Unbeknownst. To. Me. That's kidnapping, Emma, in every sense of the word."

"But they just didn't tell us," she whispered. "I know it was a terrible lie. I have even thought about telling the bishop so they will be shunned. But—"

His half laugh, half snort echoed around them. "*Shunned?*"

"Yah. It means the members of our district will turn their backs to them until they repent and—"

He shot his hand up, stopping her explanation. "Trust me, kiddo, I know all about the way the Amish work. The way they govern."

"The Amish do not *govern*," she protested. "When one is baptized they vow to—"

"Remain Amish. To live *in* the world but not *like* the world. I know. I got it. But there are laws in this country that everyone must follow. Including the Amish. And when people break them, there are consequences—consequences that are, thankfully, blind to hats and beards. In theory, the jurors should be as well."

The rhythmic tapping of her booted toes against the carpet broke through the mental roar kicked off by his words. Shifting her hand from her stomach to her knee, she pressed down until the motion stopped. "I-I don't feel well right now."

Like the overhead lights the English flicked on and off with a switch, the anger Brad wore bowed to concern. For her. He covered the gap between them with two long strides, and squatted down beside her chair. "What can I do? Do you want some water? Some air? What?"

"Maybe some . . . *air?*"

"You got it." He bounced back up, strode toward the window, and lifted it up a few inches. "How about some water, too?"

With her leg steady, she returned her hand to her stomach. "Yah."

He stepped over to his desk, tapped a button on a small brown box, and, when Sue Ellen's voice appeared through it, he asked for a water. Less than a minute later, Emma had her water, and she and Brad were alone once again.

"Look, kiddo, I didn't mean to upset you. The whole reason I put my guy on this is so I can focus on us. So let's let him do his thing while we do ours, okay?" With purposeful steps, he returned to his chair and swept his hands toward the top of his desk. "So, shall we get back to this?"

Nodding, she reorganized the items to match the order in which she'd found them and then picked up the picture of the dandelion from her eleventh birthday. "Sarah and I would always race to see who could blow on these the fastest. I would always win until Sarah got bigger. Now, it does not take Sarah many puffs, and Annie is very good at it, too. Once, it took Annie only one big puff!"

"Sarah and Annie—those are Wayne and Rebeccah's, right?"

Wayne and Rebeccah's . . .

"Yah. Sarah is sixteen. Annie is eight."

"And there are how many others?"

"Three. Jakob, Jonathan, and Esther."

Grabbing a pen from a holder to his right, Brad jotted something on a small notepad and then shoved it off to the side. "Okay . . . So the dandelion picture . . ." His chair creaked as he leaned back against his chair. "I'm not sure why, but the English—as you call us—don't just blow on dandelions when they turn white like that. We *make a wish* while we blow."

"A wish? Why?"

"I don't really know. It's just something kids, and sometimes even adults, do. It's like wishing on a birthday candle, though I'm not sure it holds as much weight. Depends on who you ask. But my mom taught me to make a wish every opportunity I had. So birthday candles, dandelion fluff, pennies in fountains, and the wishbone from the turkey on Thanksgiving were all fair game as far as I was concerned." He tented his fingers beneath his chin and grinned. "Of course, Ruby thought I was crazy the first time I handed her a dandelion and told her to make a wish and blow."

She looked from Brad, to the picture, and back again. "Did she?"

His laugh eased the last of the tension from her body, allowing her to finally relax into the back of her own chair. "She blew, but she didn't make a wish. So I handed her another one and told her to try again. That time, she supposedly made a wish, but she kept her eyes open."

"I don't understand."

"Wishes don't work if you don't close your eyes." Dropping his hands, he lurched forward, plucked up the picture, and gazed down at it, the skin around his eyes crinkling with amusement. "So I picked up another one and, that time, *I* made the wish. Closed my eyes and everything.

"When I was done, I opened them to find I'd been successful in scattering the fluff and that Ruby was watching me with the biggest smile, her head cocked just like this." He tilted his chin a hairbreadth. "When I told her that's how she was supposed to do it, she asked me what I'd wished for. I told her I couldn't tell her, or it wouldn't come true."

"Did it?" Emma asked. "Come true, I mean . . ."

Righting his head, Brad took one last look at the picture and then set it back down on the desk in front of Emma. "On your eleventh birthday, when I set this reminder of that special moment on the grave, I'd have said no. But now, with you sitting here? Yeah, it came true. In a form very different than I imagined when I made it, but it's still true, nonetheless."

She hovered her fingertips above the dandelion stem and

tried to imagine a younger Brad sitting in a field of dande-lions with the girl from her locket. When she had a fuzzy version of it, she looked up. "What was your wish?"

"For Ruby to be part of my life forever."

"But she's not," Emma protested.

A softer yet no less genuine smile reclaimed his lips. "In the sense I envisioned as an eighteen-year-old, no, she's not. But having you here"—he splayed his hands around the office—"in my life, changes that."

Emma pulled her hand away from the picture and braced it on the edge of the desk. "But I am not Ruby."

"But you're a living, breathing part of her, Emma. And there are times, when you look at me the way you are right now, it's like looking at Ruby all over again. Like all the bad stuff never happened." He reached out, patted the top of Emma's hand, and then leaned back in his chair once again. "I'd consider that an answered wish, all things considered."

She took another sip of her water and then set the bottle on the floor. "Did she try again? After you showed her how to do it?"

"You mean with the wish?" He returned her nod with one of his own. "She did. Don't know what she wished for, but I know she kept her eyes closed even after the fluff was scattered. Like whatever she was wishing for was taking a little time.

"I teased her about it when she was done. Asked her if she was wishing for an ice cream cone. But right before we came across all those dandelions, we'd been dreaming out loud about what I might want to do for a career, and what we'd like our one-day house to be like. I guess that's why I've always figured it had to do with one or both of those."

It was a lot to take in. A lot to add to the image she'd managed to conjure of the encounter. Swapping the picture for her twelfth birthday present, she held up the bubble wand. "And this?"

"I surprised her one day with a jar of bubbles. We practically used the entire jar that same day. I showed her how to make double bubbles, and she showed me how to make really long ones. We laughed a lot that day. And she jumped, too . . ."

"Jumped?"

"Ruby would do this little jump when she was excited about something—bubbles, skating, it didn't matter. If she was happy, she did her little jump."

She placed the wand next to what remained of the carnival ticket and moved on to the rock with the sparkly heart drawn on it. "Did Ruby draw this heart?"

Resting his left foot atop his right knee, he nodded. "She sure did. My cousin left a sparkly marker at my house the previous day and I gave it to Ruby. Next thing I knew, she was drawing that heart on a rock she found at the pond and giving it to me. Kept it in my room at Mom's for years. When I came back on your birthday that year to leave my annual gift, I decided to leave the rock because it wasn't more than a week after she drew that heart that she told me she was carrying you."

Emma snapped her attention off the rock and onto Brad. "Were you scared when she told you about me?"

"Nope. I was excited. As far as I was concerned, you being on the way just made us more real somehow. In a good way. Besides, it was just one more reason for us to get married like we wanted to—or like *I* wanted to, at least." Brad dropped his foot back to the ground with a thud. "So, what's next?"

"Next? I . . ." She followed the path of his finger back to the desk and the items she'd all but forgotten as his words had transported her back to a time when Ruby was alive and Emma had been on the way . . .

"The red and black checked napkin, right?" Brad prompted. At her nod, he slid the piece of cloth in her direction until she relinquished the rock in its favor. "Remember that picnic I told you about? The one I put together to show her what an English picnic was like?"

"Yah . . ."

"She planned one a week later. To show *me* what an *Amish* picnic is like." His gaze lifted to the wall just beyond her head but seemed to fix on something far beyond his office. "I guess I'd tucked the napkin in my pocket at some point along the way and didn't realize it was there until I was back home afterward."

Emma pulled the napkin close and tried to imagine Ruby packing it inside a lunch pail along with the food she'd surely prepared. "You spent so much time together. Did my grosselders know about you?"

Shaking his focus back into the room, he looked at Emma. "At that point, no. Eventually, they had to. But you have to remember, when we met, Ruby hadn't officially been baptized yet, so it's not like she was breaking any vows or anything by spending time with me. Still, I know they weren't pleased once they learned of my existence for obvious reasons. . . . I know I wasn't that Gingerich guy and that my involvement with Ruby put the kibosh on that. . . . I know I wasn't *Amish*. . . .

"But you can see, from all of this"—he spread his hands wide to indicate the collection of memories spread across his desk—"that we had something special. Something real. Something worth sticking with. Different doesn't have to mean wrong."

A soft yet staccato tapping sent their collective focus toward the now open office door and Sue Ellen's wide eyes peeking into the room. "Boss? I'm sorry to interrupt, but your mother called and asked me to let you know she should be arriving back at her place around five and she's hoping you'll come for dinner."

Glancing at his watch, Brad pushed back from the desk. "So I've got about thirty minutes if I want to be there when she arrives. . . . Okay, thanks, Sue Ellen."

"You got it." The secretary's head disappeared from view only to return a half second later. "Oh, one more thing. I touched base with the crew and let them know you'll be out of town Monday and Tuesday and will likely want a meeting with everyone here Thursday morning. Eight a.m. sharp."

"Perfect."

"Is there anything else I can do?" Sue Ellen asked, sending a smile in Emma's direction before looking back at Brad. "For you, or for Emma?"

He shook his head and then winked at Emma. "No, we're good. But it's Friday and the crews are probably calling it a day out at their respective sites, so why don't you pack it up and head home, too. Enjoy your weekend."

"Thanks, Boss. That sounds perfect." Sue Ellen wiggled her fingers around the edge of the door in a happy wave. "You two have fun this weekend. And kiss the proud new grandma for me when you tell her the good news."

"You can count on that." As Sue Ellen pulled the door closed, Brad stood, his excitement palpable. "So, what do you say we save the rest of these stories for tomorrow? That way I can get you out to the farm, and me to my mother's place before she gets back."

She retrieved the water bottle from the floor and set it, instead, on the table. "Yah. But I can get myself home. I have my scooter."

He grabbed the bag off the shelf and held it open as, one by one, Emma put her birthday presents back inside. When the only one left was the napkin she'd set beside her water, she scooped it up and lingered her gaze on the cheerful pattern. "May I ask what Ruby made for your Amish picnic?"

Relinquishing his hold on the bag, Brad wandered over to the window, his voice taking on a seemingly faraway quality. "She made the best fried chicken I ever had, these potatoes that practically slid down my throat, and a slice of homemade bread with apple butter. When that was done, there was a slice of apple pie and two oatmeal cookies. No Frisbee, though."

It was the kind of picnic Emma would likely pack for Levi if she could. If he fancied her the way he did Liddy Mast . . .

"Penny for your thoughts?"

Startled, she looked up to find his back now flush to the window and his attention trained solely on her. "I was just thinking of a friend who likes oatmeal cookies, too."

"Levi?"

"H-how did you know?" she stammered.

"You mentioned him the other day." Bracing his hands on the lip of the sill behind him, he watched her fidget the picnic napkin between her fingers. "You said he was just a friend. Maybe someone's brother?"

"Yah. He is Mary's brother."

"And Mary is one of your friends?"

She didn't mean to laugh. But something about his question and the way in which he said it made it impossible to react any other way. "Mary is my *only* friend."

His brows, like his mouth, seemed to frown. "I don't believe that. . . ."

"It is true. Mary does not see me as others do."

"How do others see you?"

"As someone who does not belong. But I do not think it is that way with Levi. I think Levi does not see me at all." She added the napkin to the bag and pulled it closed with the string. "I will stop out at the pond on the way back to the farm and put this back inside the tree. Perhaps you can tell me about the rest of the presents tomorrow or one day next week."

He pushed away from the window and joined her at the desk, his hand coming down atop the bag as he did. "If Levi does not see you, he is blind. His problem, not yours. And the other part? About not belonging? That's about to change, I assure you of that."

Her head was shaking before he'd even finished his sentence. "It won't change. Ever. Because *I* can't change. I know this now."

"Why do you have to change anything?"

"Please. It is getting late. You must go." With the help of

her chin, she led his gaze off her face and onto the wall clock to her left.

His answering sigh was muted by his hand just before it slid down his own chin. "You're right. We need to wrap this up for now. But we will talk more about this tomorrow, okay?"

She looked past him to the window and what she could see of the February sky beyond. Soon dusk would begin to settle across a day in which she hadn't done any chores. When it did, Dat and the boys would come in from the fields hungry for a dinner she, once again, had no part in preparing.

It was only a matter of time before Sarah's and Annie's curious glances over Emma's lengthy and unexplained absences morphed into fully formed questions. Especially if she spent the bulk of yet another day away from the farm. But she needed answers. Different answers than the ones her siblings would soon have.

"Emma?" he prodded, stepping forward. "I *will* see you tomorrow, right?"

She looked down at the strong hand now resting on her forearm and then back up into the eyes of the only person truly capable of providing those answers. "Yah. Tomorrow."

Chapter 13

One by one, Emma took the eggs from Esther's quick-moving hand and added them to the same basket the task demanded each morning—a basket she, herself, had made when she wasn't much older than Esther. She tried to keep count as the little girl's hand maneuvered its way around curious chickens and through piles of straw, but Esther's running commentary on the latest additions to the barn was making even simple math difficult. Still, she was pretty sure they were up to fifteen, maybe six—

"I helped Bean clean the brown and white kitty." Esther pulled an egg through the door of the chicken coop and handed it to Emma. "Her eyes look like *this,* see?"

Emma deposited the final egg into the basket and then looked up to find the five-year-old peeking out at her from otherwise closed eyes. "You mean the kitty?" At Esther's nod, Emma stood and brushed some loose straw from her dress. "That's because she's a newborn. It takes a little while for them to open their eyes. But when she does—assuming she's a girl, of course—I bet she'll be really curious about you."

"She has to be a girl. I gave her a girl's name." After a final wave to the chickens, Esther wrapped her hand around Emma's and began to tug. "Her name is Flower, and you can't hardly hear her meow."

"What has you in such a hurry this morning?" Emma asked. "Usually *I'm* the one pulling *you* away from the chickens."

Esther pointed toward the barn. "I want you to see Flower and all the other kitties, too!"

Emma swung her gaze from the barn, to the fields, and, finally, to the side yard and Sarah. On any other morning, Emma would take the eggs into the house, make sure Esther, Annie, and Jonathan were ready for school or, in today's case, their list of Saturday chores, and then join Sarah at the clothesline or Mamm in the garden.

But it wasn't any other morning. Nor had it been any other morning since she set off for her birthday visit to the cemetery some twelve days earlier.

"Come on, Emma! Flower is waiting for me to say good morning."

She followed along for a moment, only to stop as they reached the open barn doors. "Esther, I can't. I have something I have to do today—somewhere I have to go."

The pressure on her hand intensified and then released as Esther's shoulders slumped. "I don't want you to be gone again, Emma. You keep going away and I miss you. I want to help you bake bread, I want to watch you quilt, I want to sit on your lap and hear stories, and I want you to see Flower and all of Bean's new kitties!"

Squatting down, Emma bobbed her head until the sad eyes she sought were trained solely on her face. "I'm sorry, Esther. I know I haven't been around very much. But there is someone I must see. Someone I need to know."

"Is it the man with the toys?"

She glanced over her shoulder toward the house as she scrambled for an answer that wouldn't be more of the same lies, yet also wouldn't stoke the same old medley of anger, fear, and confusion that kept her awake most nights now. It was a tricky balance, no doubt. "Yah."

"I can come with you," Esther suggested. "I like toys, too!"

"You do?" Emma teased. "I didn't know that!" Then, tapping the little girl on the nose, Emma jutted her own chin toward the open barn doors. "You know what? I could take a few minutes to meet Flower. But not too long, okay?"

Esther rose up on the tips of her shoes, spun around, and then beckoned for Emma to follow her inside, her excitement over Bean's new kittens turning her walk into more of an all-out run. "Look! Look, Emma!" the child said as she ran over to the stall in the far corner of the barn.

Sure enough, tucked neatly inside a bed of hay, no doubt created by Bean, herself, were five mounds of matted fur nestled against their mother. Each kitten appeared to be sleeping as Bean proceeded to clean those in easiest licking range. "Jakob named the white and black one Mewer. Jonathan calls the gray one Whiskers. Sarah says the black one is Jumper. And Annie says the one with the gray and black stripe right there"—Esther touched her own forehead and then pointed at the kitten now wiggling itself closer to Bean—"is Apple Pie, even though that's a very silly name for a kitty."

Following Esther's lead, Emma, too, lowered herself onto the recently mucked ground and leaned in for a closer look at the outlying kitten. "I take it this little cutie is the one you have named Flower?"

Esther grinned. "She is! I like her best!"

"You should like them all," Emma reminded gently. "They're *all* Bean's babies and they are all mighty cute."

"I do like them all, Emma! But I got to name Flower and I got to lick her, too!"

Emma drew back. "You *licked* her?"

"Yah! Bean forgot to do it, so I helped!"

Feeling her lips begin to twitch, Emma turned back toward the new kittens and did her best to stifle the urge to laugh lest she hurt Esther's feelings. "While I'm sure Bean was glad for the help, you really should let her do it. She has a lot of babies to lick right now, Esther, but she'll get to all of them. Besides, you don't want to fill your tummy with fur the way Bean does, sometimes, do you?"

Esther stilled her little fingers atop the sleeping ball of brown and white fur, her face solemn. "No. I don't want to get sick."

"Good. Then let's leave the job of cleaning to Bean, okay?" At Esther's slow nod, Emma scooped her hands beneath Flower and gently pulled the newborn kitten against her aproned overlay. "Well, hello, little Flower."

"Do you know why I named her that?" Esther climbed onto Emma's lap for a closer look. "Why I named her Flower?"

Emma took in the tightly closed eyes, the tiny little ear nubs, and the soft brown and white fur before turning her attention back to Esther. "Why?"

"Because her eyes are closed real tight like Mamm's flowers when they first pop out of the ground. When it gets warm and sunny, they all open real pretty. Just like Flower's eyes will do when she gets a little bigger."

She considered the little girl's reason and, after a follow-up glance at the other four kittens, found that it fit perfectly. "I think that's a great reason to call this little one Flower."

Esther's smile spread across her tiny face only to disappear seconds later. "I am sorry there is not a kitten for you to name, Emma. If Bean had another kitten there would be six to name. Like there is six of us!"

Biting back the urge to correct the lie they'd all been told, Emma, instead, returned the sleeping kitten to its indent in the hay and stood. "I must go, Esther."

"Can't you stay just a little while longer? Flower likes when you hold—"

The rest of the little girl's pleas fell away as the clip-clop of an approaching horse just beyond the barn doors brought Esther to her feet, as well. "Someone is here! Someone is here!"

"It certainly sounds like it." Emma took one last look back

at Bean and her babies and then followed Esther back across the barn, stopping every few feet to run a hand across the head of one of its tenants.

* Mabel, the aging dairy cow . . .
* Dusty, the field mule . . .
* Robbie, the rooster . . .

Jakob popped his head around the corner of the open door, acknowledged Emma and Esther with a nod, and pointed at the wall where Dat kept many of his farming tools. "Emma, could you grab the saw? Levi Fisher is here to borrow it for his dat."

Startled, Emma looked past her brother to the driveway beyond. "Levi is *here*? *Now*?"

"Yah. He is speaking with Dat." Again, Jakob pointed at the saw. "Seems his dat's saw got bent so bad on a fallen tree, it can no longer be used. The tree is blocking the way to Miss Lottie's house."

Emma drew her hand to her chest. "Is Miss Lottie okay?"

"Yah."

Relief sagged her shoulders as the elderly English woman filled her thoughts. Loved by many in Emma's community for her wisdom and gentle ways, Miss Lottie, as she was known by everyone, lived not more than a quarter of a mile to the east, in a small cottage-style home nestled in a field of sunflowers and overgrown grass. "That is good to hear."

"Jakob!"

Together, Emma and Jakob turned toward the back of the barn and its view of the fields Jonathan was painstakingly combing for any rocks the girls might have missed before plowing and planting could start. "I have to go, Emma. I must see what Jonathan needs."

Hooking her thumb across her shoulder, Emma took a step backward toward the tool wall, her gaze flitting between

Jakob and the sliver of buggy she could just barely see beyond his shoulder. "I will see that Levi gets the saw."

"Thank you, Emma."

She watched the twenty-one-year-old disappear from her view and then crossed to the series of hooks used to keep track of the various tools and implements used around the farm. The saw she sought hung above a row of hammers and a long piece of metal she recognized as a level. It was also several feet out of her reach.

Glancing around, she spied an empty feed bucket, carried it back to the wall, and turned it upside down atop a nearby hay bale to create a makeshift stool. She stepped on, rose up on the toes of her boots, and extended her hand as far as she could reach, coming within a finger's length of the saw's handle.

Rocking forward even more, she balanced atop the very tip of her boot and stretched a little more, the deficit shrinking to that of a mere fingertip. Determined to get the grip she needed, she inched her toes onto the bucket's rimmed bottom and extended her reach still farther, her fingers grazing the underside of the saw as the bucket tipped to the left.

She felt herself beginning to fall, but just as her predicament was beginning to register, a pair of strong arms encircled her from behind and deposited her safely on the ground.

"Whoa, Emma. I do not want you to get hurt." Setting the now righted bucket off to the side, Levi reached up to the proper hook, retrieved the saw from its resting place, and leaned it against the barn wall as he sought Emma's eyes with his own. "Hello."

Aware of the sudden warmth that claimed her cheeks, she broke eye contact long enough to catch a glimpse of her reflection in the saw's blade. When she confirmed her kapp was on straight and her dress was relatively wrinkle free, she found the smile he deserved for warding off what would have been a nasty fall. "Thank you for catching me."

"I am glad I came in when I did. You could have gotten hurt."

She shrugged away his concern and, instead, collected the saw from its temporary resting spot. "Jakob said you need to borrow this from Dat to clear a tree blocking Miss Lottie's house from the road?"

"Yah."

"Here you go." She handed him the tool. "I hope this one does not get stuck in the tree."

His deep, rumbly laugh filled the space between them. "Perhaps the Beilers will have a saw I can use if it does.

"But if that breaks, too," he added, shrugging, "I will need to buy many new saws for many people."

It felt good to laugh. Great, even. In fact, the image of a half dozen or more saw handles sticking out of a fallen tree made it so the murkiness surrounding everything about her life the past twelve days paled. And for that she was grateful.

"I am glad to see that it is back," Levi murmured.

"It?"

Lifting his free hand into view, he pointed to her mouth. "Your smile."

The last of her laughter faded as she drew back. "I do not understand."

"Your smile. It has been missing for many days."

Unsure of how best to respond, she cast her eyes down at the ground. "I did not mean to not smile. If I have been rude, I am sorry. I—"

At the feel of his hand on her arm, she stopped talking and looked up to find his warm brown eyes studying her closely.

"You must not apologize for sadness, Emma."

Two weeks ago, she'd have rushed to counteract his impression of her and her demeanor with the biggest smile she could muster. But it wasn't two weeks ago. It was now. The Emma who had always tried to please her way into everyone's hearts was gone. In her place was the Emma who finally knew she never could.

Smoothing her hands down the sides of her mint-green dress, she jutted her chin toward the saw, and then the driveway. "Now that you have Dat's saw, I really must go."

Surprise traded places with concern on his kind face. "I am sorry, Emma, I did not mean to keep you from what you must do."

"If I'm late, it is because I let Esther talk me into meeting Bean's kittens."

"Kittens?"

"Yah. There are five of them." She swept her hand and his eyes toward the back stall. "Would you like to see them? Bean had them in a bed of hay in Mini's stall, just out of reach of the mare's hooves."

"It sounds as if Bean chose wisely."

Emma led the way down the same hay-strewn path she'd walked with Esther not more than ten minutes earlier. When they reached Mini's stall, she pointed down at the still sleeping kittens. "The one closer to Bean's back foot is Flower. Esther named that one."

With the help of her finger, she introduced the others, starting closest to a sleeping Bean. "Mewer, Whiskers, Jumper and"—she cast about for the right name—"Apple Pie."

His lips twitched with the smile he couldn't hide. "*Apple Pie*?"

"I think Annie was hungry when it was her turn to choose a name."

"I think you are right." He bent down, ran his hand across all five sleeping bodies, and then flashed a sheepish smile up at Emma. "Though, if I was hungry when naming a new barn cat, I would choose Oatmeal. After the cookies you would bring to hymn sings each week."

With one final stroke, this one atop Bean's head, Levi stood. "I miss those very much."

"I do not know why." Emma took one last glance at the kittens and then motioned Levi to follow her outside. "Liddy Mast brings oatmeal cookies now."

"They are not the same."

Lifting her hand as a shield against the midmorning sun, she stopped near the back of his buggy. "Oatmeal cookies are oatmeal cookies. They are all the same."

"Then you have not tried Liddy Mast's."

"They are not good?" she asked.

His eyes dropped to the saw in his hands before slowly working their way back to Emma's. "They are not yours."

"Perhaps Liddy missed an ingredient or was busy with the wash when they were to come out of the oven. . . ."

"Two times, she has brought them, and, two times, I have tried them thinking they were yours. And two times, I have known they are not after the first bite." He sidestepped his way to the front of his dat's buggy and placed the saw on the floor. "That is why I am hoping you will point to your cookies at tomorrow's hymn sing."

She dropped her hand to her side and stepped into the shadow made by the barn. "I do not think I will be at the hymn sing this week."

"Oh?"

"Yah. I-I might be busy."

"Busy?" Levi echoed. "On the Lord's day?"

"I will go to church, of course. But it is after—when the hymn sing is to start—that I think I will be busy."

"Doing what?"

"Visiting. With . . ." She took in the house on the opposite side of the driveway and then turned away, a familiar anger lapping at the edges of her tone. "I will be spending the afternoon with *family*."

Levi started to speak but stopped as she motioned toward the road. "I must go, or I will be late. If there is anything else you need, the boys are in the field, and Sarah and Annie are in the house or"—she craned her neck to afford a view of the side yard—"rather, right there, finishing up at the clothesline."

"No, I have what I need." Adjusting his straw hat atop his

head, Levi covered the distance between them with several long strides, stopping only when he was within arm's reach. "If you are leaving the farm, I could take you to where you are going. Then you will not be late."

She looked from the road, to his buggy, and, finally, back to Levi. "Miss Lottie lives in the opposite direction from the pond."

"You are going to the pond?"

"Yah."

"How can you be late to the pond?" he asked.

"It is where I am to meet someone."

Surprise flickered across his face before being scrubbed away by his calloused hand. "The pond is not so far out of the way that I cannot drop you off. I do not want you to be late because you were getting me a saw and showing me new kittens."

"I do not want Miss Lottie to be trapped inside her home."

"She is not trapped. She was sitting on the porch reading a letter when Dat's saw got stuck in the tree. It is Miss Lottie who suggested I borrow one from Beiler or Troyer."

"But you came here . . ."

"Yah." A hint of crimson pricked at his cheeks as he leaned forward and brushed something from the top of his boot Emma could not see.

Not sure what to make of his odd behavior, Emma took another step toward the road. "I really must go."

Her words brought him upright once again. "Wait right there. I will get the buggy and I will take you."

Five minutes later, they were on their way, Levi's mare, Hoofer, faithfully pulling them in the direction of the pond while Emma looked out over the farms of their Amish brethren. She saw the Troyer boys combing the fields for the same rocks that held her brothers' attention one farm south. At the Weaver farm, the laundry was already on the clothesline.

And at the Schrock farm, the bench wagon to the side of the house meant the family was inside, preparing their home for the next day's church service.

"Do you ever think about it being different?" she asked.

Levi pulled back on the reins just enough to slow Hoofer to a walk. "About what being different?"

"All of it." Emma splayed her hands to indicate the Schrock farm on their right and the Troyer farm on their left. "Your choice. . . . The way the Amish live . . ."

"No. I made my choice. I am Amish."

It was such a simple answer—one she, too, would have given just two weeks earlier. Because, prior to her birthday, she hadn't thought about life outside the Amish fold. She'd had her opportunity to experiment with an English life during Rumspringa and she'd opted against it on any large scale. She'd carried around a phone, but never had anyone to call. She'd taken off her kapp a few times while walking along the county road, but had always put it right back on her head not more than twenty or thirty steps later. Because, ever the pleaser, she'd hoped her steadfast commitment to the life would have made Mamm smile.

A sigh, born on yet another example of her naivete, perked Hoofer's ear and brought Levi's focus back on Emma. "Do *you* think about making a different choice?"

It took a moment to catch up with his question, but, when she did, Emma traveled her eyes back to the land around them. "I didn't . . ."

"You say that as if it has changed."

"Because it has. *Everything* has."

The clip-clop stopped with his tug. "You know what would happen if you were to leave the church now. You have been baptized, Emma. You have chosen this life."

"I know." Soft green fabric oozed through her fisted fingers only to flatten against her skin in tandem with the breath she hadn't realized she'd been holding. "But this was never meant to be my world."

Feeling the weight of his confusion on the side of her face, Emma looked back at the Schrock farm, her need to find a distraction settling her sights on the bench wagon. "I am sure Waneta and the girls are busy preparing food for tomorrow. Jakob hopes they will make chess pie. He says Waneta's is best."

"I do not know about Waneta's chess pie, but I do know that this *is* your world, Emma. It is mine, too. We are Amish. We live an Amish life."

She swept her gaze back to his. "You would not be Amish if your mamm and dat were not Amish. You are Amish because *they* are, because that is the life you were shown. But what if they were not Amish or one was not Amish, and no one told you that until after you had been baptized? Would it still be your world?"

"If I had been baptized, yah." With little more than a shift of his hand and a click of his tongue, the buggy lurched forward, the steady clip-clop of Hoofer's feet shattering the charged silence.

Together, they rode along, the mare's hooves the only sound between them as they approached the lone bend in the road between her farm and Miller's Pond. She could sense Levi wanting to speak, to ask questions about their odd conversation, but, in the end, he said nothing.

Still, she slanted a look at him when they came out of the bend, his widened eyes a precursor for the response now making its way past his lips. "Emma! That is the truck! The truck you were asking about at the last hymn sing!" He slowed the buggy to a crawl. "The one that stops at the cemetery each January with the sign on the door."

"I know."

Bobbing his head left, then right, Levi strained to make out details, but the late-morning sun made it difficult to discern much of anything beyond the truck's presence on the side of the road. "Someone is sitting inside. I wonder if it is the same

Englisher that I see standing inside the cemetery. The one who looks down at one of the graves."

"Yah. It is. His name is Brad—Brad Harper."

Levi shifted his full attention onto Emma. "But I did not tell you his name. . . ."

"You told me enough that I was able to find out the rest myself."

"Do you want me to stop? We could ask why he is here, why he comes to an Amish cemetery each year."

She lifted her hand from its resting spot atop her lap and waved a greeting toward the truck. "I know why he comes."

"You do?"

"Yah. He told me."

With yet another tug, Hoofer came to a stop a few buggy lengths away from the truck. "You have spoken to the Englisher?"

"Yah."

"When? How?" Levi split his attention between the man now exiting the truck and Emma. "*Why?*"

"The day after you and I spoke at the hymn sing, I rode my scooter to New Holland. An Amish boy working at a restaurant told me how to find Harper Construction. For many hours I sat next to a shed behind the building just waiting to see him come out. When he did not, I went inside to see if I was right."

They both turned, in unison, toward the crunch of gravel and the man stepping out from the side of the truck. "I do not understand," Levi said, glancing back at Emma. "Why did you go inside to meet the Englisher from the cemetery?"

"I needed to see if he was the one—the one who had been leaving things beside my mamm's grave all these years."

Levi's inhale echoed across the road, slowing Brad's steps in return. "Your mamm's grave? But—"

"Rebeccah Lapp is not my real mamm," she managed past the lump making its way up her throat. "And Wayne Lapp is not my real dat."

"Emma, how can you say that?"

"Because it is truth—a truth they did not tell the bishop, or the church, or *me*." Aware of the anger sharpening her tone, she took a deep breath and lifted her face to the sun. "I am sorry, Levi. I do not mean to get angry. None of this is for you to worry about."

"I do not know what to say."

"That is because there is nothing to be said."

Releasing his right hand from rein-holding duty, he hovered it above hers before draping it across the back of the seat, instead. "I am a good listener. Even Mary says so."

"Hey, Emma! I was just leaving a voicemail for my attorney friend when you guys came around the corner." Brad stepped alongside the buggy, nodded once at Levi, and then held his hand up to Emma. "But you're here now so let's get going. There are some people who are mighty excited to meet you, young lady."

Levi stiffened on the bench beside her, earning himself a backward look from Hoofer. "But you wanted to go to the pond," he reminded Emma.

"You are right. I did. To meet *him*," She pointed down at Brad and then, placing her hand inside the Englisher's, stepped down to the ground, the hem of her dress swirling against the top edge of her boots. "Thank you for the ride, Levi. Please tell Miss Lottie hello for me."

Chapter 14

Even though her shivering had little to do with the February chill, Emma was grateful when, at the flick of Brad's fingers, heat began to emanate from the slats in front of her seat.

"That'll have you warmed up in no time." Returning his hand to the steering wheel, he slid a peek in her direction. "So, who was that, just now? In the buggy? Was that one of Rebeccah's?"

"No. That was a friend."

"He didn't look too pleased to see me."

Pulling the flaps of her coat closer to her body, she shrugged. "It was not you. It was me. I should not have told him those things."

"Things? What kind of things?"

She looked out at the countryside, the farms and animals whizzing by so fast she could barely register which family lived where. "I told him you are my birth father. He did not know."

"Well, then, welcome to the club."

"Club?" she asked, shifting her attention to Brad.

"It's just an expression, kiddo. In this case, it means your friend didn't know just like you and I didn't know." A series of quick vibrations from the cup holder between them had Brad apologizing and reaching for his phone. "Brad here."

She turned back to the passenger side window and noted

that the homes were growing larger while the land grew noticeably smaller. Here, there were no cows grazing, no Amish
pitching hay or preparing the soil for the spring crops, and
no clothes drying in the cold winter sun.

"Okay, okay, slow down. I know you're excited, but don't
worry. We're officially on the way. In fact"—his sudden pause
drew Emma's attention back to him and the single word he
mouthed: *mom*—"we're coming up on Shady Pine right now."

Emma turned in time to see a wooden sign, mounted atop
two stone pillars, with the words SHADY PINE written across
the center. Beyond the sign was a narrow road that curved
around a grove of trees, vanishing from sight.

"That's right. Five minutes. Tops. See you then." He set
the phone back in the cup holder and grinned at Emma. "I
wish you could have seen your grandmother when I told her
about you last night. For the first few minutes after I was
done speaking, she looked at me like I was from another
planet. She might have blinked a few times, but that's it.
Then, as it all began to sink in, she started screaming—*good*
screaming. From there, we moved into a mixture of questions, tears, and planning."

"I do not want to make someone cry," Emma said, duck-
ing her gaze down to her lap.

The index finger of his right hand nudged her focus back
to start. "Not all tears are bad, kiddo. And even the ones that
were because of sadness came and went. My mom is a multitasker. Always has been."

"Multitasker? That is not a word I am familiar with."

"My mother thrives on doing many things at one time.
Last night was about the shock, and joy and sadness and
anger—each of which came and went depending on the question she asked and the answer I gave. When I finally headed
out to my own place, she was sitting at the kitchen table
making lists and deciding the order in which to call people."
He slowed to a stop at a four-way intersection and then continued on, the scenery outside the window holding little in-

terest for either of them. "Today will be about meeting you, soaking you up, asking more questions, and then sitting down together over a meal. And while I know it will probably be a little daunting this first time, I'm confident you'll grow to love her and the way she does things. Everyone does."

It was all so much to process. The sights out her window . . . Being in a shiny black truck with her English birth father . . . Hearing him describe the woman who was her grossmudder . . .

She felt the car begin to slow again, only this time, instead of stopping because of a sign or traffic light, they turned right and headed down a street with neatly kept homes on either side. "What about your dat? Will he be there today, too?"

"He took off before I was a year old. Apparently two kids in as many years was more than he bargained for." At the next crossroad, Brad turned left and then pointed Emma's attention to the lone house on their right. "There it is. The house I was living in when I met Ruby."

Pressing her forehead to the window, she took in everything she could about the house on her right. The powder-blue exterior . . . The pretty white and powder-blue curtains she could glimpse at the windows . . . The billowing flag depicting a snowman anchored into the ground to the left of a walkway . . . The ceiling-mounted swing nestled in a corner of the porch that appeared to look out over a small frozen pond . . .

Emma sat up tall, craning her neck as far to the left as possible. "Is that where you took her to ice skate?" she posed. "Like the snow globe?"

He stopped, mid-nod, his widening eyes sending her attention back to the house and the woman stepping out onto the porch with a smile as wide as any Emma had ever seen.

"Is-is that . . . *her*?" she managed on the heels of a hard swallow.

This time when he nodded, he followed it up with a squeeze

of her hand that was both reassuring and terrifying all at the same time. "C'mon, kiddo. Let's go meet your grandmother before she bursts."

She could feel the woman watching her as Brad opened the passenger side door and ushered her onto the walkway leading to the house. Somewhere in the distance she heard a child's voice and a dog barking, but the most prevalent sound of all was that of her heart pounding inside her ears.

Somehow, during the ride, she'd managed to detach herself from their plans. She knew they'd been driving here, that she was to meet a grossmudder she'd known nothing about, but knowing that and actually being less than a dozen steps or so from it happening were two very different things. One, easy to ignore; the other, completely daunting.

"Oh would you look at you!" Scurrying down the porch steps, Delia Harper clamped her hands together beneath her chin, her blue eyes ricocheting back and forth across Emma's face. "My dear, you are the perfect mixture of your mamma and your daddy, what with those big blue eyes and that spray of freckles across the bridge of your nose."

Delia dropped a hand to her chest in conjunction with a fleeting glance at her son. "Good heavens, Brad, I can't believe this is happening."

"Well, believe it. Because it is." Brad leaned over, kissed the sixty-something on her forehead, and then swept his arm toward Emma. "Mom, I'd like you to meet Emma—your granddaughter. And Emma, I'd like you to meet your grandmother . . ."

Waving his introductions away, Delia stepped forward, scanned Emma from the top of her kapp to the tips of her boots, and, after barely a moment's hesitation, pulled Emma in for a hug. "Oh, sweet girl, welcome. You are the answer to a prayer I thought was ludicrous to make. But . . . here you are. Alive and well and"—Delia stepped back, her eyes intent on Emma—"so *very* beautiful."

"I am Amish," Emma corrected via a raspy whisper. "I am plain."

Delia drew back. "You may be dressed in Amish attire, dear, but you're far from plain. You are, after all, my granddaughter, are you not?" the woman teased, her words peppered with a laugh that reminded Emma of birds chirping on a sunny spring morning—light and calming. "That alone means there's a little zip hiding inside you somewhere."

"I do not use zippers. Or buttons. It is the Amish way."

Delia's eyes narrowed only to widen back to normal size after a beat or two of silence. "I wasn't talking about a zipper, dear. I was talking about *zip* . . . spark, mischief, that sort of thing. It's my house specialty."

"And she's not kidding." Brad winked at Emma and then gestured toward the steps. "Well? Shall we go inside? Get warm?"

"Yes! Let's!" Linking her arm through Emma's, Delia steered them to the steps, across the porch, and through the front door with its snowflake-adorned wreath. Once inside, she instructed Brad to take Emma's coat and then turned to Emma as he did. "Would you like a tour of the house first, or would you rather sit and warm up? I could make you a mug of peppermint hot cocoa if you'd like—I have some ready to go right now."

Brad arranged Emma's coat atop the hanger and deposited it into the hall closet alongside his own, his eyes sparkling. "Mom makes the best hot chocolate you'll ever have, Emma. It's one of the things I missed most when I went on my little—"

Delia stymied the rest of his words with a splayed palm. "*Today* is about *happy*. *Today* is about getting to know my granddaughter, isn't that right, Emma?"

Without waiting for a reply, Delia pushed closed the closet door and nudged Brad from her path. "You get Emma settled in the living room and I'll be along in just a few minutes with the hot cocoa."

When Delia was out of earshot, Brad lowered his voice to

a level only Emma could hear. "How much do you want to bet there'll be cookies, too?"

"I do not need cookies," she countered.

"I suspect you'll change your mind after you try one. They're pretty incredible."

Mustering a smile, Emma followed him down the hall, turned left, and froze.

"Emma?" he asked, turning back at her still feet. "Are you okay?"

She knew she should answer, or, at the very least nod, but aside from having heard her name in conjunction with a question, she wasn't aware of anything except the sitting room in which they were standing. Unlike the largely barren front room at the farmhouse that was used most often for church service every six months or so, this room invited people to come . . . *and stay.* Maybe even spend a few hours if the barn chores were all done.

"Look at all the books," she whispered, stepping forward, her gaze skittering down shelf after shelf of the kind of stories that so often called to her from the rack inside the English store. Pushing past the hesitancy she didn't want to feel, Emma ran her fingers across the spines of several books before being distracted away by a framed photograph of a younger Brad and—

Grabbing onto the edge of the nearest shelf for support, she staggered back a step. "Is that . . . That's . . . That's *Ruby!*"

"It is." He came up beside her, plucked the frame from its resting spot, and pulled it into book-reading range. "My mom took this of us the day we went to the carnival."

"That is the torn ticket you gave me when I turned thirteen?"

Brad nodded, his gaze still riveted on the photograph. "Yes. There was a fireman's carnival about twenty minutes north and we stopped here on the way because I'd forgotten my wallet. I remember being antsy to get there and not real excited about the delay Mom and her camera caused. But I'm sure grateful for it now."

"Can . . ." Emma stopped, swallowed, and tried again, her voice a perfect match to the tremble in her hands. "Can I see it, please?"

"Of course." He handed her the frame and stepped in behind her as she took it. "It's like looking at yourself, isn't it?"

She knew she should say something, but she couldn't. Her eyes, her thoughts, her everything was on the picture in her hands.

An eighteen-year-old Brad stood on the left, his dark blond hair so like Emma's. The subtle wave he sported now was more of a curl back then. The sky-blue eyes they shared led her attention to the young girl standing beside him.

All her life, Ruby had been this person Emma could only imagine—a person her mind's eye had created to look like a younger version of Mamm, frozen in time. Yet standing there, staring down at the reality, the only thing she'd been right about was the only two ways in which Emma favored Brad. In all other ways, Ruby had been a slightly younger version of Emma.

* The same cheekbones
* The same sprinkle of freckles across the bridge of her nose
* The same full lips
* The same basic height
* Even the same narrow chin

They were all the same shared features that had mesmerized her inside the locket, but here, in a way the tinier photo hadn't, she felt the person Ruby had been. The way the young girl smiled out at Delia depicted someone with an air of confidence and a yearning for adventure. And the way she'd nestled inside Brad's arm spoke to the depth of her feelings for Emma's birth father.

"She looks so . . . happy," she managed around the growing lump in her throat.

"That's because she was. We both were."

Together, they turned toward the sitting room doorway as Delia entered carrying a tray with three large mugs, three spoons, and a plate of what Emma could see were chocolate chip cookies. "I'm sorry that took so long. I wanted to make sure everything was just right for our Emma—oh, you're looking at photographs. How lovely."

Emma relinquished the picture frame back onto the shelf and hurried to take the mug Delia offered. "Are there more?" she asked.

"More pictures?" At Emma's nod, Delia grinned. "Oh yes!"

Brad started to reach for his own mug but stopped as a series of chirps diverted his hand to the front pocket of his jeans. He slipped out his phone, consulted the screen, and hooked his thumb toward the hallway. "I'm sorry, but I've really got to take this call."

Sliding a glance at Emma, he added a shrug. "You okay for a little while on your own?"

"She's not on her own!" Delia protested, hands on hips. "She's with her grandmother! Now go—go take your call." Then, with barely a moment's hesitation, the woman shoved the mug of peppermint hot cocoa into her son's non-phone-holding hand and shooed him from the room.

When he was gone, Delia turned back to Emma, patting her over to the sofa. "Come. Sit. Let's get to know one another a little bit, shall we? Maybe by then, Brad will be done with his call and he can join us when we look at pictures."

Wrapping her hands around the mug, Emma sidestepped her way between the coffee table and the closest corner of the couch and dutifully lowered herself to its edge, her gaze darting between Delia and the bookshelf. "You have even more books than the English market."

The skin around Delia's eyes crinkled with a laugh. "And this isn't all of them."

"You have more?"

"I have two floor-to-ceiling shelves in my bedroom that are filled with books, and another three in the room I've dubbed my office." Delia settled onto the couch beside Emma, pointing at Emma's mug of hot cocoa as she did. "So? What do you think?"

Recovering her mouth from the shock of Delia's words, she made herself take a sip. "Yah. This is good." She peeked inside the cup and, when she saw only liquid, looked back up at Delia. "I do not see the peppermint stick."

"Peppermint stick?"

"Yah. To make the peppermint taste."

Delia started shaking her head before Emma was even finished speaking. "I could garnish it with a peppermint stick, of course, but I prefer the little crumbles that were on the top of the whipped cream. The peppermint *flavor* comes from the extract I put in with the milk and the cocoa. The flavor spreads out more that way."

"Perhaps I should get such extract the next time I am at the market. Annie always enjoys the peppermint cocoa I make, but perhaps she would love this more."

Delia turned so her knees were at an angle with Emma's. "You make peppermint hot cocoa, dear?"

"Yah. Every Christmas. When Annie was little—"

"Annie?"

"My sister. She is eight years old and she loves peppermint sticks and cocoa. So I came up with a way to combine both as a Christmas surprise." She took another sip of her own drink and then set it back on the tray in favor of a cookie. "I like to do that. . . . Mix things that do not always go together when I bake and when I cook. Sometimes it does not work, but many times it does."

"Do you enjoy spending time in the kitchen?"

Emma considered her answer as she broke off a piece of

her cookie and paused it just shy of her lips. "It is my favorite place to be, I think."

Delia beamed. "Like grandmother, like granddaughter, I see." Then: "What is it that you like about it?"

Lowering the uneaten bite to her lap, Emma tried to put her feelings into words—feelings she'd never been asked to explain before. "I . . . I like taking simple things, like milk and butter and yeast, and turning it into bread. I like cutting vegetables from the garden and combining it with chicken and chicken stock and making soup. I like taking a recipe that has been followed for many years and changing it to be new. I like, too, seeing a full plate of food grow empty and then be filled again. Because it is then that I know I did it right."

"Have you had formal train—wait." Delia brushed at the air. "That is a silly question. The Amish do not go to school."

"I went to school," Emma protested.

"To the eighth grade, yes, but that is only about learning basics. I'm talking about higher education. The kind that prepares you for—and teaches you about—whatever passion you want to pursue as a career. Like architecture, or fashion, or cooking."

She heard the hitch of her breath and wondered if Delia could hear it, too. "People go to school to cook?" she asked.

"Of course. And depending on where they went to school and how skilled they became, trained chefs can go on to work in restaurants all across the world."

"Is that what you did?" Emma asked. "Go to school to learn to make cookies and peppermint hot cocoa?"

"No, dear. I make those things because I like the *Mmmm*s I get in return when people try them." Delia's knowing grin sent Emma's hand back to her lap and the cookie she'd almost forgotten. "I went to school to be an interior designer but never got to put it into practice until Brad started his company."

Emma turned her full attention on the woman seated to her left. "Interior design? What does that mean?"

"It means this." Delia opened her arms wide to the room. "It means coordinating colors and creating whatever feel a client is looking to establish."

"Feel?"

"Like when you first walked into this room. Did you get any sense, any—"

"I wanted to grab a book and curl up *there,*" Emma said, pointing at the quilt-draped armchair between the window and the fireplace.

"And *that*'s what I do. I decide on a feel and make it come alive. Like in this room. I wanted it to be a haven after a long day, the kind of place where stress just rolls away, leaving you feeling warm and cozy."

"Warm and cozy," Emma repeated only to snap her eyes back to Delia's. "Yah! That is how it feels."

"Then I succeeded." Delia reached across the gap between them and tapped Emma on the tip of the nose. "And that, my dear, is what interior design is and what I went to school for."

"But it is just one room."

"In my house, yes, but I do this for clients all the time."

"They all have a cozy room like this?" Emma asked.

"If they want cozy, I'll create cozy. If they want austere, I'll create austere. If they want whimsical, I'll create whimsical. If they want a room that feels rustic, I'll create rustic."

"Do you like to do it? Your interior design?"

Delia clapped her hands together beneath her chin and grinned. "I love it. Just like you enjoy hearing people ask for more of what you've cooked, I enjoy seeing the tears when people see what I have created in their home."

"They cry?" Emma asked, drawing back.

"A happy cry, yes." Delia picked up the plate of cookies and held it out for Emma to take another. "But that's enough about me. You mentioned wanting to curl up with a book. Do you read?"

"Yah. It is one of my favorite things to do, next to cooking and baking." Emma took another bite of cookie and slowly scooted herself back against the couch. "Sometimes, when the laundry has been taken off the line and the gardening work is done, I will sit at the kitchen table and read as I wait for the bread to finish or the soup to simmer. Once I even burned the bread on the edges because I did not keep track of the time."

"Books have a way of doing that sometimes, don't they?"

"Yah."

Delia returned the cookie plate to the tray and reached for Emma's hand. "Oh, my dear, your world is about to open in ways you can't even imagine and—"

"I'm sorry that took so long," Brad said, breezing into the room. "But it couldn't be helped."

Her hand still covering Emma's, Delia looked up at her son, her mouth pinched. "Was it Nicholas, darling?"

"Yes."

"And?"

"He's going to get everything set up for Wednesday afternoon. At my office."

"Don't you think doing it here"—Delia splayed her hands—"would be less intimidating?"

"No, but we can discuss that later." Brad shifted his attention to Emma and winked. "So? What did you think of your grandmother's famous hot chocolate?"

"It is very good."

Delia neatened the leftover napkins stacked on the tray and then offered Brad a cookie from the plate. "Emma makes hot chocolate, too. For one of the other girls."

"*For Annie,*" Emma corrected.

"That's one of Rebeccah's kids." Brad's eyes, suddenly devoid of the sparkle they'd boasted seconds earlier, pinned Delia. "One of the ones that is *actually* hers, I should say."

"How many are there?"

Emma grabbed her own mug from the tray and pulled it

close in the hope of chasing the sudden chill from her body. "There . . . there are six. I mean . . . *five.* Jakob, Sarah, Jonathan, Annie, and Esther."

"I met that one," Brad said across his cookie. "The little one."

Emma looked into her mug. "Her name is Esther," she whispered. "Esther is five."

"Yeah. It's pretty obvious she worships our Emma, here."

Shock propelled Emma's gaze back onto Brad. "There is only one to be worshiped and that is God!"

Silence swooped in on the heels of her outburst only to be broken by a soft tsking sound from Delia. "Now, Emma, your father didn't mean any harm. He simply means that this little girl—this *Esther*—is clearly quite fond of you."

Then, before Emma could even blink, Delia resurrected her smile and stood. "Brad, dear, did you know that Emma has an interest in cooking and books?"

"Oh?" Brad looked back at Emma, his cheeks lifting. "Ruby liked those things, too."

"She-she did?" Emma stammered.

"Yup. And drawing. In fact, a contributing factor in why I went to school for architecture was because of her and all the houses she liked to draw."

Intrigued, Emma took a sip of her drink and studied Brad across the rim of her mug. "She drew houses? Where? Why?"

"Whenever and wherever she had paper," he said, laughing. "It started after I told her I wanted to build whole houses rather than just fix them the way my uncle did. We were lying on some grass out by Miller's Pond when I told her that. Next thing I knew, I was talking about houses with spiral staircases and big bay windows and large patios. Some of the stuff I mentioned, she couldn't picture, so I grabbed a notebook from my backpack and tried to show her what I meant by a spiral staircase and a bay window. I wasn't very good at drawing back then, but once she had a basic concept of what

I was talking about, *she* drew it. And Emma, she was good. *Really* good. It took her a while to get the hang of dimension and stuff like that, but she would erase and erase and erase until she got it right.

"In the beginning, she just drew parts—like stairs, and windows, and stuff like that. When I suggested she draw the outside of the house, she said that would be boring—that all houses look the same. And when you consider where she grew up, I could see why she thought that. So one afternoon, I drove her through some different neighborhoods so she could see that not all houses are simple farmhouses. They can be ornate like a mansion, they can have turrets, bump outs, different elevations and sizes. All homes, all different."

"Did she begin to draw the outside, then?" Emma asked.

"She did. And she got more and more creative each time. Soon, I was suggesting she could be the one who drew the homes I would build with my company—with *our* company." Brad brushed his hands over his napkin-topped knee, propped his elbows on the chair's armrests, and tented his fingers beneath his chin, his thoughts clearly taking him somewhere far beyond the confines of his mother's sitting room. "We really had a plan. A good plan. One that would have made for a nice life for the two of us . . . and, as we soon found out, you, too. But she just couldn't see it all the way through. Just pieces and parts like the stairs and the windows, and that wasn't enough."

"She stopped being able to draw whole houses again?" Emma asked.

"More like she reverted back to believing there was only one kind." Squeezing his eyes closed, Brad pulled in a deep breath, held it, and then parted his lashes in conjunction with a loud whoosh. "Well, I think that's enough of that for now, don't you?"

Without waiting for an answer, he rose to his feet and wandered over to the window. "You ever skate, Emma? On ice?"

At Delia's outstretched hand, Emma stood and followed the woman to the same window. A glance outside explained Brad's question. "Sometimes, on the way home from school when we were little, Jakob and I would walk out onto Miller's Pond in the winter and pretend our boots were skates. He would slide fast and I would slide slow. But we did not do that anymore after it cracked under my boot."

"Did you fall in?" Delia asked, mid-gasp.

"Yah. My leg got very wet and very cold."

Delia and Brad exchanged looks, their eyebrows inching upward in a mirror image of each other as Emma continued. "Jakob got me out with a stick."

"How old were you?"

"I had just turned seven."

"So Jakob was six, yes?" Brad prodded.

"Six and seven?" Delia echoed. "Rebeccah allowed two little ones to play on a frozen pond by themselves at six and seven?"

Emma rushed to defend the impression she hadn't meant to give. "We were on our way home from school. Mamm did not know we had stopped to play."

"Why was she not there to pick you up from school?"

"She was at home. Doing chores and looking after Sarah."

Delia pointed at Brad. "It's probably unnecessary, but jot that down for Wednesday." Then, without waiting for a reply, the woman lifted her wrist into view and tapped the face of her watch. "Everyone should be here soon, so I better get this tray back into the kitchen and the oven turned on for the roast."

"Please, let me help with the mess." Emma lurched forward, collecting Brad's and Delia's mugs with efficient hands. "Then I will get my coat."

Delia pulled a face. "Your coat?"

"Yah. So I can leave before everyone comes."

Closing her hand atop Emma's arm, Delia smiled. "They're coming to meet you, dear."

"To *meet me*?" Emma repeated, turning to Brad.

"You don't think your family stops with your grand-mother and me, do you?" At Emma's gaped mouth, he continued, his smile reaching all the way to his eyes. "No, kiddo, you've got an aunt, an uncle, and cousins who can't wait to meet you, either."

Chapter 15

"I do that when I'm nervous, too."

Stilling her fingers against the edge of her dress, Emma looked up to find the English girl Delia had introduced as Emma's cousin Michelle looking at her with the same kind of face Sarah wore while perusing the magazine covers in the checkout aisle of the English grocery store. "Do what?" she asked.

"Fidget. If I'm at my desk at school, I play with my pencil. If I'm riding in the car with my mom, I fiddle with whatever she has in her cup holder that day, and if I'm sitting on a couch with nothing in reach"—Michelle nudged her chin at Emma—"I play with the seam of my jeans like you're doing with your dress."

Michelle stretched out across the carpet in Delia's now empty sitting room and rested her head against the wall at her back. "So maybe that means it's just some family quirk or something, instead of some sort of weird thing like my idiot brother is always claiming."

"I didn't realize I was doing that." Emma moved her hands from her dress to the cushion on her left and the armrest on her right.

"And now you're picking at that loose string Grandma keeps forgetting to cut off."

Sure enough, a glance at the armrest yielded a single strand

of thread clasped between Emma's index finger and thumb—
a thread she rushed to abandon. "Oh. Sorry. I-I did not realize I was doing that, either."

Picking her head up off the wall, Michelle pushed her
long, dark, silky hair back over her shoulder and shrugged.
"I'm not getting on your case, Emma. Just noticing we might
actually have something in common."

"Yah."

"So I'm guessing this whole"—Michelle wiggled her fingers in the air—"*revelation* has to be even weirder for you
than the rest of us, huh? I mean, you're not just meeting a
new cousin like I am, or a new niece like my mom is. You're
meeting your *entire* family."

Unsure of how best to respond, Emma managed a nod
while Michelle continued. "So this means you don't really
have to dress like *that* anymore, right?"

Emma followed the path indicated by the teenager's purple
fingernails and swallowed. "I am Amish. This is how Amish
dress."

"But my mom says you're not supposed to be Amish. Your
mom died when you were born and since you should've been
with Uncle Brad instead of those Amish people, you're really
English." Lurching forward, Michelle grabbed a chip from
the bowl Delia had left out for them when the adults opted to
linger at the table after dinner. "My mom thinks you might
need a little while to get used to everything, but if I were you,
I'd be pulling off that head thing and running straight to the
junior department at Charlotte Russe or Forever 21 or some-
place like that."

Michelle nibbled her way around the outer rim of her chip
and then waved the rest of it between them. "Why do you
wear that bonnet thing on your head, anyway?"

"It is not a *bonnet*," Emma corrected. "It is a *prayer kapp*.
The Bible says, 'But every woman that prayeth or prophesieth
with her head uncovered dishonoureth her head; for it is one
and the same thing as if she were shaven. For if the woman be

not covered, let her also be shorn: but if it be a shame for a woman to be shorn or shaven, let her be covered.' "

Michelle's mouth gaped. "You memorized that? From the Bible?"

"Yah."

"Wow. That's crazy." Michelle popped the rest of the chip in her mouth and, after a few moments of quiet chewing, stood and made her way over to the couch. "So, will you? Take that stuff off, I mean?"

"I am not Amish because my mamm and dat are Amish. Before baptism you are being raised by Amish. You are truly Amish when you are baptized."

Kicking her shoes off, Michelle hiked her sock-clad feet up onto the couch beneath her, her eyes riveted on Emma. "And are you? Baptized, I mean."

"Yah."

"But you can get out of it, right? Since you wouldn't have been raised that way if Uncle Brad had known?"

"If I were to leave, my family and my friends could not speak with me ever again."

"But they're not your real family. Uncle Brad is . . . Grandma is . . . *I* am." Michelle gathered her hair together in a makeshift ponytail only to let it fall down past her shoulders, once again. "And everyone is pretty cool. Except my brother. But you saw that at the dinner table, right? Total. Dork."

On cue, the dark-haired twelve-year-old Delia had introduced as Kyle bounded into the room and skidded to a stop in front of Emma. "Uncle Brad said he's gonna get you ice skates and I can help teach you how to skate out on Grandma's pond!"

Michelle rolled her eyes. "Like she needs a twelve-year-old teaching her anything. Puh-lease."

Kyle's gaze dropped to the floor, prompting Emma to lean forward for his hand. "Actually, I'd like it if you'd teach me the proper way to skate, Kyle. Perhaps then I would not fall down."

"Oh you'll fall. Everyone does when they're learning. But Dad says as long as you get back up and try again, you'll get better!" Kyle slid a glance in the direction of his sister and, when she met his eye, stuck his tongue out.

"This is what having a brother is like," Michelle groaned. "Total torture."

Kyle stuck his tongue out a second time and then sat on the edge of the coffee table closest to Emma. "Do you have any brothers?"

"Two. Jakob and Jonathan."

"How old are they?"

"Jakob is twenty-one, and Jonathan is twelve."

"Like me! Cool! Maybe we can play together."

"No, you can't play with him, dork." Michelle dropped her feet back to the ground with a thud. "He's not our family. And he's not Emma's family, either. She just *thought* he was her family because his parents pretended Emma was theirs."

Emma bolted off the couch, bumping her knee against the coffee table as she did. "Jonathan *is* my family!"

"Maybe . . . Technically . . . Since the person who stole you is your aunt, I guess. But why would you *want* them to be family after what they did?" Grabbing another chip, Michelle popped it in her mouth. "*I* wouldn't if I were you. I mean, who did she think she was, doing that? She stole your dad from you! And your grandma! And a normal life! My mom says you could've been in college now—probably getting ready to graduate in May. You could be getting ready to get a job or live in the city. Maybe you'd be dating some really amazing guy."

Emma didn't know what to say. She heard the words coming out of Michelle's mouth. She was even able to process most of them. But it was as if she were standing in the barn being handed more and more chores and being told to do them faster and faster when all she really wanted to do was run down the driveway and escape to the pond.

But she wasn't home. She wasn't in the barn. And considering the night sky outside Delia's sitting room window and the time it had taken to get to the woman's house, finding her way to Miller's Pond wasn't a viable option.

Instead, she wandered over to the window and hoped the view of the very pond on which Ruby had once skated would give her the same sense of calm she found at Miller's Pond. Pressing her head to the cool glass, Emma tried to make out the spot where the grass met the water's edge, but in the dark it was hard to see. She knew, from earlier glimpses, that the pond was smaller than Miller's and lacking in the kind of large rocks and downed trees that were perfect for sitting and thinking. Although, at that moment, she'd take the bench she'd seen when she first got out of the car. . . .

Her mind made up, she turned back to Michelle and Kyle, excused herself, and headed up the hallway toward the closet where Brad had hung her coat. Yet as she approached the correct door, muted voices from the dining room had her veering closer to the wall and then stopping, completely.

"I don't know why you haven't done it already, Brad." The voice she knew to be Brad's sister, Jeanine, morphed into an almost hiss-like whisper Emma had to strain to hear. "I mean, if it were me, I'd have called the second I got my mouth up off the ground."

"Yeah, well, after I got *my mouth up off the ground* as you say, sis, I was kind of focused on Emma—the daughter I'd been told was *dead*."

"As well you should have been, dear." Delia's tone moved from empathy to reproach with the help of a hushed clucking sound. "Brad is doing everything exactly as he should, Jeanine. This is a very delicate matter. Emma's whole world has just changed. In an instant."

"I get that. So has Brad's. So has all of ours, quite frankly."

A snort she recognized as being from Brad was followed by the distinct scraping of a chair leg against the floor. "How has *your* life changed, Jeanine?"

"I have a niece I didn't get to watch grow up! My kids have a cousin they're meeting at twelve and sixteen instead of having her be there from the beginning! And instead of being someone they can relate to and look up to, she's . . . *Amish.*"

"Which means what, exactly?" Brad shot back.

"You heard them during dinner. . . . Michelle talked about going to the junior prom and her classes, and Kyle talked about the video game he got for his birthday. Emma nodded along, sure. It's clear she's a nice, polite young woman. But it's also painfully clear she didn't have a clue what they were talking about. And it shouldn't be like that! They're *cousins.* I mean, don't you remember how much fun we had with *our* cousins when we were growing up, Brad? The stuff we talked about? The trouble we got into? We got them and they got us. Always. But because of this . . . *this travesty* put into place by Ruby's sister, our kids missed out on that. Missed out on *getting each other* on that special cousin-level."

Something that sounded like a snap segued into Delia's voice. "Then it's up to us to help them have that. And we will."

"How?" Jeanine challenged. "My kids know nothing about farming! And Emma knows nothing about real life."

"I can see your attitude hasn't changed since I was dating Ruby."

"What's that supposed to mean?"

"You always thought you were better than Ruby. Always went out of your way to make her feel like she was weird."

"*She* wasn't weird," Jeanine said. "The fact that you two were trying to have *a relationship* was weird."

The sound of dishes clunking against one another was quickly followed by another snap. "Enough, Jeanine! Enough! That young woman in there is my granddaughter! I have every faith that Nicholas will see to it that justice will be served on this. I also have every faith that we can find plenty of common ground with Emma *now*—common ground that will only grow over time."

"Common ground?" Jeanine challenged.

"Yes! Michelle likes to putter around in the kitchen when I'm baking, and I know, from our conversation earlier today, that Emma likes to bake, as well. And as for Kyle, well, he's at the age where he can find something to talk about with anyone. Emma is no exception and—"

"You can just go *into* the dining room, Emma. You don't have to stand in the hallway like that."

All conversation on the other side of the open doorway ceased as Kyle skidded to a stop next to Emma. She, in turn, tried to think of a response but stopped as Brad came around behind her, his eyes framed with the same kind of worry Dat wore when an approaching storm threatened the crops. He searched her face for a few beats and then sagged against the wall. "You heard some of that, didn't you?"

Shame cast her eyes to the floor. "Yah."

Hooking his finger beneath her chin, Brad guided her gaze back to his. "How about we get your coat and head out? Maybe find a place where we can talk privately before I bring you back out to Blue Ball? Does that sound like something you'd like to do?"

Did it? She wasn't sure. The only thing she knew for certain was that the pounding in her head was rivaled only by the pounding in her chest.

Stepping around him, she flung open the coat closet and closed her hands over her winter coat, the familiar feel of the fabric beneath her fingertips a welcome one. "Yah. That is something I would like to do."

They rode in silence down one street after the other until, at last, Brad pulled onto the road that connected New Holland with Blue Ball. When they did, he looked at her across the wide bench seat and smiled.

"So . . . You met the crew. . . . They're quite the bunch of characters, aren't they?" He swung his attention back to the road and loosened his grip on the top of the steering wheel.

"My sister—Jeanine? She can be a bit of an acquired taste, but she *will* grow on you. And her husband—Ned? He's quiet, as you saw, but that doesn't mean he's not paying attention. I think he's just so used to Jeanine barreling over him in conversations that he just listens, makes his own assessments, and speaks when she's otherwise occupied. Smart man. Funny, too."

Resting her forehead against the passenger side window, she waited for the calm of the countryside to work its magic, but Brad's need to talk through the day and evening made it difficult. "Now, I know Michelle can be a bit prickly at times, but I'm told that's par for the course with teenage girls. Kyle is a cool kid. He loves to go out to job sites with me sometimes during his summer break. I had a hard hat made for him with his name on it that he thinks is pretty cool."

"He asked many questions about the farm." Emma wiped at the fog made by her breath and then sat back against the seat. "Perhaps he would like to visit it one day."

"I'm sure we can find him a farm if he really wants to see one up close. In fact, one of the sites I'm getting ready to start building is alongside a farm. Maybe I can get the guy who runs it to let Kyle milk a cow or something." He slanted a glance at her and then pointed at a series of dials on the dashboard. "You cold, kiddo?"

"Only a little."

"Then that's a little too much." With a quick turn of his wrist, a blast of warm air seeped out of the dash vents. "And my mom? She's the best, isn't she?"

"She is very kind." And it was true. Despite not really knowing the woman, Delia's very presence had quieted Emma's nerves on more than one occasion. "She has much to say."

Brad's laugh filled the truck's cabin. "My mom always has something to say. *Always*. But honestly, more times than not, she's right. It's like she has this ability to step back and read a situation and a person within seconds. And her advice? Spot on. Wish I'd listened to her sooner on a few things."

Intrigue lifted her gaze to the side of Brad's face as he continued. "Then again, hindsight is always twenty-twenty, isn't it?"

"*Twenty-twenty?*" Emma repeated.

"Twenty-twenty means perfect eyesight on its own. But the expression I just referred to means it's always easy to see things for what they are after they've already happened."

"Yah. That is how I feel about why I have never fit no matter how hard I tried. Before I learned about you and Ruby, I always thought it was me. That I did not laugh right, or look right, or talk right, or quilt right, or play right. Now I know it was never about my laugh, or my quilting, or anything I could change."

His jaw tightened along with his hand. "If I could go back and change the day you were born, I would. In a heartbeat. But, like you, I didn't *know*."

She wandered her gaze off him and onto the road, the headlights of his truck illuminating the upcoming bend even as her thoughts traveled back to Delia's house. "I did not mean to bring anger to your family."

"Anger?" Brad echoed. "You didn't bring anger, Emma! You brought joy! Unbelievable joy! Did you not see my mother's face when we pulled up? Did you not see the way she could barely take her eyes off you when it was just the three of us? Or the way she kept smiling at you—and trying to force more food on you—all during dinner?"

Emma smiled in spite of the heaviness inside her chest. "No, I saw it."

"Okay, good. As for Jeanine, I know she was probably over the top with all the questions she kept asking during dinner, but she means well. You're her niece. She's trying to learn twenty-two years in the timespan of dinner. Still, I didn't get the sense she was angry. Curious, sure. Anxious to learn more, sure. But, angry? No."

"It was the anger at the table *after* I went into the sitting room with the children."

He slowed the truck to a crawl as they approached yet another bend. "I don't know what—"

"It was about me. That I am Amish. That I am not English like you and them."

"Not English like—wait." On the far side of the bend, Brad pulled onto the shoulder and cut the engine. "So this is about what you overheard at my mom's there at the end, isn't it? When I was in the dining room with my mom and Jeannine?"

"I did not mean to hear." Emma looked from the darkened fields alongside them, to her lap, and back again, the chill she'd had only moments earlier replaced by a growing heat in her cheeks. "I wanted to sit by the pond for a little while. But when I was close to my coat, I heard anger. It was about me. About me being Amish."

"No one is angry at you, Emma. *No one*. They're angry at the circumstances—that you were raised Amish when you should have been raised by me, that none of us had the chance to watch you grow or influence your development, and that you didn't get to know any of us until now—at the age of twenty-two. They're upset by that and they want justice. We all do. And, come Wednesday—maybe Thursday, at the latest—I'm certain we'll have it."

"I heard talk of Wednesday. Why?" Emma asked. "What is to happen that day?"

Turning his body flush to the driver side door, Brad hooked his right calf onto the bench seat. "First up, I'm flying out to Florida tomorrow morning. There's a housing development down there I need to see, and I made the arrangements before you walked into my office for the first time last week. I can still back out if you need me here, or even if you just want to spend the time together. I keep trying to remind myself we have the rest of forever, but . . ."

"But you will come back, yah?"

"Of course. Tuesday night. I should be back from the airport around eight, maybe a little sooner."

"Sarah and Annie will be pleased that I will be there to do my own chores." Lifting her hand to the windowsill, Emma ran her finger along the edge. "I am sure there is mending to be done on Jonathan's pants by now."

He drew back so quickly, his head thudded against the widow. "No. Let someone else do the mending and the cleaning and the gardening and all the other things you never should have been doing."

"I am good at mending. Sarah, not so much."

"But I was thinking your grandmother would just pick you up out by our usual pickup/drop-off spot by Miller's Pond just as I would if I were here. That way you could go to church with her tomorrow, go shopping for new clothes on Monday, and then maybe, on Tuesday, you two could spend time together in the kitchen, since that's something you both enjoy."

"Tomorrow I am to go to church at the Schrocks, and I do not need new clothes. I made two new dresses for all of us just before Christmas." Emma parted the bottom edge of her jacket to reveal the green of her dress. "It is good fabric. Sturdy. It will last many years."

He started to speak, stopped himself, and, instead, looked out at the road. "Maybe Tuesday, then. I know she'd love to cook with you."

"Yah."

"Wait. Let me give you her number." Heaving himself forward, he popped open a recessed compartment she hadn't noticed and pulled out a piece of paper and pen. "Since I can't give her a number for you, I have to trust that you'll find your way to a phone to call her if you need something or want to finalize a time for Tuesday, if not sooner."

He jotted down a series of numbers and then handed the

paper to Emma. "Either way, I need you to be on the road by the pond at eleven o'clock on Wednesday morning. Gives us a little time together before we sit down with Nicholas."

"This Nicholas. You have said his name many times. Is he your friend?"

"He's my lawyer, and a darn fine one at that. Even though he's not a criminal attorney, I knew he was the one I could count on to point us in the right direction in order to minimize any unnecessary glare on you."

Looking up from the slip of paper in her hand, she tried to feign some semblance of understanding, but it was no use. She'd missed something. . . . "I do not understand."

"I want justice to come swiftly, first and foremost. But if there's a way to do it without having every news truck in the area camped outside our door, that's even better."

"What news truck?"

"Kidnapping is big news, Emma. Particularly within the market in which it takes place. But kidnapping by someone inside the Amish community? That's got the potential to go national. *Fast*. The past two weeks have been enough of a blur for you—for both of us—all on its own. I don't think we need to compound that with the circus that a national news story will bring if we can avoid it. That's why, on Wednesday, Nicholas is going to ask you questions—about your upbringing, the things you were told, the things you weren't told, that sort of thing."

"Why?"

"Because we need the facts. We need to know what you were told, how you were treated, that sort of thing."

"I was not told anything until I showed Mamm the locket," Emma reminded. "You know this."

"I do. But Nicholas needs to know, too. So justice can be served."

"Soon, I will tell Bishop King and they will be shunned."

His answering laugh was void of anything resembling

lightness or humor. "You said that the other day. That backs will be turned on them at church until, I imagine, they say, *I'm sorry, I won't do it again?*"

"Yah."

"Yeah, no . . . Sorry." He grabbed her hand off her lap and held it tight, his blue eyes holding hers with such intensity she couldn't look away. "They kept you from me, Emma. That's not okay."

Not sure what to say, or even how to slow her breath down enough to think straight, Emma looked out at the road in front of them, the momentary, yet overpowering urge to go home giving way to total emptiness.

Somewhere in the darkness, just beyond the beam of the truck's headlights, was another bend in the road, another handful of farms to pass before the turnoff to her farm.

But it wasn't her farm. Not now. Not then. Not ever.

"I don't know where I belong," she whispered.

"*I* do. You belong *with me*. You always did, and you always will."

She looked down at his hand enveloping hers once again and tried to make herself feel something, anything. But there was nothing.

"Well, I guess I should get you back. For now. I've still gotta get back to my own place and get packed for my trip. But you've got Mom's number"—he pointed at the paper atop her lap—"and I'll be back to get you by the pond on Wednesday at eleven o'clock."

She knew he was waiting for her to answer. She could feel it just as surely as she could the chill claiming every inch of her body despite the heat still blowing against her skin. Turning toward the window, she nodded.

Chapter 16

Many times, throughout the next morning's church service, Emma had been aware of Levi's glances. She'd felt them just as surely as she'd felt Annie's breath across her hand as she'd held open the Bible for them both. Once, she'd even caught him as she'd scanned the benches of men and boys in the hope the periodic tapping she heard didn't belong to Jonathan. What she hadn't been able to tell was whether Levi's expression was one of disgust or . . . *concern?*

It had been a fleeting impression that had lasted only as long as it had taken Annie to plant an elbow in Emma's ribs and Emma to return her attention to the service. But even with that reminder as to where her focus should have been, her thoughts had returned, as they had again now, to the things Brad had said in the truck the previous night. His repeated insistence and unwavering conviction that Mamm and Dat be held accountable for their lie gnawed at her heart and mind.

It wasn't that she suddenly approved of Mamm and Dat's lie. Because she didn't, couldn't. That lie had kept her from having Brad and Delia and the rest of the Harper family in her life all along. It had also left her to spend her whole life erroneously believing if she just tried harder or did more, she would finally fit with her brethren the way her siblings, and everyone else in their district, did so naturally.

But to be shunned by their community? To have backs turned to them in church and at all meals until they repented? Surely that was a worthy punishment. And while she knew their shunning would bring shame to the children, as well, it was *they* who had lied. They who had acted as if they knew better than God.

"I am sorry, Emma. For what you carry in your heart."

Startled, Emma whirled around only to watch, helplessly, as her dinner roll slipped off the edge of her plate and toppled onto the dirt driveway. "I'm sorry, I do not mean to be wasteful," she murmured.

"That was my fault. For scaring you like I did." Swooping down, Levi retrieved the roll from its resting spot, wiped the dirt onto his pants, and swapped it for the one on his own plate. "Please. You are to have mine."

"I can't ask you to eat a dirty roll," she protested.

"You did not ask, and thanks to my pants, it is not dirty anymore. See?" He lifted it for her to see and then, with a mischievous grin, took a bite. "Yah. That is good. Very, very good."

It felt good to laugh, even if it didn't last. Still, she was grateful when he hooked his thumb toward a sparsely used table on which to set their plates and eat. A glance at the food table showed that it would not be long before Mary's plate, too, was filled and she could join them. Falling into step beside Levi, Emma crossed to the vacant end of the table and lowered herself to the bench while Levi claimed the empty spot opposite. "So? Are you going to the hymn sing at Luke's when we are done eating?" he asked.

She took in the food she'd placed on her plate—the chicken, the stuffing, the corn, the roll—and waited for it to speak to her stomach, but it didn't. Instead, her stomach continued to clench and roil as it had since Brad had spoken of his anger for Mamm and Dat. "I should not have taken so much food."

"That is not so much. *This*"—he directed her eyes onto his

plate and all the same items Emma had chosen, just in larger quantities—"is much food. Which I will eat, I am sure."

Shrugging, she nudged her plate to within inches of his. "Perhaps, if you are not too full, you would like to eat mine, as well."

"That is *your* food. For *you* to eat."

"I know, but I can't. My stomach is . . ." She stopped, held her hand against her aproned front, and took a breath. "My stomach is not right."

"Is that why you looked so sad during the church service?" he asked, pausing his fork against the chicken he'd sought out first. "You do not feel well?"

She lowered her eyes back to her plate before closing them for the briefest of moments. "I-I . . . I don't know."

The smile she'd managed to chase from his face disappeared from his brown eyes, as well. "You are still troubled? About what you told me the other day?"

"Yah."

Silence filled the space between them as Levi's gaze darted to the food table and his sister before settling back on Emma once again. "Is he not kind?"

"Who?"

"The Englisher from the cemetery . . . The one you went off with in the black truck the other day . . ."

"You mean my birth father?" she whispered. At his expected nod, she, too, leaned forward. "He is very kind. And I met his mother—my grandmother, too. She likes to cook and to bake like I do."

Levi studied her as she spoke, and then, when she was done, he pointed to her plate with his chin. "Stomachs do not feel bad because people are nice. Stomachs feel bad when one is sad or worried.

"This, *here*"—he lifted his finger to the skin beside his eyes and then pointed across the table to the same location on her face—"says you are worried, while the smile you are missing says you are sad."

"That's because I—"

"It is crazy how much Isaiah King likes chicken. Lots and lots of chicken." Mary set her plate next to Emma's and hiked her legs, one at a time, over the bench. "But I did manage to beat him to the stuffing and the . . ." Mary's verbal inventory of her plate petered off in favor of bugging out her eyes at her brother. "Must you look at me like that when I'm talking, Levi?"

"Like what?" he groused.

"Like you do not want me here."

"Emma and I *were* trying to have a conversation. . . ."

Emma shrugged away Levi's frustration and slid her plate next to Mary's. "I have chicken that I am not going to eat."

"Really?" Pulling a face, Mary poked her fork into the first of Emma's two slices. "But you did not even try it yet. I am sure that it is good. Isaiah's big helping was not his first or his second."

"I am not eating it because I think it is not good. I am not eating it—or any of it—because"—Emma slid a glance at Levi—"I am not hungry."

It wasn't an untruth. She wasn't hungry. The fact that her lack of hunger was from the near constant clenching inside her stomach really wasn't important.

"Then why did you fill a plate?" Mary asked as she transferred Emma's first slice of chicken onto her own plate and then shoved the second one across the table to her brother.

Why, indeed.

To Mary, though, Emma merely shrugged. "I thought I was hungry when I put those things on my plate."

Mary sliced off a bite of meat and slipped it onto her tongue, her happy eye roll a nod to the cook. But still, Emma's lack of appetite remained.

After a few bites, Mary pointed the tines of her fork at Emma. "Sarah says you have not been home very much this past week. That you have been in New Holland many times."

"She told you that?"

"I asked why I had not seen you the few times I passed by your farm in the buggy."

"You could have asked me," Emma protested.

"Yah. But you were busy talking to Levi, and Sarah was next to me at the table putting more food out for Clara Schrock." Mary scooped up some stuffing and lowered her voice so as not to be heard by anyone beyond their table. "Did you go into New Holland to see about working at the Quilt Shop? Did they like the quilts you have made? Are they teaching you things you must know to sell them at the store?"

"I went to New Holland, but not for a job."

Mary moved on to her roll, eyeing Emma as she did. "Is this about what you told me the other day? When I walked you home? Did you go back again?"

"Perhaps Emma does not want to answer such questions," Levi challenged.

Mary shifted her full attention onto her brother. "Perhaps you should not say such a thing. *I* am Emma's friend, remember? Not you. You spend your time at hymn sings talking to—wait!" Mary relinquished her fork onto her napkin and grabbed hold of Emma's arm. "Yah! That is why I had hoped to see you outside when I drove to Katie Beiler's one day, and Miss Lottie's the next. I have wonderful news! Leroy Schrock has asked to drive me to the hymn sing today!"

"Le-Leroy Schrock?" Emma echoed, stunned. "I-I didn't know you two talked all that much."

"I had a problem with Dat's buggy the other day on my way home from town. Leroy passed by and helped tighten the wheel. It is then that we spoke." Mary's eyes shone with excitement. "He may not be good at volleyball, but he is very nice."

Emma started to speak, to string together something that sounded like the excitement she knew Mary was waiting to hear, but, instead, she pressed a hand to her mouth, murmured her apologies for her hasty departure, and ran around the side of the Schrocks' barn. There, she surrendered to her stomach's incessant churning before lowering herself to the ground and resting her head against the weathered wood at her back. Breath by breath, she steadied her hands in her lap and waited for their trembling to stop. And, breath by breath, she reveled in the cool, crisp air against her cheeks and forehead. It didn't change the feeling in her stomach, but focusing on something, anything else for even a few minutes was better than giving in to the tears she didn't want Mary to see when her friend invariably came around the corner.

Yet when the feet she'd anticipated finally came, they didn't belong to Mary. Hurrying his already hurried steps, Levi closed the gap between them with three long strides, the worry she saw etched in his face catching her by surprise.

"Here you are," Levi said as he, too, lowered himself to the straw beside Emma. "Are you okay?"

When it became clear she could not stop the renewed trembling with breaths alone, Emma wedged her hands between her legs and the ground and managed the closest thing to a true nod she could muster. "Where is Mary?" she asked.

"She got up to try to find you, but it is then that Leroy said it was time to head out for the hymn sing. She told him to go ahead, that she had to find you, but I told her to go on—that *I* would find you and bring you to the hymn sing if that is what you would like."

Tipping her chin upward, Emma took in the charcoal-colored clouds, the lack of any real sun plummeting her mood even more. "That is very kind of you, Levi, but if I am to go, I will go with Jakob. I do not want to take Liddy Mast's place on your buggy seat."

"I am not to bring Liddy Mast to the hymn sing." Levi resituated his hat more squarely atop his head and then gazed up at the sky, as well. "You did not like to hear about Mary and Leroy, did you?"

Oh how she wanted to protest, to say with conviction how

happy she was for her dearest friend, but the effort to do so was greater than she could muster at that moment. Instead, she swallowed hard, and waited for the lump she felt forming in her throat to go away.

"I know we have lost a few volleyball games when he has been on our team," Levi said, his voice quiet, "but he is nice."

Closing her eyes briefly, Emma breathed her way through yet another flip and subsequent flop of her stomach. "I do not question that Leroy is kind. We do not speak often, but I have not seen anything to tell me that is not so."

Levi's answering silence soon gave way to an inhale that matched the upward bent of his coat-clad shoulders. "Did you know that my mamm and Fannie Hershberger have been friends since they were both little ones?"

"Mary told me that once."

"Did you know that Fannie got married first?"

Unsure of his reasons for such an odd topic shift, Emma lowered her chin until his face, rather than the clouds, was her only true focal point. "No, but I do not understand why you speak of this."

"I speak of it because it doesn't matter if Mary and Leroy are to court, or who is to marry first. You and Mary will always be friends, Emma."

She didn't mean to laugh, but just the notion that she even had *prospects* for marriage was silly. Still, she appreciated his kind words and the intent behind them. "I am happy for Mary—I am. It is just that I will miss our talks at the hymn sings."

"That will not change because of Leroy."

"If they marry, she will not *go* to hymn sings and then . . ." Blinking hard against the tears she heard lapping at her words, Emma made herself stand. "Thank you for checking on me, but I should go. I do not want Jakob to leave without me."

Levi, too, stood, his hand finding its way between his chest and his suspender. "Jakob has already left. So have many."

"Oh." She sagged back against the barn. "I did not know. I am sorry if I have made you late."

"I told Mary I would find you and that I would make sure you were okay."

"And you have done that."

"Yah, I have found you, but"—he studied her closely—"I do not think you are okay."

"I want to be," she whispered. "But I do not know how to be."

"Perhaps you need someone you can talk to without worry. Someone who will listen to your troubles and help you to know what is best."

"I don't know if *anyone* can tell me that."

"I do not know, either. But if there is one who can, it will be Miss Lottie. She knows of things I do not know, even if I wish that I did." Removing his hold on his suspender, Levi swept his hand toward the line of buggies on the other side of the barn. "Come. I will take you to her now. And when you are done, I will bring you home."

"But we don't know if Miss Lottie is home. She could be out or busy or—"

"Or she could be there, happy to listen, happy to help."

Happy to listen . . .

Happy to help . . .

Emma's thoughts drifted down to her hand and the stomach that suddenly seemed a little less unsettled. "Yah. Perhaps we *could* ride out to Miss Lottie's and see if she is home."

Chapter 17

For more than a handful of years, Emma had fantasized about this exact moment. Sitting beside Levi on a wagon seat . . . His horse, Hoofer, dutifully pulling them through the countryside . . . No Liddy Mast to flutter her eyelashes . . . Mary otherwise occupied, giving them a chance to really talk . . .

Now that it was here, though, there wasn't any talking. In fact, the only sound beyond Hoofer's hooves against the finely graveled country road was the occasional command of her owner to slow down or move faster. Twice, she'd gotten the sense Levi was about to say something designed to start a conversation, but both times he'd remained silent, freeing her to remain lost in her own thoughts.

The Emma of two weeks earlier would have been mortified at the silence, no doubt trying to scramble for something, *anything* to say to make Levi see her as courting material. But that Emma was gone, shoved to the side by someone who still looked the same, yet no longer was.

"I remember once, when I was not much older than Esther, bad storms took Dat's crops." She surveyed the land to their left and right even as her mind's eye replaced the view with one from seventeen years earlier. "Dat did not question the Lord's will, but he said something about how fast things could change. When we went to bed, the wheat was plentiful and soon to be harvested. When we woke up, it was gone."

Tugging softly on the reins, Levi glanced across the seat at Emma. "Yah. I remember that storm. I was seven. I stood beside Dat in the kitchen and listened to the hail on the roof. The next morning, there was much worry about how to feed the animals that winter."

"That is how I feel right now." She inhaled the cold winter air into her lungs and released it in a smoky plume. "Only it is not crops that have changed in one night. It is me."

"You?" Levi asked over the slow but steady clip-clop of Hoofer's hooves. "You look like the same Emma to me. You have the same hair, the same"—he pulled his left hand from the reins long enough to brush at the area flanking the bridge of his nose—"freckles *here,* and the same blue eyes."

She shook her head at his words. "I do not mean those things. I mean the things you cannot see. The things that make me . . . *me.*"

"I do not think you are different."

"Of course I am different. I am not born from Mamm and Dat. I am born from Mamm's sister, Ruby, and an Englisher. And Jakob, Sarah, Jonathan, Annie, and Esther are not my brothers and sisters."

"That does not mean you are not still Emma," he said with a gentle pull of his hand as he guided Hoofer to turn left onto Miss Lottie's dirt driveway.

Torn between trying to find a way to verbalize her feelings and the ready-made distraction that was the white cottage with the wide front porch, she opted for the latter, falling silent as she did. Lottie Jenkins was a staple inside Emma's district, the elderly English woman's wisdom, quiet lifestyle, and utmost respect for the Amish way endearing her to the plain people she lived among.

For as long as Emma could remember, Katie Beiler's mamm

had been a summer staple on Miss Lottie's porch, likely sharing a moment of conversation over lemonade and baked
treats while Katie's younger siblings chased bubbles nearby
with Digger the dog. It had been such a common sighting, in
fact, that when Katie's mamm went to the Lord the previous
year, her absence from Miss Lottie's porch had been particularly jarring. But while the Beilers had spent the most time
there, many in Emma's community stopped by, as well, their
lives and troubles always seemingly lighter after time spent
on the same porch that was now no more than a few buggy
length's away.

"It is too cold for Miss Lottie to sit on the porch with me,"
she whispered as her gaze gravitated upward to the plume of
smoke rising from the simple chimney. "Perhaps it is not a
good time."

"There is room to sit and visit inside." Levi drew Hoofer
to a stop beside the hitching post at the base of the walkway
and turned to Emma. "Go. Spend some time. Share what is
troubling your heart."

Again, Emma looked at the house, and again, a hint of
calm enveloped her. "Yah. I will go." Turning back to the
handsome man behind the reins, she mustered up the smile
he deserved for his kindness. "Thank you, Levi. For the idea,
and for the ride. Now it is your turn to go. To enjoy the
hymn sing and the fun." She stopped, took a breath, and infused a lightness into her voice she didn't feel. "Perhaps you
will like Liddy Mast's oatmeal cookies better today."

He started to speak but stopped as a telltale creak drew
their collective attention back to the cottage. Seconds later, a
light to the left of the door switched on, bathing the porch in
a muted glow. "Levi Fisher? Is that you, dear?"

"Yah."

"Come in out of that cold, young man. I'll make us some
hot tea."

Tucking the reins onto the floor of the wagon, Levi stepped down off the seat and crossed around to Emma's side of the wagon. "I am going to a hymn sing, Miss Lottie, but I brought someone who would love to have some of that tea with you."

The thump of Miss Lottie's cane preceded her steps onto the porch. "Oh?"

Levi nodded up at Emma and then reached up for her hand. She took it, stepped down onto the driveway, and made her way toward the walkway. "Hello, Miss Lottie. It's me—"

"Emma Lapp!" Miss Lottie tapped the end of her cane against the wooden floor with delight. "What a wonderful surprise this is! Come in! Come in! It's nice and toasty warm inside."

Emma stepped closer, the light from the porch glinting off the upper edge of Miss Lottie's thick glasses. "If it is not a good time, I-I could go."

"You will do no such thing, child! After my breakfast this morning, I made a pie. I didn't know why, just that I was called to make one." Miss Lottie beckoned Emma onto the porch. "The Lord clearly knew you were coming."

When Emma cleared the top step, Miss Lottie peered around her, eyeing Levi across the top of her glasses. "There's plenty for you, too, Levi. It'd give me a way to thank you again for clearing that tree from my driveway."

"You already thanked me, Miss Lottie, and it was no trouble. Just neighbors helping neighbors." Then, stepping forward a half step, he trained his attention back on Emma. "If you're not ready when the hymn sing is over, I will wait right here."

"You are not to get me," Emma protested. "I can walk. It is not far."

"It will be dark. I will stop and bring you home." Nodding first at Miss Lottie, and then Emma, Levi crossed back around to his side of the wagon. With one last nod of encouragement at Emma, he climbed up to his seat, took his place behind the reins, and headed back toward the road, the wheels of his wagon squeaking and groaning with each new rut he encountered.

When Levi and his wagon disappeared from view, Miss Lottie rested her leathery hand atop Emma's arm. "Come inside, dear. We can visit in front of the fire."

"Are you . . . certain?" she eked past the lump in her throat. "It is not too dark to walk home now."

"I am certain, child. Come." Miss Lottie led the way back to the door, pulled it open, and caned her way into the hallway. Where it split, the elderly woman pointed Emma toward the tiny sitting room and its quilt-draped sofa and matching armchair. "Why don't you put a log in the fire and I'll get us some of that pie I told you about. The smell has been tickling my nose and my stomach long enough."

Emma waited for her stomach to react to the notion of food as it had after the Sunday church service, but it didn't. Progress . . .

Stepping into the sitting room, Emma took a moment to look around, the look and feel a near perfect match to the image she'd created in her mind. Although it was a room with four walls, real furniture, and a stone hearth, it was, in many ways, simply an indoor version of Miss Lottie's porch. Warm, welcoming, safe.

She reveled in the warmth emanating from the fireplace and then wandered over to its mantel and the series of framed black and white photographs that covered it from one end to the other. The pictures, themselves, were of places—a building that reached the sky, a bridge over a rushing stream, the top of a mountain overlooking a valley, and the vast ocean. In each picture was a single person—a woman—whose back was to the camera, looking out at the scene. She didn't need to look closer to know the woman was a younger Miss Lottie. The mere presence of the floppy straw hat atop the figure's head was all the proof Emma needed. Still, it was clear the pictures were taken years earlier, before age necessitated the cane that was as much a part of the woman now as the very home in which Emma was standing.

"It takes a while to get everything in here when one hand is occupied with walking, but I get it done." Miss Lottie caned her way into the room with a stack of plates and set them down on the table Emma recognized as being Amish made. "I'll be right—"

"Miss Lottie, I'm sorry," she said, snapping to. "I was so busy enjoying your pictures I did not add a log to the fire as you asked. I will do that now, and then I will get the pie and anything else you need."

"How about we switch? Everything is on a tray in the kitchen. If you can carry that in, *I* will add the log so we can get to our evening."

"Yah." Emma went in the direction indicated by Miss Lottie's finger, located the tray with its pie, forks, teacups, and teapot, and carried it back into the sitting room in time to see her host backing away from a newly roaring fire. She set the tray on the table and took a spot on the sofa, her gaze gravitating back to the picture-topped mantel. "You have been to many places."

Miss Lottie followed Emma's gaze to the mantel as she settled into her own chair. "I have."

"What was that like?" She poured some tea into each of the two cups and handed one to Miss Lottie. "To go to such places and see such things?"

"It is always an experience to see something for the first time."

Lifting her own cup to her lips, Emma stopped just shy of actually taking a sip. "Do you still go to places like that sometimes?"

"No. I have seen many things. I have had many experiences in my life that have had me traveling to many places." Miss Lottie took a sip of tea, pinning Emma with her eyes across the rim of her mug as she did. "But soon I came to see that where I feel most content, most at peace in my heart, is right here, in Amish country. So I returned."

She considered the woman's words against snatches of conversation she'd heard at Katie Beiler's marriage to Abram Zook in the fall. "You are Katie's kin, yah?"

"I am."

"Which means you were Amish . . ." Emma prodded, setting her cup back onto the tray.

Miss Lottie leaned forward, cut two pieces of pie, and deposited one onto each of their plates. "I was *raised* by Amish. I did not join the church."

"But you came back here."

"I did."

Emma took the pie plate and a fork from the woman and rested it atop her lap. "Why?"

"I was wandering in an outdoor market in San Francisco one day and I came across a sign. It said, 'Home is not a place, it's a feeling.'" Miss Lottie forked up a piece of pie and took a bite, her eyes disappearing briefly behind closed lashes. After what seemed like a minute, maybe two, the woman's eyes popped open to meet Emma's. "For days after I saw that sign, I couldn't get those words out of my head. I thought about it when I woke up, I thought about it as I was drifting off to sleep. And then, a few days later, it just hit me. I'd always felt as if I was *visiting* places I went—even places I stayed for several years. Yet when I thought back to the one place where I never felt as if I was visiting, it was here. In Blue Ball. I have never regretted coming back here for even a moment."

"I did not know you were Katie's kin until she married Abram."

"Katie and the rest of 'em didn't know until shortly before that, either. But *I* knew."

"So, it was wanting to be near them that brought you back here?"

"That was some of it, of course, but I feel as if everyone in this community is my family. It's like the sign in that market said, home is not a place, it's a feeling. The second I arrived back in Blue Ball . . . and bought this house . . . and looked out the window and saw a buggy driving by, I no longer felt as if I was visiting."

A log split, sending sparks up the chimney and Emma's thoughts to the reason she'd come. "Do you think you would feel the same if you learned you were never meant to be here from the start?"

"You mean here, in Blue Ball?" Miss Lottie asked, lowering her teacup to the armrest. "Among the Amish?"

"Yah."

"That's an interesting question, Emma—one I'm not sure how to answer. I think it would come down to choosing to listen to your head or your heart . . . anger or truth."

"Anger *and* truth," Emma corrected. "They are together, for me."

Leaning forward, Miss Lottie set her cup on the tray, folded her hands atop her lap, and nodded ever so gently at Emma. "I'm listening, child."

Emma traveled her gaze back to the hearth and the flames licking at the base of the chimney. "Everything is different now. *I* am different."

"You look the same to me."

"Because I am still dressed as if I am Amish. But I am not."

"You were baptized, dear."

"But I should not have been." At Miss Lottie's not so quiet inhale, Emma abandoned her view of the flickering flames and stood, her feet taking her around the room with no clear destination in mind. "I did not know another world."

"That is what Rumspringa is for. To let you taste the English world and its ways. Did you not do that?"

"No, I did. I wore some English clothes a few times . . . listened to English music with Mary . . . and"—she turned back as she reached the entrance to the hallway—"I even tried a cigarette outside the English grocery store, but I did not like it."

"Did you take a full year, or did you hurry back for baptism?" Miss Lottie asked, her eyes following Emma around the room.

"My Rumspringa fell between baptisms for the bishop, so it was a little more than a year. But I knew after six months."

"Then what is different now? Have you met an English man?"

She whirled around, her face hot. "No!"

Miss Lottie's shoulders sagged with relief. "That is good."

"Not in the way that you mean," Emma clarified. At Miss Lottie's pointed look, she rushed to explain. "I have met an English man, yah. But not in a courting way."

Wandering over to the window, she parted the pale yellow curtains with her hand and peered out at the road, a series of flashing orange lights in the distance letting her know the day of worship and visiting at the Schrocks had come to an end. Soon, the hymn sing, too, would end and Levi would be arriving to take her home. . . .

She rested her forehead against the cool glass for a few long moments and then turned back to the woman patiently waiting for Emma to explain the unexplainable.

"The Englisher is my dat. My *real* dat."

Reaching up, Miss Lottie readjusted her glasses against her eyes as if the enhanced view might change what her ears had heard. But after a slow inspection of Emma's face, the elderly woman squared her shoulders with a hearty breath. "I did not know that, child. I didn't come back to Blue Ball until you were closer to four."

"I did not know until two weeks ago," Emma said, her voice wooden even to her own ears.

A peek at Miss Lottie pointed to surprise as the reason for the room's sudden silence, save for the quick pops and slow crackles from the fireplace. Eventually, though, the woman spoke, her voice so hushed Emma was forced back to the sofa just to hear.

"What made your mamm tell you now?" Miss Lottie asked. "After all this time?"

"I saw the picture—the one of my real mamm. And that is when I knew."

"Your . . ." Miss Lottie stopped, cleared her throat, and tried again. "Your *real* mamm?"

"Yah. Ruby. She is dead. I killed her."

"Killed her?" Miss Lottie echoed.

"Yah. It is while she was having me that she went to the Lord."

"But I thought Ruby was your mamm's sister."

"And I thought Mamm did not smile at me because I reminded her of a sad day. But it was not that. She does not smile when she looks at me because I am the *reason* for that sad day."

Miss Lottie moved her hands from her lap to her armrest, her eyes never leaving Emma's. "I don't believe that, child."

"What? That she does not smile at me?" Anger tightened Emma's jaw. "I am not the one who lies! That is Mamm and Dat! They told my real dat that I died with Ruby! Every year on my birthday he has come to the grave to visit with Ruby and me. But I was not there! I played. I went to school. I had birthdays. I grew. I went on Rumspringa. I was baptized. In all that time, Brad did not know I had lived, and I did not know I was his and Ruby's child."

Now that she'd started, she couldn't stop, the details she'd pieced together since the morning of her birthday pouring from her mouth with nary a breath in between. "I have a grossmudder who likes to cook just like me . . . and cousins who are very different but only because I was raised in a home where I did not belong. A home where—when I would look across the table at dinner—I would see bits of Dat and Mamm in everyone else. Dat's eyes in Jakob's . . . Mamm's in Annie's and Esther's . . . Dat's chin in Sarah's, and Mamm's nose in Jonathan's. But my eyes did not look like anyone's. My hair was different, too. It was all just more ways I did not fit. But it was not me! It was not that something was wrong with me! It is because I did not belong at that table! Dat was not my dat! Mamm was not my mamm! The children were not my . . ."

Dropping her head into her hands, Emma gave in to the sobs she could no longer hold back—gut wrenching, shoulder heaving sobs that drenched her cheeks and made it difficult to draw full breaths. But as she wiped her eyes in an attempt to see through the torrent of tears, Miss Lottie was suddenly beside her, pulling her close. "Oh, Emma. . . . It's okay, sweet child. . . . Let it out. . . ."

And so she did. She cried for the mother she'd never know, she cried for the father she barely knew, she cried for the family that was never supposed to be hers, and she cried for herself—for the life she thought she had and wasn't sure she should.

Soon the sobs gave way to quieter tears and, finally, sniffles that filled the time between cracks and pops of the fire. "I don't . . . I don't know where I . . . belong," she said between the last few hitched breaths. "I don't know where I *want* to belong."

Slowly, gently, Miss Lottie released Emma from her arms just enough to be able to afford eye contact. "You have had your world turned upside down in a matter of two weeks, Emma. The only way you can know those things is to get information."

"Information?" Emma wiped her face with the back of her hand. "What kind of information?"

"Get to know your birth father. Get to know your grandmother. Get to know your cousins. Learn their world. Soak it all in. And, while you're doing that, pay careful attention to what"—Miss Lottie touched Emma's chest with her finger—"your heart is saying. Then, and only then, can you answer those questions about where you belong."

"It has already been twenty-two years," she protested between leftover sniffles.

"You're right, Emma, it has. You can't erase all that and accumulate twenty-two years of new knowledge in a matter of weeks. Not when it's all still so raw. Decisions made in anger are never good decisions, Emma. Never. You must give it, and yourself, more time."

"But do I even have a choice?" she asked. "My real family is English. Isn't that what I should be now, too?"

Miss Lottie pushed her glasses higher on her nose and then gathered Emma's hands inside her own. "I don't know the reasons behind the decisions your parents—Rebeccah and Wayne—made. Only you and they know that, but—"

"There is never a reason to lie, Miss Lottie. The Bible says, 'Lying lips are an abomination to the Lord, but they that deal truly are his delight.' "

"That is true, certainly. But the Bible also says, 'He that answereth a matter before he heareth, it is folly and shame unto him.' "

She stared at Miss Lottie. "But they lied, Miss Lottie! And no, I *don't* know why!"

"Have you asked?"

"No. I do not need to ask. Lies are never good, never right."

At the approaching clip-clop of Levi's horse, Miss Lottie squeezed Emma's hands one last time and then released them in exchange for her cane. "Remember, Emma, anger does not make for good decision making."

"I will try. . . ." Emma smoothed her skirt down against her legs and then stood, her eyes making short work of the uneaten pie on her plate. "Oh, Miss Lottie, I never tried your pie. I just got so busy telling you—"

Miss Lottie stilled the rest of Emma's sentence with a gentle finger. "Shhhh . . . It just means you must come back and see me. Soon."

Chapter 18

Emma settled back against the tree and tried not to think about Sarah's face as she'd passed the clothesline and the basket of clothes waiting to be hung with nary an offer to help. But while that memory invoked a knot inside her throat, the one of Mamm's disappointment as, Mamm, too, had looked up at Emma, stirred an anger she didn't want to feel in her special place.

No, Miller's Pond had always been her happy place—the place where something as simple as watching a butterfly flitting around in the spring, or a colored leaf floating down to the earth in the fall brought her a sense of peace. Here, she could be herself without self-critiquing her every move and non-move. Here, she could cry if she wanted to cry, or laugh if she wanted to laugh. And here, she'd been able to pretend what the truth had been all along—that the trinkets she'd added to the drawstring bag in her hand each year were, in fact, her birthday gifts.

Thanks to her time here, at the pond, and later at Brad's office, she now knew the reason behind the gifts left through her fifteenth birthday. She'd hoped they'd get to the last few items the day she'd met her grandmother, but it hadn't happened. Instead, she pulled the last six presents out, one by one, studying each one closely. The plastic covered bridge . . .

The small, red rubber ball . . . The yellow spinny thing on a stick . . . The baseball with the ink markings on it . . . The dried flower with the blue and pink ribbons tied around the stem . . . And, finally, the whittled bird . . .

When they were lined up, side by side, across the top of the rock on which she sat, Emma ran her fingers across each and every one, her thoughts visiting a time Brad had brought to life in her head—a time when Ruby was alive, and Emma's birth parents had been able to convey thoughts to one another with little more than a glance. Thanks to Brad, Ruby was becoming more than just kin she'd never met—kin who had died too young and whom Mamm still mourned. Now, Ruby was someone who'd looked like Emma, laughed softly, looked happy in a photograph, learned to skate, planned picnics, rode rides at an English carnival, drew pictures of houses, made wishes, had been in love with Brad, and seemed to be happier in his English world than she'd been in her own.

Scooping the last present up off the rock, Emma took in the carefully whittled bird—the wings poised to indicate balance, the eyes cast downward as if observing something below, and a tiny worm inside its partially open beak.

"That bird needs a baby!"

Sucking in her breath, Emma turned to find Esther not more than five feet away, heading in her direction. In the little girl's left hand was her lunch pail, and in her right, a small picture book Emma recognized from her earliest school days. "What are you doing here?" Emma traveled her gaze past the five-year-old to the path that wound its way around the far side of the pond. "And where are Jonathan and Annie? They should be with you."

"I peeked at the pond through the trees"—Esther pointed to the narrow break between the trees that otherwise hid their location from the road—"and I saw you! I asked Annie if I could walk the rest of the way with you and she said yah!"

Esther set her lunch pail and book on the ground and

clambered onto the rock by Emma's feet, her large brown eyes fixing on the bird once again. "Did the nice man give it to you?"

"Nice man?"

"Yah. He spreaded all his toys on the rock the other day."

"*Spread*," Emma corrected.

"I liked the horse best!" Esther inched her way across the rock toward Emma, her finger guiding Emma's attention back to the whittled bird. "Since we don't have six kittens, you could name the bird. . . ."

She looked a question at the little girl only to shake it away as the answer dawned all on its own. "You did such a good job naming Flower, I think *you* should name this bird, too."

"Are you sure?" At Emma's nod, Esther's ever-present smile widened even more, revealing the sizeable gap where two of her top front teeth were missing. "I want to name her Emma, just like you!"

"Emma?" She looked at the bird, wiggled it ever so gently, and then pretended to make it fly over to Esther. "Emma is a *girl* name," she said in a squeaky voice. "I want a *bird* name."

Giggling, Esther rose up on her knees to address the wooden bird. "But you have a worm in your mouth."

"Yah. I am hungry."

"But you will not eat it," Esther said, her brows dipping down in a sudden burst of seriousness. "You are carrying your worm like the bird in Dat's barn."

Then, abandoning her conversation with the whittled bird momentarily, Esther fixed her eyes on Emma. "Jakob says it is good Flower and the other kittens cannot climb yet because they might eat the baby birds in the nest."

"Are you sure they have hatched? It is not spring yet."

"Yah! There are two babies! And the mamm bird brings them worms! I saw her!"

Emma lowered the now-silent wooden bird back to her lap and, with the index finger of her free hand, tapped her little sister's nose. "You will have to show me the nest when we go back to the house."

"Yah. But I still want to call that one"—Esther pointed at Emma's lap—"Emma."

"Why?"

"Because if I were a baby bird, you would bring me worms just like that bird!"

Leaning her head back against the trunk of the tree, Emma listened to her own laugh as it echoed around them. "Oh? You think I would give you a worm, do you?"

"Yah! Because you love me and you taked good care of me."

"*Take,*" Emma corrected, sitting up. "And you are right. If you were a baby bird, I would bring you worms."

Esther pointed at the bird. "Can I sit there? For just a little while?"

"You mean on my lap?" At Esther's nod, Emma moved the bird to the rock and pulled the little girl into cuddle range. "I always have a spot for you to sit, little one."

"Even if you *leave*?" Esther whispered.

"Leave?" she echoed, loosening her hold on Esther. "I am not . . ." Breathing back the rest of a sentence she knew she could not say, Emma straightened her shoulders against the tree and pointed at the sleeve of the little girl's dress. "Would you quit growing, please? Because pretty soon there will not be enough fabric in the store to make the dresses you seem to be outgrowing faster than I can make them."

Lifting the bird off the rock, Esther held it to her chest and rested her cheek against Emma. "I tolded Annie and Jonathan you would not leave. I tolded them you *do* like us. But Annie tolded me you don't anymore. She tolded me that's why you do not help with the chores, and why you don't sit next to me at dinner all the time."

Esther shot her chin up, eyes wide. "She tolded us you yelled at Mamm one day!"

"*Told*." She knew, in the moment, it didn't matter if Esther's grammar was correct, but drawing attention to it bought Emma time to breathe her way through the sudden dizziness.

"Did you, Emma? Did you yell at Mamm?"

She knew the consternation on Esther's face. It was the same expression, she, herself, would have worn at the notion of any of her siblings ever raising their voice to Mamm. But that was before—before she knew everything about her life had been built on lies.

"Emma?"

Snapped back to the moment by the worry in Esther's voice, Emma lingered a kiss atop the little girl's kapp. "Why do you tiptoe over to see Bean's kittens?"

"Because they are babies. I do not want to wake them if they are sleeping."

"That is a good reason." She breathed in the medley of earth and apples that clung to her sister's hair and then sat back. "I have reasons for things that I do, too, Esther. And right now, there are some things I cannot talk about. But I will . . . soon. Can you wait for me to do so?"

Esther started to nod but stopped to look up at Emma, instead. "You *do* like us, don't you, Emma? Even if there were no more kittens for you to name?"

Somehow, despite the tears she felt gathering in the corners of her eyes, Emma still managed a laugh. "I do not need a kitten to name when I have a bird to share mine."

She picked up the bird and turned it to face Esther once again, her voice adopting its earlier squeaky quality. "Thank you for naming me Emma, little girl. I like my new name."

Giggling, Esther scrambled back onto her knees to maximize eye contact with the whittled creature. "I named you that because I *love* Emma."

"That is good," she said, moving the bird in for a wooden beak kiss. "Because Emma loves you, too. Never, ever forget that."

*   *   *

She'd tried for Esther. She'd tried for Jakob and Jonathan, Annie and Sarah. But nothing about sitting at the dinner table with Mamm and Dat had felt right. On the surface, it had been like any other evening meal—heads bowed in prayer, plates of rolls and potatoes and meat being passed around from person to person, and the sharing of stories from the day. But that was where the similarities had ended for anyone who dared to truly see.

Some of that could be put on Mamm and Dat and the un-easy glances they sent her way every time the conversation around the table lagged in a way that made Emma's silence almost deafening. Some of it, too, could be put on the anger Miss Lottie had warned her about, yet she couldn't shake.

For twenty-two years, these two people had told her an untruth—that she was their child. That single lie had led to the telling of more. To Jakob. To Sarah. To Jonathan. To Annie. And to Esther. Because despite what they all believed, Emma was not their sibling. She was still kin, sure, but not in the way they'd all believed or in the way they still believed.

And every day that went by with her knowing a truth they didn't, she, too, was part of that lie. But until she could tell them without her anger spilling into places it didn't belong, she needed to wait.

"Emma? I think the plate is dry enough to put away."

Halting her hand, mid-squeak, she looked up to find Sarah studying her from the top of the single step stool. "Oh. Yah. Here." She passed the now dry plate to her sister to add to the cupboard and turned her attention to drying up the counter around the sink.

"I do not know why you do not help with the laundry or the mucking or the baking anymore," Sarah said, closing the cupboard door and stepping down off the stool. "I do not know why you do not speak at dinner. But I do know you are making Mamm very sad and that is not good."

Emma stopped wiping to stare at Sarah. "You think *I* am making *Mamm* sad?"

"Yah. You do not see the way her smile disappears when you walk out the door without saying what you are doing or where you are going. You do not hear her crying when she says she is quilting."

"Something that is not there cannot disappear."

"What do you mean?" Sarah asked.

"You said Mamm's smile disappears when I walk out the door. But Mamm does not smile at me when I am here, so I do not know how it can disappear when I leave." She draped the wet dishcloth across the oven handle and then turned back to Sarah. "And if she is crying in her room when she is to be quilting, it is because of her choices, her lies."

"Emma!" Sarah stamped her foot on the wood plank floor only to startle herself with the answering noise. Flustered, the sixteen-year-old glanced over her shoulder toward the hallway, waited to see if a reprimand would follow from the vicinity of the front room, and, when it didn't, turned back to Emma, her voice dropping to a whispered hiss. "I do not know why you are this way. I saw Levi bring you home last night. That should make you happy, not like . . . *this*."

"*Like this*?"

"Yah. Angry . . . Mean."

Sarah's words snapped her back a step. "I am not *mean*."

"The Bible says, 'Honour thy father and mother.' But you are not. You are saying things you should not say about Mamm!"

"It is not just Mamm. It is Dat's lie, too."

"Emma!"

"Listen to me, Sarah." Stepping forward, Emma gathered her sister's hands inside her own. "The Bible says many things. It says to honor thy father and mother, but it also says 'Ye shall know the truth and the truth shall make you free.' That is what I *am* now, Sarah. . . . That is why I leave and do not say where I go. Because I am *free*—free of lies that should never have been told. And soon you will know the truth about them, too."

With one big pull, Sarah wrenched her hands free, her expression a mixture of fear and defiance. "Maybe it is good that you go, that you do not help with chores as you once did."

Chapter 19

She saw the described car the second it came around the bend. The slow pace, combined with its periodic stops and starts, a clear indication the driver wasn't entirely sure where the path to Miller's Pond was located. For the briefest of moments, Emma actually considered stepping back into the protection of the trees and letting the car drive right by, but considering she was the one who had requested the visit in the first place, it wouldn't be right.

Instead, she stepped forward, waved at the driver she couldn't quite see yet, and waited as the car hurried to a stop on the opposite side of the country road. When the window lowered to reveal the expected face, Emma crossed the finely graveled road to the driver's door.

"Thank you for coming. I hope it is not a bother."

Delia's hand shot through the opening to grab Emma's. "If you had seen my face when I got your call, dear, you would know just how much of a *non*-bother this is." Then, with her soft blue eyes searching Emma's, she squeezed. "Are you okay?"

Shrugging, she pointed at the other side of the car and, at Delia's emphatic nod, looped around the front and slid into the passenger seat. When she was settled, with the seat belt fastened across her shoulder, she gave into a sigh. "It is all too much to think about. This *who is* and *who is not* my family stuff. I don't know what to think, and when I *do* think, I do not like the anger that I feel."

"Do you want to talk about it?" Delia asked.

Did she? She wasn't sure.

So much had changed. Who she was . . . Where she came from . . . Where she belonged . . . But somehow, amid all that change, she wanted, no *needed,* to feel as if something—some aspect of herself—was still the same. Yet there she was, sitting in a car with her newly discovered English grossmudder. How could anything ever be the same again?

Aware of a burning in her eyes, Emma turned and looked out her window, the fields she'd glimpsed from this spot nearly every day of her school years soothing her heart with the kind of familiarity she felt every time she—

Emma sat up tall, her focus skipping back to Delia. "Could . . . could we bake together?"

Delia drew back only to have her whole face lift with a smile. "Oh, Emma, I can't think of anything I'd rather do." Placing her hand on the gearshift, the woman divided her attention between the road and Emma. "Do you want to teach me something you like to bake, and I'll teach you something I like to bake?"

"Yah!"

"Then let's head to the store, shall we?" At Emma's emphatic nod, Delia closed her window against the chilly day, made a U-turn back in the direction she'd come, and let loose a happy squeal. "From the moment Michelle was old enough to hold a spoon I tried to cultivate a love of cooking and baking in that child. She always liked to watch, always liked to be nearby for any extra chocolate chips or blueberries that didn't make it into the cookies or muffins I was baking. But beyond that, she's never had any interest in recipes and actually baking. So this is going to be a real grandma-dream-come-true for me."

She sensed the Amish fields giving way to property and

houses owned by the English to her right and left, but all she could really see was the dough they'd soon be making from the generations' old recipe she'd tweaked and changed until it was her own. "Where do you get your recipes?" Emma asked on a whim.

"All sorts of places. Magazines. Online recipe sites. Friends. Family. If it has ingredients I like, I'll give it a whirl." Delia turned right at the first traffic light and continued. "Many of our favorite recipes have come about that way. How about you? Where do you get your recipes?"

"Some have been handed down from my mamm and my grossmudder. But they do not stay the same."

Delia stopped at the next light and peered at Emma. "Meaning?"

"The recipes are good as they are—they have fed many mouths for many years. But I like to change them. Sometimes the change is little—like a bit more salt, or a splash of vanilla where there was none. But sometimes, in changing little things, I find that I can change even more. When I am done, it is no longer someone else's recipe. It is mine."

"And the change?" Delia prodded. "Is it well received?"

The last of the tension she'd been harboring in her shoulders faded away as she rested her head against the seatback. "Plates are always empty and tummies are always full when I make something new. Even Esther's."

"Esther is the youngest, correct?"

Emma smiled as an image of the little girl popped—fully formed—into her thoughts. "Yah."

"You two are close, aren't you? I can see it in your face and hear it in your voice every time you say her name."

It was something she'd never really thought about, yet the reason for that closeness was really quite simple. "With Esther, I do not have to try to change," she said. "I can be me."

"You can't be you with the other children?"

Emma felt the car slow in advance of the turn into the grocery store's parking lot and let her gaze travel ahead while her thoughts stayed with Delia's question. "I love them all, but there is something special with Esther. It is why I am most afraid to tell her about all of this."

"Will that be soon?" Delia asked as she pulled into a parking spot not far from the market's door.

"It must be, even if Mamm does not agree."

An audible inhale from behind the steering wheel pulled Emma's gaze back onto Delia. "I don't think *Rebeccah* is in any position to argue anything with you right now, dear."

"Right now, it is just me who knows of Mamm and Dat's lie." Emma returned her chin, if not her thoughts, back toward the window. "I do not think she wants the others to know. But I do not want to tell lies the way she does."

Delia's answering smile held no sign of humor. "Trust me, sweet Emma, Rebeccah has far bigger worries on the horizon than what those children know, I can promise you that."

Desperate to reclaim the lightness she'd felt not more than five minutes earlier, Emma unlatched the seat belt and wrapped her fingers around the door handle. "Could we go inside? I just want to think about baking, if that is okay?"

"Of course. You're right." Delia pulled her keys from the ignition, tucked them into her purse, and opened her own door. "Let's leave the unpleasantness to those who created it and go have some fun, shall we?"

With little more than a few finger points at two or three cabinets, Emma moved around Delia's kitchen with ease, gathering requested ingredients for Delia's favorite recipe and familiarizing herself with the many English trappings available to Emma in making her own. When everything they needed was assembled across the top of the counter, Delia nudged her chin at a red-capped bottle.

"I've never made apple cinnamon bread before," Delia said, tying her apron into place.

"We are to make white bread. The cinnamon and apples are for the apple butter we will put *on* the bread."

Delia brought her hands together with a quick clap. "I love apple butter! But I've always heard it's very labor intensive, no?"

"Not with that"—Emma pointed at the slow cooker she'd found on Delia's shelf of pots and pans. "It will still take many hours, but it will be delicious with the bread." After little more than a brief hesitation, she, too, tied one of Delia's aprons across her dress. "At home, it must sit on the stove for a long time, with much stirring."

Ingredient by ingredient, they created the simple dough for Emma's bread. While it rose in its bowl by the kitchen window, they sliced apples and chatted. When the apple butter was turned over to time, they punched and kneaded the dough and then left it to rise once again.

As it did, they moved on to Delia's recipe—a white chocolate pastry puff that required whisking, melting, and occasional samples enjoyed off the edge of mixing spoons and fingertips. When Emma suggested melting some dark chocolate to drizzle across the top, Delia grinned.

"You remind me of her right now," Delia said as she scooped up the latest dirty bowl and carried it over to the sink.

Emma gathered up the used mixing spoons and followed. "Who?"

"Ruby." Delia squeezed a drop of dishwashing soap into the bowl and turned on the water. "Your mother. She was just like you are now whenever I'd catch her drawing during a visit."

Intrigued, Emma set the spoons into the bowl and waited for more. Delia didn't disappoint.

"You've been floating around this kitchen since the moment we unpacked the groceries from the store. And once we actually started, that joy you told me you feel when you bake was every bit as tangible as that bonnet."

"It is a prayer kapp," Emma corrected quietly. "I like to bake. It makes me happy."

"I can see that. And that's what drawing did for your mother."

Emma picked up a dishcloth to Delia's sponge and waited to dry the first of many things they had dirtied. "Do you mean the drawings she did of houses?"

"I do."

"That was not just for my . . . *father*?"

"The drawings?" At Emma's nod, Delia handed her the first bowl and moved on to the next. "The first house she drew was for herself—so she could get a better idea of Brad's dream to build homes. But as he talked about different features he wanted to do and different looks he wanted to create both inside and outside, she really seemed to enjoy drafting new versions. Soon, it became apparent she had the kind of ability that made her a natural for a career in architecture.

"Next thing I knew, they were planning their one-day business, with Ruby as the architect, and Brad as the builder. They even came up with a name for their business."

Emma stopped drying. "What was it?"

A sad smile tugged at the corner of Delia's mouth as she scrubbed at a spot near the bottom of the bowl. "Imagine Homes."

Before she could ask why, Delia continued, the woman's voice almost wistful. "They used to say that to each other. He'd say something like, *imagine a fireplace with a long, narrow window on each side. . . .* Or she'd say something like, *imagine a house built around a flower garden.* Sometimes the things they'd throw out would get them laughing, and sometimes it would have Ruby reaching for paper and a pencil while Brad talked the idea through into something workable.

"Believe it or not, even as young as the two of them were at the time, they really had some great ideas. So much so, I truly believed Imagine Homes would exist one day, with Ruby drawing the designs, and Brad making them come to life all over this town."

"But he did not call his company Imagine Homes," Emma said, swapping the now dry bowl for the next wet one. "It is Harper Construction."

Delia reached for the pile of spoons but stopped and shut off the water instead. "He did that at my suggestion. I wanted him to look forward, instead of backward. To really embrace this venture as his own. Though, even with the name change, he still made sure Ruby was part of it even if he's the only one who ever actually sees it."

"A part of the company?" At Delia's emphatic nod, Emma lowered the partially dried bowl back to the counter. "But how? She is dead."

Delia wiped her hands across the front of her apron and reached for Emma, her eyes sparkling. "Come. I have something very special to show you."

Chapter 20

Sitting on the couch, waiting, it was hard to look at anything besides the photograph of a young Brad and Ruby on the way to the carnival. Sure, she saw snippets of herself in Brad's hair and eyes, and Ruby's everything else, but that's where the connection ended. In fact, if not for a handful of lunches and a single family-style dinner, the curly haired boy with the ear-to-ear grin would be as much of a stranger to Emma as the girl smiling warmly at his side.

"I'm sorry that took so long, Emma," Delia said, breezing into the room with a burgundy-colored folder in one hand, and a dark brown leather book in the other. "It seems I need to move *clean office* a smidge higher on my to-do list for this week and—"

Delia's gaze landed on Emma's face, quickening her steps to the couch as it did. "Emma? Is something wrong? You look a little . . . *upset.*"

"I do not mean to be upset," she said, looking between Delia and the mantel, her voice barely more than a rasp. "It is just that . . . I don't know what to feel."

Depositing the folder and book onto the coffee table, Delia sat down and draped her arm across Emma's shoulders. "Oh, sweetie, this is time to be happy! You've found us and we've found you! It's an answer to many, many prayers!"

"I did not say such prayers."

"That's because you didn't know. Those people kept us from you and you from us."

Those people.

Mamm and Dat.

Only they weren't really—

Shaking off the troubling thought, Emma lifted her finger and Delia's attention back to the picture. "I do not know them. They are strangers to me. But I would not be sitting here without them."

"Brad isn't a stranger anymore, Emma." Delia hooked her finger beneath Emma's chin and guided Emma's gaze back to hers. "Little by little, the two of you—and all of us—are going to build something very special, I just know it."

"Yah."

Delia watched her for a few moments and then reclaimed the brown book from its temporary resting spot on the coffee table. "Brad told me the two of you have been working your way through the little memories he's been leaving at the gravesite each year, yes?"

"There are six more I still do not know."

"And when he gets home tonight, maybe you two can rectify that. Or, better yet, once tomorrow is behind you both."

"Tomorrow?" Emma echoed. "Do you mean this man I am to talk to?"

"Nicholas. Yes."

"I do not know why I must speak to him."

"Because he has to know everything as it happened. He needs facts."

"But I can speak to Bishop King alone. When I do, our community will shun them," she said, her voice rising. "I will tell him as soon as the children have been told. Backs will be turned to them until they repent!"

"*Backs will be turned to them?*" Delia cupped her mouth

only to let her hand fall back to the still-closed book. "That isn't enough, Emma."

"It is awful to be shunned! Your friends and your family cannot look at you, or speak to you! And if they do, they can be shunned, too!" Emma turned toward Delia, her knees scraping against the coffee table. "My friend, Mary? Her uncle Barley was shunned once for using electricity inside his home. Mary could not speak to him or look at him for weeks."

Delia started to speak, stopped, and, after several long moments of silence, tapped the cover of the book. "The other day, when you saw *that*"—she pointed to the picture on the mantel—"you asked if I had more pictures of Ruby. Perhaps you would like to see them before we get to the reason I brought you into this room in the first place?"

"There are more? In there?"

"There are, indeed." Her smile back in place, Delia opened the book to the first page, her fingers immediately moving to the edge of the first photograph—a picture of a tired house Emma found vaguely familiar. "This is the house Brad was helping repair when he met Ruby for the first time. So, when I suggested putting all his pictures into an album he could look at whenever he was missing Ruby, he said it had to start with this one."

Emma studied the front porch . . . the front windows . . . the dilapidated looking house . . . the—"Wait! I know this house! It is different now. It has fresh paint and the porch is not lopsided like this. And that woman"—she pointed to the person standing on the porch, peering out—"does not live there now. Miss Lottie does!"

"Is she Amish?"

"No. Well, I mean, she was raised by Amish, but she did not join the church. I think she said she moved into this house when I was a little younger than Esther." She leaned in for a closer look, her mind's eye replacing the house in front of her with the tidy cottage she'd sat in just two days earlier. "She is kin to the Beilers and she is very wise."

Delia turned the page, her own soft inhale barely noticeable against Emma's. "He borrowed my camera the first time he went to the ice cream shop because he wanted to take a picture of Ruby for me to see."

"I know this shop! It is still there!" At Delia's nod, Emma pulled the book partially onto her own lap to get a closer look. "This picture? It is when Ruby came outside at the end of the night, isn't it?"

"Brad told you . . ."

"Yah. He told me he waited for two hours for her work to be done. He is right," she said, studying the picture. "Ruby was surprised to see him when she came out. Her eyes are very big like Mamm's get when she is surprised, but there is a smile there, too."

"There's more."

Page by page, they made their way through the album, the images Brad had recorded matching many of the stories he had shared. But as much as she enjoyed having the visual to go with the story, it was the faces, themselves, that held her attention most.

"I realized, the other night, after you left, that we didn't take any pictures. I guess we were all so in the moment, none of us thought of grabbing a camera." Delia relinquished her hold on the edge of the album long enough to squeeze Emma's hand. "We'll have to rectify that so we can start a new album—one with you and your father . . . and me, too."

Emma drew back. "I do not take pictures. The Bible says, 'Thou shalt not make unto thyself a graven image.' It is the Amish way."

"*Ruby* took pictures," Delia said, sweeping her hand back to the album.

"Ruby had not been baptized yet. I am." Emma swung her gaze between the photo in the album and the one on the mantel and then released a quiet sigh. "I should not even be looking at these pictures."

"Every child has a right to know their parents, dear. Since Ruby is gone, these pictures are your way to know her."

She knew she should argue, but she couldn't. Delia was right. She needed to know. To see. And who would punish her for looking, anyway? Mamm and Dat?

Leaning forward, she nodded at Delia to continue, and, once again, she soaked up everything the woman had to say about each and every picture. When they got to a picture of her birth parents sitting in a field surrounded by white fluffy dandelions, she looked up to find Delia watching her. "Did you take this picture?" Emma asked.

"No. See how it's taken from down low?" Delia pointed Emma's focus back to the picture. "Technology has gotten much better since this was taken, but Brad basically put it on video mode and then I pulled several still frames from it for this album."

She didn't really understand, but, still, she nodded as Delia turned to the next page and the series of pictures showing Ruby blowing on the dandelion. In the first shot, Ruby's eyes were open; in the second shot, one was closed and the other was peeking out at Brad with such a silly expression Emma couldn't help but laugh. And in the third picture, Ruby's eyes were closed and dandelion fluff scattered in the air.

"I wish I could know what she wished for that day," Emma whispered as much to herself as Delia.

"While I can't know for certain, I might have a guess." Delia pointed to the folder on the table. "Shall we take a look at that now?"

Emma looked down at the album and the handful of pages that still remained. "There are more pictures, yah?"

"There are. And we can get back to those. But this will speak to what I said earlier, in the kitchen. About Brad keeping Ruby part of things with the company even now. Even after . . . *everything*."

Sliding the album across her lap and onto the cushion to her left, Emma turned her attention to Delia and the folder with the same Harper Construction logo used on Brad's truck. "I have seen these at the office. Near Miss Sue Ellen's desk."

"You're right. Only *those* folders are different from this one in that they're missing one very special floor plan." Flipping the folder open, Delia pulled out a letter with the same Harper Construction logo across the top and set it aside in favor of the drawing on the next page. "Floor plans are what customers look at to decide which house suits their needs best—meaning, does it have the right number of rooms, does it have the bay window they want, or the office they need, et cetera.

"Each floor plan has a name to make it easier for people to reference. Like these ones." Delia took out a handful of floor plans and splayed them across the top of the folder. "The Emerald is a two-story with a bonus room over the garage. The Sapphire is a one-and-a-half story home with a formal dining room and a second-floor laundry. The Amethyst is a ranch with a split bedroom setup, meaning, the master suite is on one side of the home and the other two bedrooms are located on the other end. The Turquoise is a ranch-style home with a mother-in-law suite in the basement that can be accessed through a separate entrance, depending on the lot's grade. And then there's The Diamond. It's the one with all the bells and whistles."

Emma drew back. "Why would people want bells and whistles in their house? That would make it hard to sleep."

Delia's laugh brought a smile to Emma's lips, too. "That's just an expression, dear. It means that it has all of the extras that people want—the best of the best, so to speak." Feature by feature, Delia moved her finger around the floor plan, tapping out each item she listed. "Planning desk, center island, farmhouse sink in the kitchen, wet bar in the living room for entertaining, double bay windows in the dining room, French doors with alcove in office, switchback staircase to access the second floor, Jack and Jill bathroom between bedrooms number three and four, with each of those bedrooms having its own separate alcove for a sink, the second bedroom having its own bath, and, of course, the master suite with built-in fireplace, his and her large walk-in closets, separate tub and shower in the master bath, et cetera."

"There are many things in this house," Emma murmured.

"There's also a finished lower level." Delia's finger moved down the page to another set of drawings. "With a media room, a game room, another wet bar, a fifth bedroom, full bath, and storage space. It really is quite a house. I think they've built six or seven of these so far since Brad added the plan to the packet."

Emma smiled and nodded politely and then slid her attention back to the album. "Could we look at the rest of the pictures now?"

"Wait. I haven't gotten to the whole reason I'm showing this to you in the first place. The one thing you won't see in the packets at the office." Delia restacked the floor plans, set them off to the side, and reached into the folder once again.

Seconds later, Emma was staring down at a floor-plan-like drawing and trying to remember how to breathe. "This . . . this says *The Ruby,*" she whispered, post-swallow.

"It does."

"But . . ." At a loss for words, Emma simply stared at Delia and waited.

"That's the drawing—or, rather, a *copy* of the drawing Ruby wanted to be the first house Imagine Homes built."

Emma recognized some rudimentary features thanks to the previous floor plans, but still she was grateful when Delia's finger took over the tour. "Ruby didn't want a long front hallway. She wanted people to feel welcome the moment they stepped inside. So that's why the door opens into the family room. She wanted lots of windows because she told Brad she felt most at peace when she was looking out at the wide-open fields and the sunny sky."

"I . . . I like that, too," Emma murmured.

Nodding, Delia moved on, her finger moving to the right. "She wanted a large kitchen."

"To bake in?"

"To sit with family and visit," Delia corrected. "And she wanted lots of windows in the kitchen, too. That way you could nap in your cradle where it was warm and sunny, and she could be nearby, preparing lunch."

Emma drew back. "*Me?* But I was not born!"

"You were on the way when she made this drawing, dear."

"But—"

"Your pending arrival factored into almost everything here." Moving her finger toward the sketch of the second floor, Delia pointed to each of the four rooms. "She wanted all of the rooms to be together, and she wanted them simple. She said bedrooms were for sleeping. The rest of the house was for being together."

Emma's gaze skipped back to the first floor and the family room that seemed almost notched in two. "What is that line, there?"

"For some reason, Ruby wanted the front room to be quite large, but Brad did not agree. He said it was wasted space for the everyday and suggested a divider of sorts that could divide the space but allow it to be open and large for"— Delia shrugged—"special parties or whatever it was that made Ruby want such a large room."

"It is what she was used to," Emma murmured. "Amish homes have a large room that is used for hosting church. Each family only hosts a few times a year, but the room must be large enough to accommodate benches with many people when they do."

If Emma's words registered at all, they didn't last long as Delia's finger jumped to the front of the house. "Ruby also wanted a wide front porch, one that wrapped around the front and sides of the house. She wanted to be able to knit or quilt in a chair, or simply sit on a comfortable porch swing, and be able to see you wherever you were. And these boxes here? On the first-floor windows? Those are flower boxes."

It was hard to picture an actual home when all she could see was lines, but somehow she could. The simple house with a wide front porch and rocking chairs . . . The view of a pretty summer sky from inside the front room . . . The faces from the mantel-topped picture looking down at a newborn Emma sleeping soundly in a cradle by a kitchen window . . . Ruby's loving smile directed on no one but—

Fisting the tears from her eyes with her left hand, Emma pushed the drawing and folder back onto Delia's lap with her right. "I need you to take me back to Blue Ball. Now."

"Take you back? But-but why?" Delia closed the folder and tossed it onto the coffee table. "I thought we were having a nice time! I thought I could make you dinner, we could try your bread and my pastries, and we could look at the rest of the photo album! I thought, too, that if you were still here around seven, you'd get to see Brad for a little while before it was time to take you back to the farm. I mean, I know you'll be together tomorrow, but it's going to be such a stressful day in a lot of ways and it might be nice to have a little quiet, carefree time first."

"I need to go back."

Delia's whole being sagged. "Emma, dear, if I did something to upset you, it wasn't intentional. Maybe I should've waited and let Brad show you your mother's drawing, but you were asking so many questions about Ruby and the company that—"

"Please. I need to go back," Emma insisted. "I need to pack my things."

For a moment, the silence born on her words was so deafening, Emma actually pressed her hand to her chest in an effort to quiet her pounding heart. But it didn't matter. Delia's answering gasp drowned out all. *"Pack your things?* Emma, does this mean you're ready to start your new life here? With your father and me?"

"Yah. . . . I mean, *yes.*"

Chapter 21

She watched Delia's car disappear from view and then turned toward home, the anger she'd managed to keep in check during the ride to Miller's Pond propelling her forward. Step by step, she made her way past the first of four farms, the insistent bleating of the Schrocks' goats little more than background noise for the images cycling their way through her thoughts.

* Stopping at the grave before school on her birthdays . . .
* Looking over her shoulder as she added the latest trinket to the bag . . .
* Watching her classmates play at recess and never being asked to join . . .
* Always doing more than asked at home and still never getting a heartfelt smile from Mamm in return . . .
* Standing in Brad's office, staring into eyes that looked just like hers . . .
* Flipping through photographs, trying to memorize everything about two people who, for all intents and purposes, were strangers, yet also her parents . . .

"Good evening, Emma."

Startled off the edge of the road, Emma looked up to find Levi Fisher smiling back. "Levi! I did not hear you coming!"

"I see that." He tugged Hoofer to a stop beside Emma and readjusted his hat. "Soon the sun will be down and it will be quite cold to be out walking."

"I am not out walking."

Dragging his hand down his face, Levi sat back in his seat. "You are out, and you are walking."

"Yah, I am walking. But it is only to get to Dat's farm."

"I could give you a ride if you would like."

"But you live the other way," Emma said, pointing in the very direction they'd both come.

"I do."

She waited for him to say more, but when he didn't, she took the hand he held out to her and climbed into place beside him on the buggy seat. "It is very kind of you to drive me home. Thank you."

"It is my pleasure."

With a quick, yet firm jiggle of the reins, Hoofer began to walk, the mare's gentle pace and sure steps a stark contrast to the anger Emma was just four farms away from unleashing. Still, she took advantage of the quiet that fell around them to steady her breath and try to unfurl her fingers from the fist she couldn't seem to relax no matter how hard she tried.

"Do you see that cow? There?" Levi guided her attention toward a Holstein grazing in the Troyers' field. At her nod, he broke out in a grin. "Found it sitting outside our front porch week before last. Came out after lunch and there it was. Staring back at me like *I* was the one who didn't belong."

"But you live more than a half mile that way," she said, hooking her thumb over her shoulder. "Why would a cow go so far from home?"

"Dat said it must have smelt Mamm's cooking."

Her laugh mingled with Levi's only to fade away as he continued, his words taking her on a journey past his front porch and a neighbor's cow to his dat's fields. "The rocks have been cleared from the fields and soon we will begin the planting. The days will be long when we do, so I am trying to help Miss Lottie with some repairs now, while I can."

"Repairs? What kind of repairs?"

"The floor in her living room has many creaks, and one of the railings on her front porch is not tight."

"Do you like to do such things?" she asked.

"Yah. I like to work with my hands. Perhaps, if Miss Lottie would like, I can build a shed for her gardening tools since she does not have a barn. I could make it look like a small house. I think Miss Lottie would like that, yah?"

"I think she would like that very much."

"Did it help to speak with her the other night? You were so quiet when I picked you up, I did not want to interrupt your thoughts with questions."

Something about his voice, his very demeanor, snapped her attention back to his face. "If I did not thank you for bringing me to Miss Lottie's, I am sorry. I—"

"You thanked me, Emma. Many times."

"Good." She looked again at the fields and breathed in the cold winter air. "And yah, speaking with Miss Lottie was nice."

"That is good, though you were missed at the hymn sing."

This time, her laugh was void of anything resembling humor. "I do not know who would miss me. Mary was with Leroy, so there would be no one to speak to, no one to miss me."

"I missed you." With a gentle pull, he slowed Hoofer's pace still further. "No one makes the kind of oatmeal cookies you make."

"You still didn't like Liddy's cookies?"

"It is as I have told you, Emma, Liddy Mast makes oatmeal cookies, but she does not make them like yours," Levi corrected. "No one does. Not even Mamm."

She felt her mouth growing slack and covered it with a quick swallow as, once again, he continued. "But it is more than just oatmeal cookies that I missed. I missed looking over to check on Mary and seeing your smile. It is something I look to see at every hymn sing now."

"My . . . my smile?" she echoed.

"Yah."

She saw Levi's mouth still moving, knew he was still saying things she probably wanted to hear, but at that moment there was only one voice she heard.

"There were so many things I loved about Ruby, but her smile? It was the best. Distracting as all get-out, but wow."

Brad had liked Ruby's smile. . . .

"I missed hearing you laugh when Mary said something funny. It does not matter who I am talking to or what I am doing when I hear that sound. I always stop and listen." Levi's own soft laugh rumbled past his lips. "And I missed watching that little jump you do when your team wins at volleyball."

She stared at Levi. "I jump?"

"Yah. When you hit the shot that wins."

"Ruby would do this little jump when she was excited about something—bubbles, skating, it didn't matter. If she was happy, she did her little jump."

Emma pressed her hands to her cheeks in an effort to cool their building heat. "I did not know I did such a thing."

"You do."

In lieu of words she didn't have, Emma looked out at the dusky fields, the familiar landscape calming her nerves. Closing her eyes for just a moment, she breathed in the scent of thawing earth and imagined the way it would change as the temperatures warmed and crops began to grow.

"I spent the day with Delia," she whispered. "She is my English grossmudder."

If he was surprised by her admission, he kept it to himself. Instead, he guided Hoofer to the edge of the road and brought the buggy to a stop. "Was it a good visit?" he asked, resting the reins atop his legs.

"It was. We baked together. I showed her how to make my bread and apple butter—" She sucked in the rest of the word, only to wave away the worry. "No, it is okay. It still has many hours. It will be fine."

"*I* like apple butter," Levi said.

Something about the earnestness in his voice made her giggle. "I must bring you some."

"Yah." He fiddled with the reins for a moment before tucking them to the side in favor of shifting his full attention to her face. "You did not look like Emma when I saw you back there."

She started to protest but stopped as the reality she'd been denying long enough, pushed itself to the forefront of her thoughts. "I am Emma—*this Emma*—because of Mamm and Dat. They raised me to be Amish because they are Amish. But Brad is my birth dat. He should have raised me. He wanted me. They *both* wanted me—Brad *and* Ruby. But Ruby died having me, and Mamm and Dat told Brad I died, too. If they had not done that, he would have raised me. If she'd lived, I would be English. If he'd known I'd lived, I would be English. . . . I would have gone to an English school, maybe even college. . . . Maybe I would cook in a fancy restaurant the way Delia said. . . . Maybe I would know important people and travel to many places in the world. . . . I would not wear a kapp"—she pointed to her head—"and I would drive a car instead of a buggy."

"Do you *want* to go to college and cook in a fancy restaurant?" Levi asked.

"I don't know. I have never thought of such things. College is for English, not Amish. Being a chef in a fancy restaurant is for English, not Amish. Traveling the world to see many places and many countries is for English, not Amish." She took in the streaks of mauve and pink in the western sky and tried to gather her words into something neat and tidy. "I am only Amish because of lies. If there had been no death and no lies, I would be English."

"When you were little, yah. But you chose to be baptized," Levi reminded. "That was no one's choice but your own."

"It was made because I was not shown another life."

"That is what Rumspringa does. It shows you another life."

"It shows another life to one who is *Amish*. But it is not the same—not as it would be if the English world is the only world I ever knew." She sat with her own words for a moment, only to shrug them away as the reason she was there, in his buggy instead of eating dinner with Delia, pushed its way to the front of her thoughts. "Ruby drew a house for us to live in."

"She drew a house?"

"Yah."

"Tell me."

And so she did. She told him about the floor plan Ruby had drawn. She told him all the little details Ruby had included with Emma in mind. She told him about the window in the kitchen and the way Ruby had wanted to put Emma's cradle there. She told him about the front porch and how Ruby had wanted a swing there so she could watch Emma playing. And she told him about the smile she knew Ruby would have had for her if Ruby had lived—a smile Mamm never seemed to have for Emma in the way she did for her real children.

"That is why I am leaving. Why I am going to go home, pack my things, and say goodbye to Jakob, Sarah, Jonathan, Annie, and"—her voice grew hoarse—"Esther."

"Say goodbye?" Levi shifted on the seat to face Emma. "Why? Where are you going?"

"I should never have been *here*." She swept her hands outward. "I should not be Amish."

"But you *are* Amish, Emma! You chose the Amish way when you joined the church! We all did!"

She blinked against the tears she didn't want him to see. "Yah. I did choose to be baptized. But I knew only lies. I did not know who I was."

"You were Emma then, you are Emma now." Slowly, tentatively, Levi reached for her hands only to pull back at the last second. "My dat always tells me to think before I do. To think of the good and the bad that will come with each choice I make. Sometimes, I want to just choose. Sometimes, I do not want to spend so much time thinking. But when I do as Dat says, and I think about the good and the bad my choice will bring, I see things I did not see at first. Things it is important for me to see."

"They *wanted* me, Levi. They wanted to build a house for us to live in—as a family."

This time when he reached for her hands, he didn't stop, the feel of his warm skin against hers stealing her breath from her lungs. "Just *think,* Emma. Please. Think about the good and the bad that will come if you do this. Then, if you still feel it is right for you to leave the Amish way, you must leave."

Chapter 22

She was waiting at the usual spot when Brad drove up at eleven o'clock the next morning, the absence of anything resembling a suitcase at her feet clearly registering on his face the moment he stopped the car.

"Hey there, kiddo." He stepped onto the road, squeezed her hand in greeting, and motioned toward the thicket of trees at her back. "Is your stuff back there? By the pond?"

Casting her eyes down at the drawstring bag beside her feet, Emma shook her head.

A flash of movement sent her eyes back to Brad in time to see him check his wristwatch. "Okay . . . That's okay. As long as we're in and out of there inside ten minutes, we'll still be able to have a little catch-up time together before Sue Ellen starts calling to find out where we are."

Dropping his hand to his side, he motioned toward the truck with his chin and grinned. "So come on. Let's make this official and get your stuff."

"I have not packed my things," she said.

He stopped, mid-step. "Why not? My mother said that's why she took you back earlier than planned yesterday. Because you said you wanted to get your stuff together."

"Yah. That is what I said, what I thought I was going to do. But I didn't."

His gaze traveled down the road toward the farm only to

return to hers, all signs of lightness gone. "They gave you a hard time, didn't they?"

"No. I did not tell them."

He cupped his hand over his weighted exhale but said nothing.

"Miss Lottie says it is not good to make decisions in anger."

"Miss Lottie?" Slowly, he dropped his hand to his side to reveal lips that were twisted in controlled anger. "Who is Miss Lottie?"

"I have spoken of her before. She lives closer to the Beiler farm. She is English."

"Does this *Miss Lottie* know the truth?"

Emma nodded. "We spoke the other night."

"And that's what she had to say? Decisions shouldn't be made in anger?"

"Yah." Emma wandered over to the truck and stared at her reflection in the driver side window, the hooded eyes and somber expression she wore reaching into her very being. "Levi says I should think of the good and the bad when I am to make a decision."

"There is no bad to leaving that house, Emma. What they did to you . . . *to me* . . . *to my mom* . . . *That* is what's bad, not trying to make it right after twenty-two years of lies!"

She didn't need her reflection to know the tears were there, hovering in the corners of her eyes. She could feel them just as surely as she could the disappointment emanating off her birth father. "I'm sorry," she whispered. "I will leave. Soon."

He took a few steps toward the trees, only to double back just as quickly. "I'm not upset with you, Emma. Please know that. I'm upset about the whole situation. I just want it to be behind us so we can get to immersing ourselves in each other's lives the way we should have all along. The way we *would* have if none of this had ever happened."

"Yah."

A second glance at his watch had him scooping up the

drawstring bag and guiding her around the front of the truck to the passenger side. "As much as I know there's more to say, we really should be heading over to my office. Sue Ellen can order us in an early lunch and I can tell you the story behind the rest of your birthday presents. Keeps her from getting all angst-y that I'm not there, and has us right where we need to be, when we need to be there."

"I will do my best to answer your friend's questions," Emma said, fastening her seat belt.

"That's all we can ask, kiddo. So, don't stress, okay?" At her nod, he closed her door and crossed back to his own side of the truck. Once he was settled and they were on the way to New Holland, he flashed a grin at her that rivaled the February sun. "So Mom told me about your cooking session out at her place yesterday. She even gave me a slice of your bread with some of that apple butter on top and—"

Groaning, she dropped her head in her hands. "The apple butter. I forgot about that when I left. It must be ruined by now."

"Nope. Mom set an alarm on her phone so she would get up and shut off the slow cooker when it was time. Then she transferred everything over to some sort of container."

"What kind of container?" she asked, sitting up.

"I don't know. Technically, the apple butter wasn't exactly done when I helped myself to some for my bread, but I couldn't help myself." A long, low whistle filled the truck's cab. "I gotta say, Emma, that stuff was amazing. Maybe even better than Ruby's."

Pride she knew she shouldn't feel warmed her cheeks, forcing her to look out the window until she got her emotions in check. "It is just apple butter."

"There was nothing *just* about that stuff *or* the bread. And my mom said you made some suggestions for her pastries she'd never considered before and it made them a million times better."

"I am sure they would be good without my ideas."

"And they always were—one of my favorites, in fact. But she's right, they were better last night. Much better." He let up on the gas as they approached a traffic light, his attention flitting between the line of cars slowing to a stop and Emma. "Mom says you show signs of having some really amazing instincts in the kitchen with everything from tastes to process."

"I like to cook and to bake. It makes me happy."

"That's how I feel about what I do, and how Mom feels about what she does. It's called a passion." When the light turned green, they lurched forward with the line of cars. "Perhaps cooking and baking is *your* passion, Emma."

"It is just something I do to help at home."

"But maybe, with some proper training, it's something you could do for a career." At the four-way stop, he turned left toward Harper Construction. "Like I did when I went away to school for architecture."

She waved at his words much the way Dat's horse swished his tail at the pesky flies that frequented the barn. "I do not have enough schooling to go to college."

"You don't now, sure. But I can get you a tutor. And I'm sure, if we look, we can find cooking classes that don't require any sort of degree." He turned into the Harper Construction parking lot and claimed his usual spot by the back door. "And if you like it enough to pursue it, I'm sure I can find a friend who has an in at one of the bigger restaurants. Or, better yet, you could open your own catering business or your own bakery, or even your own five-star restaurant one day. Of course, I'd help you get it off the ground with funding and whatever else you need."

She was pretty sure she smiled. If not, maybe a nod? She wasn't entirely sure. All she knew for certain was that her head was beginning to spin and her heart was beginning to race. Reaching down, she wrapped her hand around the top of the drawstring bag and hugged it to her chest, the need for something familiar impossible to ignore. "Can we really look at the rest of the gifts when we go inside?" she asked as she followed him from the car and up the back steps. "There are only six left."

He glanced back at the lot, took in the lone sedan not far from his truck, and then pushed open the door. "Sure thing. Let's just check in with Sue Ellen and make sure everything is still a go with Nicholas and—"

"Brad! Emma!" Sue Ellen abandoned her desk chair to greet them, her warm, welcoming gaze lighting on Emma. "It is good to see you again, sweetheart." Then, turning her attention to Brad, Sue Ellen tapped her watch. "Everything is on schedule for one o'clock. I've set up the conference room for three and I made sure the video feed is ready to go so there are no glitches there."

"Thank you, Sue Ellen." Brad reached into a silver tray marked *inbox*, extracted a small stack of envelopes and pink sticky notes, and tilted his head toward his office door. "Emma and I have some things to go over, but if you could order in some lunch—maybe some sandwiches or pizza or something—that would be great. Oh, and if Nicholas arrives early, let me know that, too."

"Of course." Sue Ellen turned her smile back on Emma. "Enjoy your time together."

"Thank you." She smiled across her shoulder as Brad ushered her into his office and over to the chair opposite his desk. When she was situated with the bag on her lap, Emma loosened the opening, reached inside, and felt around until she found the covered bridge left on her sixteenth birthday.

"I remember when I found this one," she said, holding the gift up for Brad to see across the stack of mail he was slowly picking his way through. "It reminded me of the covered bridge on the road to Bird in Hand."

"Then I picked well." He separated the envelopes into two different piles and then sat back, tenting his fingers beneath his chin. "Ruby loved to walk down the embankment and sit on the rocks just below the bridge after a hard rain. The first few times, I figured it was just her place to think—like Mom's bench out by the pond always was for me growing up. But when I asked her about it, she said she liked to sit there and listen. She said the sound of the water rushing across the rocks in the creek bed made her feel closer to God.

"I didn't really get it until she sat me down on the grass and covered my eyes with her hands."

"I feel that way by the pond sometimes, too. When the air is perfectly still you can hear everything that is from God— butterfly wings, frogs croaking, and the birds singing." Emma turned the bridge over in her hands. "If I am upset, His sounds give me peace."

"I went there after Ruby died—after I thought you had both died." Brad separated his hands from one another and dropped them to their respective armrest. "The water had frozen, but even if it had been spring and the creek bed had been swollen from a hard rain, I'm not sure I would have heard anything over my anger."

"Anger?"

"Oh yeah."

"*At me?*" she whispered.

He drew back so fast his head actually thumped against his seat. "You? Why on earth would I have been angry at you?"

"Because Ruby died having me."

"No. I wasn't angry at *you*. Never you." Splaying his hands, palms out, he leaned forward. "You know what? Let's move on, shall we? What's next?"

She searched his face for anything to indicate his words didn't match his true feelings, but when she saw nothing, she pulled out the small, red rubber ball that had been waiting for her on Ruby's grave the day she'd turned seventeen.

"Ahhh, yes. The rubber ball and the spinner."

"This?" She pulled out the yellow spinny thing she'd gotten the following year and, at his nod, set it on the table next to the ball.

"I took Ruby to an arcade one day. We knew you were on the way and I wanted her to see some of the fun stuff I got to do as a kid. So we played Skee-Ball and all sorts of games. When we were done, we took the tickets to the counter and picked out silly stuff—the ball and the spinner being the ones we had the most fun with."

She dove her hand into the bag again, this time producing the baseball with the blue smudges from her nineteenth birthday. "Why did someone try to write on a baseball?"

"Because that's the baseball I smacked clear out of the ballpark for my team not long after I met Ruby. She came to watch me play and so I stepped up my game. Hit that ball farther than any other ball I'd ever hit. So I signed it like a professional ball player would."

She studied the ball carefully, smiling as the top of the B and the bottom half of an H suddenly made sense. "I see it now. At least a little bit."

"What's next?"

"My twentieth birthday and this dried flower with the pink and blue ribbons tied around the stem."

"That's the flower I gave Ruby after she told me about you. And since we didn't know if you were a boy or a girl, I had the florist put a pink ribbon *and* a blue ribbon around it."

A quick tap on the partially open door brought Brad to his feet and Emma's attention onto Sue Ellen. "Boss, Nicholas just called. He'll be pulling into the lot in about two minutes."

"We'll be ready." Stepping around his chair, he snuck another peek at the clock. "Is that lunch order going to have enough for all of us?"

"Yes."

"Perfect. Thanks, Sue Ellen." Then, turning back to Emma, he pointed at the bag. "We should be able to get in the last one before he actually gets in here."

Reaching into the bag one last time, she produced the whittled bird. "Esther has named this Emma. Because she says if she were a baby bird, I would bring her worms."

"That's how I saw Ruby being with you. Nurturing and loving—hence, the mother bird. I just believed she could do that in my world, too." He stepped around the desk, motioned her to his side, and led her out to Sue Ellen's desk in time to see a tall blond man walk through the front door with a pad of paper under one arm and some sort of silver contraption in his opposite hand.

"Nicholas, my friend! I see you're running early as always."

Grinning, Nicholas shifted the silver contraption to his left hand and extended his right for a shake Brad returned in short order. "I figured we could go over a few things before we bring in the chief." Then, turning his attention onto Emma, his jaw slacked open.

"You'd swear she was Ruby, wouldn't you?" Brad prodded.

"Seriously. Whoa . . ." Nicholas shifted his hand to Emma. "Hi, Emma, I'm Nicholas—Nicholas Forrester. I've known your dad, here, since we were two."

Not entirely sure what to say, she settled for a nod and a smile as the man took one more head to toe sweep before looking back at Brad with an even wider grin. "Lucky for her, the only thing she seems to have gotten from you are your eyes."

"Ha . . . Ha . . ." Brad sent his gaze to the ceiling, only to drop it back to Emma with a wink. "I've been taking this guy's abuse for a lot of years."

"And you're a far finer man because of it." Nicholas peeked around Brad to acknowledge Sue Ellen as she walked into the room from the direction of the back door. "Is that takeout I see in your hands?"

"It is. Sandwiches from Melly's. The delivery boy just dropped it off."

Nicholas pumped his hand in the air. "This-*this* is why I really should stop by and see my buddy Brad more often. He feeds me." Shifting his hand back to his pile of things, he offered a more appropriate greeting to Sue Ellen and nudged his chin toward the conference room. "I imagine we'll be in there?"

"Yes, and everything is set up."

"Speakers and video recorder good to go?"

"I tested it all this morning." Sue Ellen set the bags of food on her desk and shifted her attention to Brad. "If you guys want to get started, I'll get this stuff ready."

"Perfect. Thanks, Sue Ellen." Placing his hand on the small of Emma's back, Brad guided her toward a room off the building's front hallway.

The room, itself, was fairly small. Just enough room to hold a long rectangular table with six chairs—two on each side, and one on both ends. A single window, overlooking the road, infused only snippets of light into the room through the partially closed blind. In front of the window, pointing toward the table, was a camera mounted atop a tripod. On the wall, in multiple frames, hung the various floor plans Delia had shown her the previous day. A quick inspection, though, showed no sign of The Ruby.

"Let's put Emma here"—Nicholas directed Brad to the chair the farthest from the window—"that way we're not moving her around the table unnecessarily."

"Emma?" Brad pulled out the chair and motioned her over. When she was seated, he took the chair to her left while Nicholas took the one to her right.

"So, Emma, I'll be recording your words with this voice recorder"—he lifted the silver contraption off the table—"during this first session for my own records. Is that okay?"

Emma scanned the table and chairs before settling her sights on the tripod positioned in front of the window. "Is-is that a camera?" she asked, pointing.

"It is," Nicholas said, setting the silver contraption back down. "But it's not on. This voice recorder is fine for our chat."

She lowered her hand back to her lap. "I am told you want to talk about what they did . . ."

"I do, indeed. So, are you good with the recorder?"

She looked to Brad for approval, and, at his nod, gave one of her own.

"Okay, so let's get started." Clearing his throat, Nicholas positioned his notepad in front of him, consulted a notation on the upper right-hand corner, and then pressed a button on the silver box. "The date is February 10th and I'm here with Emma Lapp. Emma, when were you first told Brad Harper was your father?"

"I-I was not told. I knew when I saw him. When I came to his office to ask why he put things on my birth mother's grave."

Nicholas made some notions on the notepad and then moved on, his tone brisk. "How long did you know the deceased Ruby Stoltzfus had been your mother?"

"I did not know until my birthday. When I found the locket Brad left with her picture inside. When I asked Mamm later that morning, she told me about Ruby—how she had gone to be with the Lord while giving birth to me."

"Until that day, Rebeccah and Wayne Lapp had always said they were your birth parents?"

She stopped, mid-nod. "I do not remember them saying those words. I just knew them to be Mamm and Dat."

"And Ruby? How did they refer to her?"

"I knew her to be Mamm's sister, who died when she was eighteen."

Nicholas jotted something down and then returned his attention to Emma. "Were you told how she died?"

"No."

"Did you ask?"

"No! I did not want to upset Mamm. Speaking of Ruby, thinking of Ruby, visiting Ruby's grave . . . it all made Mamm sad. *My birthday* made Mamm sad."

Nicholas leaned forward. "Your birthday made Rebeccah Lapp sad? Why?"

"Because Ruby died on my birthday."

"So, you knew that part?"

"Yah. It is on her grave at the cemetery."

"Yet you never asked how she died?" Nicholas asked, again.

"No."

"Did the other children in the house . . . I think there's"— again Nicholas consulted his notepad—"*five* of them . . . ever ask how Ruby died?"

"No. Everyone wanted to see Mamm smile. Such questions would keep her sad."

"Do you think the children knew you were not their birth sibling?"

She blinked against the tears she knew were seconds away from escaping down her cheeks and willed herself to answer the question. "No."

"When Rebeccah and Wayne introduced you to people, did they refer to you as their daughter?"

Had they?

She couldn't be sure.

"They would call me Emma."

"Is that different than the way they'd introduce the others?"

"No. But we do not need to be introduced to people we already know."

Nicholas allowed a half smile. "Fair enough." He flipped to the next page in his pad and looked back up at Emma. "I want to ask you about an incident when you were seven. I understand you fell through some ice and that no adults were present at the time, is that right?"

She slanted a glance at Brad only to follow his eyes back to Nicholas. "I-I was on the way home from school with Jakob. We should not have been on the ice."

"How long were you in the water before you were rescued?"

"Only my leg fell in. Jakob helped me out with a stick, and we walked home. Mamm warmed me with blankets and scolded me."

"She scolded you?"

"Yah. We were not to be on the pond alone."

"Was Jakob scolded as well?"

"No. I was older."

"You were seven," Nicholas said.

"Jakob was six."

The man jotted some notes and then looked up at Emma once again. "Were you treated like the other children in the house?"

"Mamm did not smile at me the way she did the others. Before the locket, I thought it was because I was a reminder of a sad day. Now, I know I was not just a reminder. I am the reason."

Brad's chair creaked as he leaned forward and snapped at Nicholas to turn off the recorder. "Whoa, whoa. You need to stop saying that, Emma. You are not the reason Ruby died. Having you in a house with people who aren't trained in proper medical care is what killed her, not you. You have to know that. You *need* to know that."

Oh how she wanted to believe him. To know she wasn't responsible for her birth mother's death and Mamm's heart-ache. . . .

"You know what?" Brad sat up and shifted his focus back to his friend. "Since we're ahead of schedule anyway, what do you say we take a break, have some of that food from Melly's, and then get back to the rest of your questions?"

Setting his pen atop his notepad, Nicholas shrugged. "Works for me. Though, really, I don't think I need to ask anything else. Emma has done a great job answering everything so far. I'm sure she'll be fine with the chief's questions. We'll just need to make sure the camera is on her face and set to record, and then we can—"

"Camera?" she echoed, looking from Nicholas to Brad and back again. "I cannot have my picture taken. I am Amish."

"Emma, please," Brad said around a moan. "This is not the time or place for that. It was this, or the police station. And Chief Wilton is a good man; his questions will be very much like the ones Nicholas just asked."

Emma braced herself against the edge of the table. "I-I cannot talk to the police! It is not the Amish way!"

Reaching forward, Brad covered her hand with his own. "I know that, kiddo. That's why Nicholas suggested doing this by way of video. We figured it would be less intimidating for you."

"But it is not the Amish way," she repeated, pulling away.

"This isn't about being Amish, Emma. This is about reporting a crime and seeing to it that justice is served."

"But that is what Bishop King will do. He will see to it that Mamm and Dat are shunned."

Brad splayed his palms. "Oh no . . . No way . . . Keeping my child from me—and me from her—for twenty-two years is due way more than a momentary snub." He grabbed her hand off her lap and held it tight, his blue eyes holding hers with such intensity she couldn't look away. "Not only did I miss out on everything—your first smile, your first rollover, your first word, your first step, your first birthday, your . . . *everything*—I can't recapture any of it by way of pictures or videos because the Amish don't take pictures."

"*I* can tell you some things."

"Some, yeah. But not everything. Not the things I should have seen with my own two eyes, not the things I should have experienced all on my own."

"But—"

"Emma, Rebeccah and Wayne stole a baby! They stole you! That's not okay. They shouldn't be allowed to walk around like they did nothing wrong, like they didn't just strip us of time we'll never get back . . . memories we missed out on making . . . milestones we didn't celebrate together! Rebeccah and Wayne belong in prison, Emma—for a long, long time!"

"Prison?" she said, pulling her hand from his grasp once again. "You-you mean jail?"

"Yes. Prison . . . Jail . . . Locked away for the rest of their lives . . ." Exhaling through pursed lips, Brad raked his fingers through his hair. "That's where kidnappers *belong*, Emma."

She started to stand, but a sudden bout of dizziness kept her from actually gaining any momentum. Instead, she gripped the edges of the table and waited for the room to stop spinning.

"Maybe I should give you two a few minutes?" Nicholas asked, pushing back his own chair.

Brad waved for him to stay put. "No. No. She can do this. I know she can." He draped his arm around Emma. "Emma, they're bad people, they have to be punished."

Chapter 23

She heard the crunch of his tires as he backed down the driveway, but she didn't turn. Instead, she lifted her fist to the door and knocked as hard as she could. "Miss Lottie?" she called, her voice hoarse with tears. "It is Emma. Emma Lapp. I-I need to speak—"

The door swung open, knocking her off balance and into the arms of the elderly English woman. When the woman swayed from the unexpected force, Emma jumped back, the apology she'd uttered again and again on the drive over making yet another loop past her lips.

"Shhh . . . Shhhh . . ." Miss Lottie summoned her inside enough to be able to close the door and then pulled her close. "It's okay, child. I'm here."

Seconds gave way to minutes as Emma gave into the torrent of tears she was powerless to stop. As she cried, Miss Lottie rubbed her back, telling her *everything is going to be okay . . .* to *have faith . . .* to *trust the Lord.*

She heard the words, knew they were supposed to comfort, but they fell short. Still, she tried her best to get her emotions under control if for no other reason than the fact her tears had soaked clear through to Miss Lottie's skin.

Stepping back, Emma wiped the back of her hand across her cheeks, her gaze slipping to the floor. "I am sorry, Miss Lottie. I did not mean to make you all wet like I did."

"Oh, child, my dress is fine. Nothing a sit near the fireplace won't fix." Hooking a finger beneath Emma's chin, Miss Lottie searched her eyes before abandoning them in favor of a full head to toe inspection. "Are you hurt?"

"No."

"Your parents? The children? Are they hurt?"

Emma squeezed her eyes closed against the faces she'd been unable to shake from her thoughts since the meeting with Nicholas and eked out another no.

"Then everything else is small potatoes—remember that." Miss Lottie reclaimed her cane from its resting spot beside the door and led Emma down the very hallway she'd walked just three days earlier.

The living room looked very different in the limited winter sunlight streaming in from the windows off the back of the house. The welcoming feel was still there, but something about the change in lighting and the distant tap-tap of a hammer made Emma feel fidgety and ill at ease. "I should not be here, interrupting your day. I-I should go."

"I was knitting, dear. I can knit while you talk, if I want to. But I don't. I'd much rather visit with you." Miss Lottie pointed Emma to the same couch she'd occupied on Sunday evening and then claimed her armchair. "Let's save that piece of pie I owe you until after we talk. I get the sense that's what you need most right now, anyway."

Emma nodded, pulled the nearest throw pillow onto her lap, and exhaled a wobbly breath. "He wants them to go to jail."

Miss Lottie's brow arched above the rim of her glasses. "He?"

"Brad. My birth father."

"I see. And by them, you mean Rebeccah and Wayne?"

She swallowed, hard. "Yah. He says they kidnapped me and that kidnappers belong in jail. His friend Nicholas asked me many questions today. He wrote some things down on paper, and he pressed a button, too."

"A button?"

"It was on a small box. It was silver. He pressed the button when we talked, and he pressed it again when we did not."

"So, he was recording you . . ."

"Yah. That is what he said." She startled at the snap of a log in the hearth, the pillow tumbling off her lap and onto the floor. Two rapid apologies and one grab later, it was back on her lap. "He asked things—about Mamm and Dat. Things they said to me when I was little, if they were good to me, and many questions like that. I did not mind answering his questions. I-I thought he just wanted to know, like Brad—my birth father—did. I didn't understand why Nicholas wanted to record what I said, but Brad said it was okay."

"Go on, child."

"It was time to eat, so Nicholas stopped asking questions. That is when Brad mentioned the police. That the policeman would ask me questions after we ate. I said I did not want to talk to the police—that it is not the Amish way—but Brad said it was important. He said Mamm and Dat committed a crime when they kept me and did not tell him I had been born. And that is when he said they were to . . . to . . ." She stopped, wiped a fresh round of tears from her cheeks, and made herself breathe in and out until she could continue speaking. "That is when he said they were to go to jail."

Miss Lottie sat up tall, her wrinkled hands gripping the armrests of her chair. "Did the police arrest them?"

Emma drew back, horrified. "*Arrest them?* No! Why would they do that?"

"Because that's what will have to happen in order for them to go to jail."

"No! I-I did not talk to the police. I ran outside. I ran down the road. I was almost to the end of the first road when my birth father stopped in his truck. I told him I did not want to talk to the police. I told him I couldn't."

"And what did he say?"

She traveled her thoughts back to the memory of Brad's

eyes, hooded and tired, looking back at her through the open passenger side window, the disappointment they'd conveyed leaving her more confused than ever. But when she'd asked to be taken there, to Miss Lottie's, he'd grudgingly consented.

The sound of her name on Miss Lottie's tongue yanked her back into the room in time to hear the woman's question repeated.

"He said he'd give me a little time to get used to the idea, and then we'd try again with Nicholas and the policeman." Pushing the pillow back onto the couch, Emma stood, then sat, then stood again. "I told him I would leave the Amish . . . That we would have new days to spend together . . . That it is okay if he does not have pictures of me as a little one because I can tell him things I did. I told him Bishop King would shun Mamm and Dat, that having backs turned to them was enough. But Brad does not think it is enough. He said they had no right, that they robbed him of me! He says it must be jail."

"I see. . . ."

"But Esther is too little to go to jail, Miss Lottie! Jonathan and Annie, too! Soon Sarah will be baptized, and Jakob? It won't be long until he is courting. They cannot go to jail."

"They wouldn't."

Emma sidestepped her way between the coffee table and the couch to claim a seat closer to the elderly woman. "You do not think Mamm and Dat will go to jail as Brad says?"

"No, if he pursues this, they likely will. But if your mamm and dat go to jail, the children will not."

"But that is where Mamm and Dat would be."

Miss Lottie leaned forward, captured Emma's hands inside her own, and shook her head. "If your parents go to jail, the children will stay behind."

"Stay behind? You mean at the house? But how? Mamm and Dat would not be there. . . ."

"How old is Jakob now, dear?" Miss Lottie asked. "Twenty?"

"He is twenty-one."

"Then I suppose he could petition the court to take responsibility for the others, but it would likely be a hard sell. Esther is still so young. . . . Do your parents have kin still in the area? Siblings? Parents? Anyone?"

"Two of Dat's brothers live in upstate New York. One of his sisters is in Shipshewana, the other in Holmes County. Mamm's brothers are scattered around, too. The closest one, Jeb, lives in the western part of the state with his wife and their eight children."

"Eight children?" Miss Lottie tsked softly beneath her breath. "So, there is no one here? In Blue Ball?"

"Not kin, no."

"So they'd have to move in all of those cases."

Emma looked down at her hands inside Miss Lottie's and quietly pulled them away, their sudden dampness necessitating a wipe on the sides of her dress. "I don't understand. Who would have to move?"

"Your siblings. They will need someone to go to if Jakob can't take them. Somewhere that will satisfy child services."

"Child services?"

"That's who will place them into foster care if need be."

This time, when Emma jumped up, she hit the edge of the coffee table with her shin, the quick stab of pain barely noticeable against the roar in her head. "That cannot happen. They belong with Mamm and Dat," she protested.

"I agree, but if your mamm and dat are in prison, someone will have to care for them, Emma. I'm not sure how successful a twenty-one-year-old would be in getting custody of four younger siblings."

"But . . ." Emma strode over to the window and its view of her brethren's fields in the distance, the stark browns of a winter's earth chilling her from the inside, out. "What should I do, Miss Lottie?"

"Do you want them to go to jail, child?"

"No. Of course not."

"Is that just because of the children?"

Resting her forehead against the glass, she considered the woman's question, her anger leapfrogging with . . . *sadness*? "No."

"Why?"

"I-I do not know."

"Perhaps, when you discover the reason for that answer, you will know what you must do."

"What happens if I *don't* know what to do?" she asked, turning around.

Miss Lottie waved her back to the couch. "You will. In time."

"But I *don't* have time," Emma protested. "Brad said he will give me a few days to think, but if I still cannot talk to the police, he will talk to them, himself."

Plucking her glasses from the bridge of her nose, Miss Lottie rubbed her worried eyes. "Then use those few days wisely, child."

"What do you mean?"

"What did you do when you found out about Ruby and Brad?" Miss Lottie asked, sliding her glasses back into place.

"I found him."

"And then?"

"I have spent time getting to know him and my grandmother. There is much to learn. But I am learning a little, and they are learning a little."

"I imagine you ask them questions? And they, you?"

"Yah. Many. There is much to learn."

"Have you asked your mamm why she did what she did? Why she didn't tell you about Ruby and Brad?"

"There is nothing to ask! There is no reason to do what she did!" The second she spoke, she dipped her head in shame. "Miss Lottie, I am sorry. I do not mean to speak that way to you."

"You're angry, child. You're also human. But so, too, is your mamm. Remember that."

Emma snapped her eyes back to Miss Lottie. "She didn't tell me Ruby was my real mamm! She had Dat tell Brad I did not live! For twenty-two years, I didn't know, and Brad didn't know! For twenty-two years, I didn't know why I couldn't make Mamm smile the way the others could!"

The hurt, the anger, and the confusion were back, only this time, instead of manifesting themselves in tears, alone, they claimed her voice, too, thickening it until her words were little more than rasped breaths, hitched out between sobs. "How? How could she do that, Miss Lottie? How could she do that to me?"

"There is only one person who can tell you that, dear. But you have to ask . . . and then you must listen. It is the only way you will have the answers you need to do what is right. For you."

Chapter 24

She was sitting by the kittens when she heard Mamm's footsteps, a sound she'd once welcomed as an assurance of safety. Yet, now, after everything, anger and dread were all she felt. Anger over the lies. Dread at the thought that Brad was right and Mamm and Dat belonged in jail.

"Sarah said you were out here." Closing the straw-covered gap with tentative steps, Rebeccah Lapp reached down and ran her calloused fingers across first Bean, and then each of her babies. "Esther talks most about this one," she said, stalling her hand on the brown and white mound lying farthest from Bean. "She has named it Flower because—"

"When she was first born and her eyes were closed real tight, it reminded Esther of your flowers when they shoot up out of the ground, and that when they finally opened, they'd be warm and sunny like your flowers always are." Bracing her hand against the side of the stall, Emma stood, her gaze on everything in the barn but Mamm. "I know. Esther tells me things, too. She loves me."

"Of course she loves you, Emma. You are her big sister." Rebeccah straightened to a full stand, her step forward toward Emma quickly negated by Emma's step back. "I have tried to give you space the past two weeks, to let you learn what you need to learn and—"

Emma's humorless laugh earned her more than a few curious glances from Dat's horses. "Learn what I need to learn? You mean to learn about my real dat and my real grossmudder? My aunt and my cousins? The people I knew nothing about until I found the locket Brad left for me at Ruby's grave? *Those* people?"

"Emma, please."

"You had Dat tell him I died!"

Rebeccah started to speak, only to stop and bow her head in shame.

"How could you do such a thing?" Emma yelled. "How could you tell such a lie? He *wanted* me! He wanted *a life* with Ruby and me! And you? You did not even love me enough to smile at me!"

Whipping her head up, Rebeccah stumbled backward, the thump of her back against the half wall startling Jakob's horse. "Did not love you? Emma, why would you say such a thing?"

"Because it is true. It has been that way for as long as I can remember!"

"Emma! That's not—"

"I remember when I was younger than Esther is now, wanting so much for you to smile at me the way you did Jakob, but you did not. Soon, you smiled at Sarah, and then Jonathan, and then Annie, and then Esther. But never me.

"For so many years, *too* many years, I thought it was because I had come into the world on the same day you lost your sister—that my birthday, *my birth* reminded you of a sad day and that is why you could not smile at me the same. But that is not all it was, was it? It was not because I was a reminder. . . . It is because I was—I *am the reason,* aren't I?"

Rebeccah flew a trembling hand to her mouth only to let it slip down her chin in horror. "Ruby didn't die because of you. She died because of that boy!"

"You mean my father?" Emma countered, her voice shrill.

"Because of him, Ruby was in a family way when she wasn't married!"

Emma turned, her hands clenching her hips. "I am not here because of Brad alone! Your sister was part of it!"

Pain skittered across Rebeccah's face, pushing her back a step. "Ruby was young. . . . She made mistakes. . . ."

"Mistakes?" Emma echoed. "You mean *me*?"

"You should have been born to a Mamm *and* a Dat."

"You are right, I should have been! But you and Dat did not let that happen. You made decisions about my life that were not yours to make," she rasped. "And why? So I could wonder why you never smiled at me?"

Rebeccah stepped forward, and again, Emma stepped backward, maintaining the distance between them. "I smiled at you, Emma."

"*This* is not a smile." She emulated the wobbly smile she'd seen on occasion. "People do not have tears in their eyes when they are happy!"

The smile she'd just tried to demonstrate flashed across Rebeccah's face. The tears that sprang to her eyes, however, remained as she matched each of Emma's steps until the back wall of the barn eliminated the distance once and for all.

Extending both her arms, Rebeccah bookended Emma's shoulders with her hands and waited until Emma's eyes were on hers. "I smiled right here"—she touched her chest—"every time I looked at you, Emma. But if it did not always show it was because I was afraid this day would come."

"This day?"

"The day I might lose you."

Feeling her breath begin to saw in and out with the kind of emotions she didn't know how to process, Emma closed her eyes, only to open them at the feel of Mamm's hand on her cheek. "Emma, you are not the reason Ruby died. And you are not the reason I was sad. Ruby died because something was not right with her heart. If I am sad when I think of her, it is because she was my sister . . . and because she never got to know you, or hold you the way I have. And Dat? He held you even before I did. When I was tending to Ruby, he held you as his own."

"But I wasn't his own. I was Brad's!" She wriggled free of Rebeccah's hand and stepped around her to return to Bean and the kittens. Bean, clearly aware of their presence, was licking her babies while keeping a wary eye on the activity happening just beyond their makeshift bed. Emma wiggled her finger at Bean and then spun around as Mamm began to speak again.

"You are very much like her, you know. Having you has been like having a little bit of her still here. The same sweetness, the same joy, the same love of home and family. Sometimes, when you are baking something in the kitchen, your smile is so like hers—so full of joy and excitement. And the way you are with Esther? Ruby was like that with your uncle Jeb when he was little—always kind, always patient. She would have made a good mamm."

Emma shifted from foot to foot. "Perhaps, with her, I would have fit."

"Fit?"

"I have never fit, anywhere," she said around the tightening in her throat. "Not here, not at school, not at hymn sings . . ."

"Emma, you have always fit here. *Always.* And at school, the children did not refrain from playing games with you because they did not like you. They didn't play with you because you would stay inside helping the teacher. When you finally went outside, it was almost time to stop playing."

"How-how do you know?" she stammered. "You . . . you weren't there."

"Because I spoke with your teacher. That is why I gave you cookies to bring, so you would go outside sooner. But you didn't. You stayed inside and put a cookie on every desk while the children played. You did not want to make those who did not bring cookies to share feel poorly." Step by step, Rebeccah made her way back to Emma. "And the hymn sings? I think you fit better than you realize."

"You cannot know that."

"Perhaps you are right. But I know *you*, Emma, and I know you are quiet. I know you can get lost watching a butterfly or a frog. I know you look to see the smiles that come when people try your cookies and cakes. I know whenever you saw a frown or a hint of sadness on anyone's face—even someone on the other side of a room—you wanted to fix it, as if *you* were the reason they were not happy and—"

Rebeccah pressed her hand to her lips as a single tear rolled down her cheek. "Oh, Emma . . . I did that to you, didn't I? I-I made you think that anything short of laughter was your fault."

"No, Mamm, I—" And then she stopped. She was doing exactly what Mamm said. "Maybe. I do not know."

Lowering herself to the ground beside Bean, Emma ran a soothing hand across Flower's back and waited for the repetitive motion to calm her thoughts and her breath enough to continue. When she was fairly certain any lingering shake wouldn't manifest itself in her voice, she looked back up at Mamm.

"You will be shunned for keeping me," she whispered. "Maybe even worse."

"Bishop King knows, Emma. He has always known."

"The bishop has . . . *known*?" At Mamm's nod, she pulled her knees to her chest and tried her best to make sense of everything. Something was missing. Something—"Why didn't you tell me about them?" she asked. "Why did you let Brad think I'd died with her?"

"Because Ruby wanted you to be raised Amish. It was *her* wish."

A swell of renewed anger pushed her legs back to the

ground with an audible thud. "I don't believe that!" Emma countered. "I have seen pictures of my real mamm and dat together. She loved him!"

"Maybe you are right. I don't know. She did not speak of him with me until you were on the way. The only thing I can tell you for sure is that she wanted to raise you in the Amish way."

"How? How can you know that?" she demanded. "Ruby died!"

Rebeccah's shoulders lifted in a pained shrug. "She chose baptism just one month before you were born."

"She chose . . ." A deafening roar filled her ears, making it difficult to think let alone speak. But still, she tried, skipping ahead to the only part that mattered. "But then, she couldn't be with my father."

"It was her choice, Emma. For her and for you."

The snap of a twig from somewhere off to her left stole her attention from the afternoon sun shimmering atop the pond and sent it skittering toward the man now picking his way around old branches and stumps for the meeting she'd walked a quarter of a mile to request.

Much like Esther needed all the pieces of her wooden puzzle to create a farm, Emma needed all the pieces of the past in order to know her future. And from what Emma could tell, Brad held the second-to-last piece.

"Sorry your call went to my voicemail, kiddo. I tried you back as soon as I got out of the shower and saw that you had called, but the phone just rang and rang."

"I did not stay." Emma slid the drawstring bag into the center of the rock to clear a spot for Brad to sit, and, when he did, she looked back over the water once again. "I am sorry I got so upset yesterday."

"You've been through a lot. We all have. And I probably should have warned you about the video call with the police chief sooner than I did, but I guess I wanted to try and spare you as much of the nasty stuff as possible."

"You mean like sending Mamm and Dat to jail?"

"That's—wait . . . Does that mean you're ready to talk to the chief?" he asked.

"No." The sound of his weighted exhale propelled her gaze back to the pond long enough to gather her breath and her courage. "I did not know Ruby chose to be baptized. That she wanted to raise me in the Amish way."

"Okay . . ."

"Why?"

"I don't know, I guess you can only cram so much into two weeks."

She took one last look at the pond and then turned so the only thing in front of her was Brad. "I mean why did she choose to be baptized when she knew I was coming? When she knew baptism would mean she could not share a life with you?"

"She didn't want to lose Rebeccah and Jeb and her parents."

"But she wouldn't have. Ruby hadn't been baptized when she learned I was coming. She could have lived a life with you and still spent time with her family."

Brad pushed off the rock, picked a small stick up off the ground, and snapped it against the edge of the rock. "That is what I told her. Time and time again. I talked about the company we wanted to open, the floor plans she could design while you slept, and the house I would build for us as soon as I could.

"Those first months after we found out she was pregnant, she seemed all onboard with everything. She even drew up the house she wanted me to build. It was much plainer than the other ones she'd drawn, so I told her to draw it again. I told her to think big, think fancy, and think splashy because our baby was going to grow up having the very best in life—the best toys, the best schooling, the best clothes, best car in the high school parking lot, et cetera."

She made herself nod as if she understood, but she didn't.

"I would have raised you to be a princess, Emma. And I would have treated Ruby like a queen."

A princess . . .

A queen . . .

"But she didn't draw it again, did she?" It was a silly question considering Emma already knew the answer. She'd seen the drawing. Seen the large front room Ruby had wanted yet Brad had insisted on dividing . . .

"No, she didn't. So I just figured I'd change it when I built it. But I never got the chance to do that because, a few weeks later, she told me she wanted to be baptized and to raise you Amish." He tossed the stick a few yards and then raked his now-free hand through his hair. "And that is when she told me we were over. That her decision meant we could not be together.

"We argued. Or, rather, I argued. I reminded her of all the things she could have and be in the English world. I even reminded her that different doesn't mean bad. But it didn't matter. She didn't want any of that. She wanted better for you, she said."

He flicked his hand in Emma's direction. "As if an eighth-grade education and being out of touch with the here and now is better somehow."

She sat with his words for a moment, letting them roll around in her thoughts. "When Ruby made an Amish picnic for you, did you enjoy it?" she finally asked.

"Very much. The food was great."

"Was that the only date she planned?"

"No. We came here, many times. She taught me to skip rocks; how to catch a butterfly so it would still fly when I let go. And that field of dandelions I told you about? We found that when we were out in this area, just walking around."

"Did you enjoy those things?"

He shrugged his assent.

"The Amish see the big and fancy," she said, quietly. "It is all around us. It cannot be pretended away. It is just not the way the Amish choose to live their lives. You say different is not bad, and you are right, I am sure. But simple, as Ruby showed you, is not bad, either. I have had a good life so far. A *happy* life. I had warm food in my stomach, a bed to rest my head, and family who love me."

"*Love?*" he spat. "You think keeping me from you is *love?*"

"I think trying to honor Ruby's wishes for my life was love."

"Ruby was dead, Emma."

"Not in Mamm's heart, she wasn't."

"Nor in mine. But Rebeccah has had a living, breathing link to Ruby in you for twenty-two years." He lowered himself back down to the rock and, ever so gently, tucked a stray wisp of hair back inside Emma's kapp. "Now it's my turn."

"Please don't put them in jail," she whispered. "For me. *Please.*"

Chapter 25

For the second time in less than three weeks, Emma made her way toward the simple white farmhouse with the wide front porch. A quick peek in the barn as she passed revealed little more than a few curious horses, a sleeping barn cat, and an old buggy wheel in need of repair. The tap-tap of a hammer from somewhere just beyond the barn piqued her curiosity, but, still, she kept walking, her need to figure out the final piece of the puzzle leading her to the one person who'd always understood her, even when she didn't always understand herself.

Mary Fisher had been her friend since the beginning, enabling them to carry on a tradition started by their mamms. They'd chased each other around the pond when they were toddlers, sat beside each other as they learned to read, raced each other to the part of their post-school-day walk that required one to go left and one to go straight, and kept each other's innermost secrets. But perhaps, more than all that, Mary had a way of seeing things Emma could not always see.

Taking the porch steps two at a time, Emma fast walked across the wood planking to the dark green door she'd helped Mary paint the previous summer. In spite of the heaviness in her heart, the memory of Mary's howl when Emma accidentally painted her toe brought a fleeting and oh-so-needed smile to her lips. The raw day would prevent them from sitting outside today, but an empty stall in the equally empty barn would certainly work, too—

"Emma? Is that you?" At the familiar voice and the equally familiar flapping it always seemed to kick off inside her stomach, Emma stepped out from behind the upright and waved at the handsome twenty-four-year-old heading in her direction with a hammer in one hand and a level in the other. "Dat left with Mamm and the girls in the buggy not more than twenty minutes ago."

She tried to hide her answering slump, but if the way Levi's eyebrows dipped with worry less than a blink later was any indication, she'd failed. Miserably. Before she could come up with something to placate him, though, he settled himself on the second-to-last step and patted Emma over to the top one. "I know I am not Mary, but I am good at listening, too. Maybe even better."

Her laugh stirred a matching one from Levi as she heeded his invitation. "I think it is good that Mary cannot hear you say such a thing."

"I think you are right." He brushed a piece of straw from his pants leg and then swiveled on the step so Emma was his view. "Have you decided what you will do?"

And just like that, any residual laughter on her part ceased, wiped away by the tug-of-war that had become her life. "I thought I had . . . before I talked to Mamm."

Something sparked behind Levi's eyes. "So, you will stay?"

"I know I should be able to answer such a question, but what seemed so easy two days ago, is not easy now. Miss Lottie said not to make a decision in anger. But without anger, there is only"—she looked out at the barn—"confusion."

"I am listening."

And so she told him. She told him about Brad's steadfast belief that Mamm and Dat belonged in jail. She told him how Miss Lottie convinced her it was time to talk to Mamm. She told him how Mamm's lack of smiles toward Emma over the years had both nothing and everything to do with Emma. She told him Ruby had chosen to raise Emma in the Amish way and how she'd confronted Brad with that information. And last but not least, she'd told him how Brad had finally, *finally* relented on the notion of jail provided Mamm and Dat didn't interfere in his relationship with Emma ever again.

His slow, thoughtful nod when she got to the end let her know he'd been listening. The quick touch of his hand on hers let her know he cared even if her answering gasp made one of the barn cats rethink his approach and scurry behind a bush, instead.

"It is good that you know these things," Levi said, catching and holding her gaze with his. "It is when you know things, you can decide things."

"Three days ago, I wanted to punish Mamm for keeping me from Brad. He is my only living birth parent and I should know him. But now that I know the truth about everything, I see that Mamm was doing what Ruby wanted her to do. And me? I am a link to Ruby for Mamm, and a link to Ruby for Brad. But I cannot be both, just as I cannot be both English and Amish."

Again, he nodded. And since his hand had never left hers, he simply tightened his grip. "Whatever world you choose, Emma, I will choose it, too."

"Whatever world I . . ." She looked from Levi, to his hand on hers, and back to Levi. "What are you saying, Levi? *What* do you choose?"

"I choose you and me. To be together."

"Together?" she echoed.

"Yah."

She stared at him, waiting for some outward sign he was teasing, but there was none. Just a tender smile that was trained solely on Emma. "But-but I'm not Liddy Mast!"

"You're right. You are Emma Lapp."

"I know but—"

"You are Emma Lapp," he repeated.

"But I'm not sure what that means. . . . Who I am, anymore . . ."

Levi quieted her words with a gentle squeeze. "You are still the same person you have always been, Emma. You are kind. You are sensitive. You are caring. You are good at volleyball and baking cookies. You are a fine sister, a fine daughter, and—"

"How can I be a fine daughter when I am so confused?"

"You are a fine daughter *because* you are confused," he said, his voice thick.

She stared at him. "That does not make any sense."

"You have taken time to get to know your birth father, yah?"

Emma nodded. "Yah. I have learned many things, but there is much more to learn."

"And your mamm?" Levi asked. "Have you learned things about her?"

"Do you mean Ruby or . . ." She stopped, swallowed, and steadied her voice. "*Mamm*?"

"Both, I guess."

She considered Levi's question. "Yah."

"And?"

"I love them both. Brad and Dat, too."

"Then that's the only real difference I see about you, Emma. You have more people to love, and more people to love *you* now."

Emma ran her fingers across the back of the now-closed photograph album and looked up at Brad and Delia, the love in their eyes making her smile tremble even more. "Thank you for letting me look at the rest of these pictures. They help me to see Ruby in a way I never could have without them."

"I'm glad, dear." Delia rubbed Emma's back in smooth, even circles. "She was happy with your father. Very happy."

She could see how they thought that. Ruby's smile in each and every picture was proof. It was also proof that the decision Emma had come to was the right one. For Emma.

"Mom and I talked about it and we know transitioning from an Amish life to an English life is going to take some time. We know you'll make it fine, but we also know it will be filled with unknowns for a while. So that's why we thought maybe it would be best if you and I move in here, with Mom, until you get more comfortable. Then, and only then, we can move to my place—*our* place."

"Or just stay here," Delia added, resting her cheek against Emma's shoulder. "I certainly have the room *and* the books to keep you busy."

Emma let her answering laugh accompany her gaze as she took in the cozy sitting room that had made her feel at home on her very first visit to Delia's home.

* The floor-to-ceiling bookshelves filled with more books than the English grocer . . .
* The photographs of Brad as a baby and a young man . . .
* The happy little knickknacks she'd come to know the origin of thanks to the warm and welcoming woman sitting beside her . . .
* The window with its view of the pond Ruby had skated on . . .
* The mantel with the framed picture of her birth parents, together and smiling . . .

Somehow, Emma could see the room as it might look in two years, five years. The pictures and the books would still be the same, but in her mind's eye there would be new things on the shelf, too. Perhaps a framed picture drawn by one of her own children . . . The skates she hoped to own one day lying beside the window . . . Her husband seated beside her on the couch while Brad added a log to the hearth . . . A plate with Delia's pastries and her own bread sitting atop the coffee table . . .

"If there is something you want to change or add, we can do that. This is your home, too, Emma." With the gentlest of fingers, Brad turned Emma's chin until he was the only thing she saw. "We want you to feel as if you fit here—with us. Always."

Just for a moment, as she stared into the eyes she'd yearned to see her whole life, she wished someone would take a picture. But as quick as the thought came, it disappeared. She didn't need a photo album to remember this moment. This man, and his mother, were part of her life to stay.

"Emma? Did you hear me? We want you to know that you fit here. . . ."

She found Brad's hand with her left and Delia's hand with her right and squeezed both. "I know. And I do. But I also fit in Blue Ball. With Mamm, Dat, and the children. And with Levi."

"Levi?" Brad echoed.

"He has asked to court me and I have said yes."

"To court you? As in the Amish tradition . . ."

"Yah."

Brad's eyes left Emma for Delia, only to return with a hint of anger. "Emma, I told you if Rebeccah and Wayne interfered in any way, I will not be able to honor my promise to you."

"This is not about them—not in the way you mean, anyway. Levi was willing to leave his vows to be English *with* me if that is what I wanted," she said.

"Then do it!" Brad said. "He can come work with me!"

"That is what Levi said, too."

"Good! And *you* can do what you love, too. You can open a restaurant and people will come from miles to eat what you make!"

The image his words created in her thoughts quickly bowed to another, better one—one responsible for the smile she felt tugging at the corners of her mouth. "I am counting on that."

"Then I don't understand. . . ."

"I do not want to leave my Amish ways, and I do not want to leave my family."

"*We're* your family, Emma," Brad protested. "Your *real* family."

"It is nice to look at you and see my eyes, and my same hair. It is nice to look at pictures of Ruby and see my chin and my nose. But Mamm and Dat? And the children? They have made me who I am, too." She looked from Brad to Delia and back again, the love she felt for them setting off a stream of tears she didn't bother to wipe away. "I need *all of you* in my life—in the *simple* life Ruby wanted for me and for herself."

"Ruby's choice doesn't have to be your choice, Emma."

She smiled at her birth father. "You are right, it doesn't. But I'm not making this choice because of Ruby. I'm making this choice for *me*. For *my* life. I do not need *many* tables full. I need only *one* table full—my own."

"But you haven't given me a chance to show you what it can be like here. . . ."

"I don't need you to. I know my life. It is like it was with Ruby. Her smiles in your English world were different than her smiles in simpler times. She smiled here, by your pond, but her smile with the bubbles and the dandelion? They were bigger, happier. Because *that* is where she fit best. I know I have said I didn't fit in Blue Ball, but that is because I was looking to others instead of inside to my own heart."

"But I just found you, Emma," Brad pleaded. "I don't want to lose you again. I *can't* lose you again."

"You won't, you can't. I am your daughter." She released her hold on his hand to wipe the tears from his eyes. "And you, Brad Harper, are *my dad*. Forever and always."

Eleven Months Later

"You are not peeking, are you?"

Emma stopped moving and turned her temporarily sightless eyes in the direction of her husband's voice. "How can I peek if your hands are covering my eyes?"

"I don't know. Your dad told me to be sure you cannot see."

She tried to make a face, but when her mouth was determined to smile as it was at that moment, there was little she could do to make it stop. Three months earlier, in front of God and their families, she'd become Emma Fisher. It had been a surprisingly warm day for late October, a fact Delia hailed as Ruby's part in the special day.

Emma knew she wasn't to think such things, but still, during quiet moments alone, she couldn't help but believe Delia was right. After all, Emma had been able to have what Ruby couldn't—a family that knew no bounds. A family where she had both a dat and a dad.

"Are you ready?" Levi called.

"Yah. I am ready. And I am right here, next to you, so you do not have to be so loud."

Levi's laugh filled her ears. "I was not asking *you*."

She drew back into Levi's chest, but his hands remained firmly in place. "Who? Who else is here?" she asked.

In lieu of an answer, Levi dropped his hands to a *ta-da* she recognized as belonging to her father. "Dad? Where . . ." The words drifted away as her uncovered eyes came to rest on the two-story home no more than three buggy lengths away.

She took in the three front steps, the wraparound porch with the view of the Amish countryside on one side, the driveway on the front, and a small pond on the other. She took in the flower boxes on the first floor, the dark green shades of the second-floor windows, and the man standing next to it all with a tool belt around his waist and the smile she could never get enough of seeing.

"Dad?"

"It was a little too big to leave by the grave, but what do you think?" Brad Harper asked, stepping forward.

She rubbed her eyes, took in the house again, and then locked gazes with the man slowly closing the gap between them. "This . . . this is *The Ruby,* yah?"

"It is, indeed."

"But you have never built one."

"I have now." Brad clapped a hand on Levi's suspender-clad shoulder. "With Levi's help, of course."

She looked from Brad, to Levi, and back to the house, her mind's eye skipping ahead to the inside she'd yet to see. "Is . . . is it the way she drew it inside, too?"

"Why don't we go inside and you can tell me if it's the same or not."

For the briefest of moments, she couldn't move, the notion of stepping inside almost more than she could handle. But it didn't last long. Soon, she was fast walking across the earthen driveway, up the porch steps, and through the front door.

Two steps in, she froze.

Somehow, someway, Levi and her father had managed to take a simple pencil sketch and transform it into something with walls and paint and . . . *life.* Stunned, Emma inched forward, her eyes scanning the room for the simple details that had been so important to her birth mother all those years ago.

* The fireplace to her left . . .
* The large windows overlooking the Amish countryside . . .
* The accordion divider tucked into the wall to
  accommodate church . . .

"It's Ruby's house," she whispered, looking from Brad to
Levi and back again. "You built Ruby's house."

"Ruby designed it, and Levi and I built it, but it's *your*
house . . . yours and Levi's," Brad said, grinning.

"Ours?" she echoed. "But—"

"Happy birthday, Emma."

Bookending her face with her hands, she took everything
in again, the joy bubbling up inside her making it difficult to
breathe. "I do not know what to say."

Brad laughed. "Then look first, talk second."

"I am looking. . . . It is . . . It is *wonderful.*"

"There is more to see, kiddo."

"*More?*"

"Surely you need a place to make all that amazing food,
don't you?"

She sucked in her breath. "Is it the kitchen Ruby drew?"

"Why don't you see for yourself?"

In need of no directions, Emma crossed the living room to
the small linking hallway she knew would take her to the
kitchen. Sure enough, as she stepped inside, her eyes moved
immediately to the large window Ruby had envisioned as the
perfect napping spot for her infant.

She tried to imagine the young girl she'd seen so many
times in photographs, tucking Emma's infant self into a sun-
drenched wooden cradle and showering her chubby cheeks
with sweet kisses. . . .

"I think your mother would be very pleased to know that
one day soon, our grandchild will be sleeping in that very
same spot," Brad said, his voice thick with emotion. "God
willing, of course."

She stole a glance in Levi's direction long enough to trade knowing smiles before turning back to the window and the slightly different image that was now just a little less than seven months away—

Something that sounded a lot like an Esther giggle floated into the room and sent her attention skittering toward a pile of brightly wrapped boxes stacked atop the large center island. Before she could fully process the sight or formulate anything resembling a question, a flurry of faces entered the room from the door Ruby had marked *pantry* so many years earlier.

* Dat . . .
* Jakob . . .
* Sarah . . .
* Jonathan . . .
* Annie . . .
* Esther . . .
* Delia . . .
* Mary . . .
* Levi's Mamm and Dat . . .
* Miss Lottie . . .

Stunned, she stumbled back into Levi's waiting arms. "What . . . what is this? Why are you all here?"

As if one, all eyes, including Emma's, turned back toward the pantry door as Mamm stepped her way through the crowd of Emma's loved ones with a birthday cake in her hands and a smile as bright as the sun on her face.

"Happy birthday, Emma."

ACKNOWLEDGMENTS

Writing is, by its very nature, a solitary act. I spend months sitting in front of my computer screen, losing myself in my characters' worlds. Still, there are some people who make the journey to a book's completion all the more fun for me.

That said, I'd like to thank my friend Tasha Alexander. The nugget for this story came while visiting her in the most peaceful place I've ever visited. Being able to play the "what-if" game with her for a few hours that same day made it all the more fun.

A huge thank-you also goes to my family for their patience, understanding, and willingness to eat leftovers while I tapped away on this book.

And, finally, I must thank you, my readers. Your kind emails and enthusiasm for my books keep me doing what I'm doing.

A DAUGHTER'S TRUTH

Laura Bradford

ABOUT THIS GUIDE

The suggested questions are included
to enhance your group's reading of
Laura Bradford's *A Daughter's Truth*.

DISCUSSION QUESTIONS

1. In the blink of an eye, Emma's world changes. Not because of her own choices, but because of the choices made by those around her. Have you ever had your life significantly impacted because of the choices of others? Can you share?

2. While talking to Emma the first time, Miss Lottie references a sign she saw in a San Francisco outdoor market that said, "Home is not a place, it's a feeling." It's a sentiment that eventually leads the English woman back to her childhood roots in Amish Country.

   Is there somewhere (besides your physical house) that always feels like "home" to you? Where you feel the most like yourself? Where?

3. Levi's advice to Emma when she's on the brink of leaving everything behind is to "think before you do." If you could give one piece of advice about life to someone, what would it be?

4. All her life, Emma has yearned to see herself in someone. For Emma, it's about something tangible she can see. Whom do you most resemble, appearance-wise, in your family? Do your interests/abilities resemble anyone's?

5. Mary has always been Emma's safe harbor—the person who has been by her side every step of the way, and truly knows Emma's heart without Emma having to say a word. Do you have a friend like that? How long have you known her/him and how did you meet?

6. What do you think was the turning point for Emma—the moment or series of moments that helped her choose the right life for herself?

7. Do you think Emma makes the right decision in the end? Why/why not?

Connect with Us

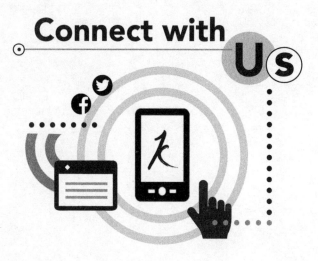

Visit us online at
KensingtonBooks.com
to read more from your favorite authors, see books
by series, view reading group guides, and more.

for sneak peeks, chances to win books and prize packs,
and to share your thoughts with other readers.

facebook.com/kensingtonpublishing
twitter.com/kensingtonbooks

Tell us what you think!

To share your thoughts, submit a review,
or sign up for our eNewsletters, please visit:
KensingtonBooks.com/TellUs.